Banderos, The Last War: Book Six

SYLVIE GRAYSON

For information write to
Great Western Publishing at
sylviegraysonauthor@gmail.com
http://www.sylviegrayson.com

ISBN: 978-1-7750405-9-0

First Great Western Publishing paperback printing April 2019
10 9 8 7 6 5 4 3 2 1
Great Western Publishing is a registered trademark of Sylvie Grayson.
Cover art by Steven Novak novakillustration@gmail.com
Printed in the USA

You can contact +Ms. Grayson at sylviegraysonauthor@gmail.com or visit her website at www.sylviegrayson.com and sign up to follow her or receive her newsletter.
You can also follow her on BookBub https://www.bookbub.com/profile/sylvie-grayson
You will be the first to hear the latest on new book releases, book giveaways and author presentations.

Other books by SYLVIE GRAYSON -

<u>Sci/fi fantasy</u>

The Last War Series

Khandarken Rising, Book One

Son of the Emperor, Book Two

Truth and Treachery, Book Three

Weapon of Tyrants, Book Four

Prince of Jiran, Book Five

Banderos, Book Six

The Sovereign, Book Seven

Go to her website to sign up to follow her
www.sylviegrayson.com or follow her on BookBub
https://www.bookbub.com/profile/sylvie-grayson Check out
her Facebook page https://www.facebook.com/sylvie.grayson
or contact her at sylviegraysonauthor@gmail.com

Also by SYLVIE GRAYSON
<u>Contemporary suspense, romance and murder</u>

The Lies He Told Me, Book One

Ran Man, Lies He Told, Book Two

Don't Move, Lies He Told, Book Three

Game Plan, Lies He Told, Book Four

Legal Obstruction

Suspended Animation

My Best Mistake

Moon Shine

False Confession

Prairie Storm

Dead Wrong

DEDICATION

This book is dedicated to my husband, Brian Higgins, who has encouraged and supported me on this writing journey. Without his care and backing, I would never have gotten to Book Six. Thank you so much.

- Sylvie Grayson

Banderos,

The Last War:
Book Six

CHARACTERS

Adoni – Full name Adoniram, from Legitamia, sookie family, now works in Khandarken with Loyal Hawker

Anatoliy – assistant to Leader Cownden Lanser of Khandarken

Balsom, Ms- secretary for Governor Frank Maude

Banderos – Gerwal, father of Banderos family, strongman in unclaimed territory between Jiran and Adar Silva

Banderos, First – eldest son, groomed to take over from Gerwal, head of the family military

Banderos, Second – clever and kind, died at age 7 falling from the top of the compound wall

Banderos, Third – died an infant, a few days old

Banderos, Fourth — works with First, same mother for first four children

Banderos, Fifth = works with First, no one trusts him, even Gerwal

Banderos, Sixth = died in his bed, aged twelve

Banderos, Seventh-

Banderos, Eighth= same mother, Fifth through Eighth

Banderos, Ninth= a scholar, mentored by Gerwal's scribe, married, two kids

Banderos, Tenth-=

Banderos, Eleventh= herder, with the cattle and sheep

Banderos, Twelfth= herder, works with Eleventh

Banderos, Thirteenth= runs the bakery, married with 3 kids, same mother Ninth to Thirteenth, pale skin, light green eyes, sandy hair

Banderos, Fourteenth= captain of the border station guards

Banderos, Fifteenth= works at the border stations, and with the roaming guards

Banderos, Sixteenth= died in a fight with First a few years ago

Banderos, Seventeenth= works the vegetable crops in the compound

Banderos, Eighteenth= works with Seventeenth in the vegetable gardens

Banderos, Nineteenth- a loner, admires Angel,

same mother Fourteenth to Nineteenth, dusky skin, dark hair

Banderos, Angel= only daughter

Banderos, Twentieth — died an infant

Banderos, Twenty-first, Twenty-second, Twenty-third — triplets all died as infants

Banderos, Rascal-

Banderos, Runt-

Banderos, Baby — Angel through Baby had the same mother

Banderos, Willa – Gerwal's 6th and current wife, no children

Boz — Shandro Penrhy's counsellor and advisor

Carlton, Emperor – Aqatain's only legitimate child, is attempting to regain the Empire

Chinata /China – Princess, Aqatain's illegitimate daughter by Maa, married to Prince Shandro Penrhy

Farmer, Abe — owner of Farmer Holdings with his sister, Beth, fighting arts mentor, married to Julianne Adjudicator, Little Harry's daughter

Farmer, Bethlehem- sister of Abe, owner of

Farmer Holdings with him, married to Dante Regiment, one son

Hawker, **Jade** – father to Loyal Hawker, uncle to Beth and Abe Farmer

Hawker, Loyal – cousin to Abe and Beth Farmer, works undercover for his uncle, Governor Frank Maude

Hawker, Ms – Loyal's mother, sister to Governor Maude of the Southern Territory

Lanser, Cownden — Aqatain's illegitimate son, was Chief Constable of Khandarken, now Leader of the country

Lanser, **Jessalyn**- mother of Cownden Lanser, sister to Judson Lanser

Lanser, Judson– Advisor to Emperor Carlton, uncle to Cownden Lanser

Learmonth, Jack- head of distillery and hotel chain family

Maa – woman who established and runs the Sanctuary in north-east Khandarken, mother of Chinata

Major Paynter – in the military of Emperor Carlton

Malahide – right hand for Major-General Dante Regiment

Maude, Frank -- Governor of Southern Territory in Khandarken, uncle to Loyal Hawker

Nazur, **Olaf** – senior Nazur, strongman holding territory to the west of the Banderos land

Nazur, **Orde**- son of Olaf, anxious to take over the territory

Penrhy, Shandro – Prince, Sovereign of the Penrhy tribe

Regiment, Dante– Major-General in Khandarken military, son of General Paulo Regiment

Regiment, Paulo –General of Khandarken military

Scribe, **Reginald**- works for Paulo Regiment

Shafoneurs – tribe to the south of the Penrhys in Jiran

Stuke, **Damian**- son of Dr Stuke, married to Fanny Master, in the military

Waite – works undercover for Major Dante Regiment

Weisner – tutor at the Banderos compound

Hawker

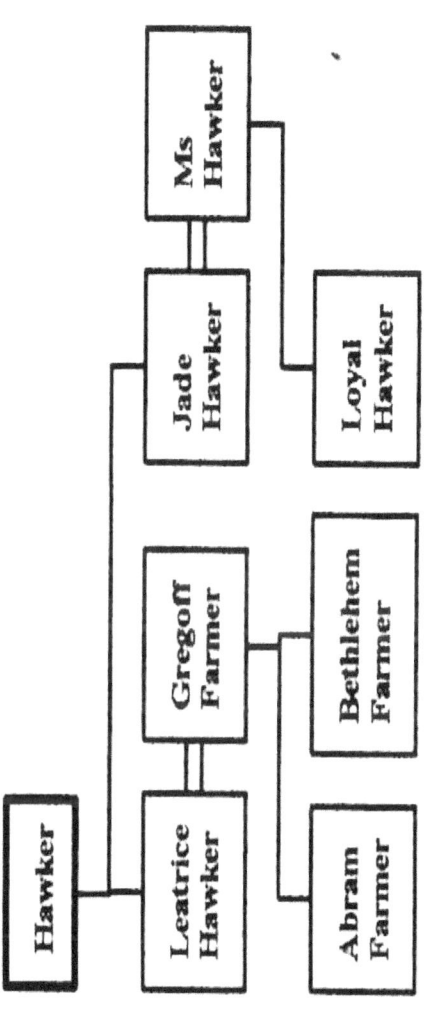

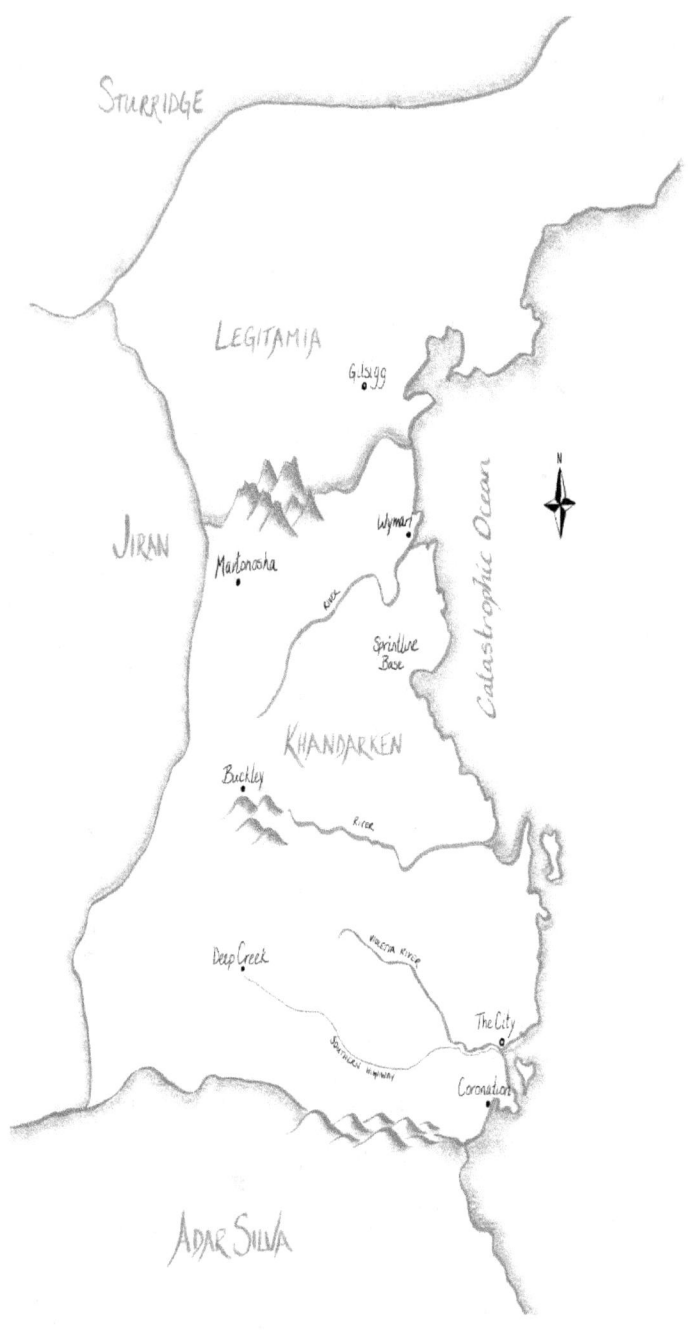

Chapter One

In the unclaimed territory south of the Jirani plains, Loyal Hawker steered his dusty transport to the side of the track. It was early spring, and the sun was pale in the morning sky. They'd been travelling for several days, following his sales route through this thinly populated area on the journey toward Sommerset, capital of Adar Silva. He scanned the irregular line of houses and shacks that made up the so-called village of Hafford. This was where he and Adoni were to meet up with Damian Stuke.

He glanced over at his assistant. Loyal hadn't known Adoni long, but the young fellow was quick and clever, and in the past had proved surprisingly skillful in a firefight. He was from the regions of Legitamia, north of Khandarken along the Catastrophic Ocean. His sallow skin and slanted eyes were an unusual sight here in the south.

"We stop in Hafford for the night," Loyal said.

"The bar has a couple of rooms in the back that are usually available for rent."

They both turned to stare at the shabby building—walls made of stacked poles, roof of some kind of thatch and a muddy path leading to the half-door that stood open to the elements.

"And," Loyal added, "Stuke shouldn't have any trouble finding us."

"Sounds good." Adoni shrugged his hawker's jacket over his shoulders. "Are the supplies safe?" He pointed to the sales goods secured on the roof of the transport and in the small trailer behind.

Loyal shrugged. "As can be. There's not much traffic around here." As a travelling seller, he had managed to cover a lot of territory through the new countries that had sprung up out of the remains of the Old Empire. He was used to dealing with the constant exposure and risk of theft.

The village was situated on the plain at the edge of a thin forest, with numerous trails criss-crossing the roads that serviced it. This was not one of Loyal's usual ports of call as he made his sales rounds. His specialty was medical equipment and supplies, along with the talc mined at Farmer Holdings by his cousins in south Khandarken, and the colouring agents manufactured from it.

But he had recently expanded his route. Since his alliance with Major Dante Regiment and the Khandarken military, his main objective as he travelled had shifted from sales to the gathering of information. To his surprise, he'd become an undercover agent, working with his uncle Governor Frank Maude of the Southern Territory of Khandarken. As a result, his field of operations was constantly increasing. There were persistent rumours about this area—talk of dispossessed gathering and organizing, of unrest and possible uprising. This was one of the reasons Damian Stuke was scheduled to meet them here.

Adoni opened the door and stepped out as Loyal shut down the transport engine and closed the holograph map on the frontboard. Ahead of them the village meandered in a slightly irregular pattern— shops, restaurants and houses intermingled with service barns and sheds on either side of the makeshift street.

Approaching the tavern, Loyal walked up a couple of stone steps and through the half-door. He glanced around. A long plank against the back wall served as a counter. The floor was made of bare boards, slightly dusty, and the one plexi window looking out on the strand was smudged and blurred. The barkeep looked up from behind the counter and gave him a nod of recognition.

Loyal had been here before. His singular appearance, pale blonde hair in tight curls on his head and down the long sideburns, along with a tall, broad-shouldered lean frame made him readily recognizable. There were tables loosely scattered around the space, two of which were already occupied. Stuke was not yet here.

Loyal moved up to the heavy plank to tap a coin on the surface. "Two ales, my good man."

The attendant nodded, then his gaze sharpened as he caught sight of Adoni coming through the door. He glanced nervously about the interior at the occupied tables and focussed on a thin stooped fellow in the corner who seemed to be totally fascinated by the bottom of his probably empty tankard.

The barkeep quickly poured the ales and set them on the bar, taking the coin from Loyal's hand. "There you go, gentlemen. No roughhousing in my bar," he warned.

Loyal raised his eyebrows. *Was this a signal of some sort?* What roughhousing was the man talking about? He grabbed both tankards and made for a seat against the far wall. Stuke, who also worked with Major Regiment, was scheduled to arrive shortly. They'd be able to keep a close eye on the door from this spot as they waited for his arrival.

Adoni dropped into his chair with a long sigh. "Looks good, boss," he said and raised the tankard. "To your health."

Loyal nodded and returned the greeting. "To your health," he said and took a long draught. There was a sudden roar from behind. Alarmed, he set his drink down and swivelled on the bench to find the solitary drinker no longer staring into his tankard, but on his feet, glaring openly at their table.

"What is this, a joke?" the man blustered "By the

graves, there ain't no yellow faces allowed in here!"

The barkeep stopped what he was doing and swiftly jogged the length of the bar. "Down, boy," he gritted. "No roughhousing allowed!"

The fellow was not deterred. "Where'd you come from, you dog," he called. "Must be a Legi from up by the Catastrophic Ocean from the looks of you. How'd they let you get this far south all in one piece?"

Loyal felt the gorge rise in his throat. Often there had been comments about Adoni's appearance as they travelled his seller's route. His assistant was clearly not from around here with his unusual appearance, but never had there been such an outright attack. He glanced at Adoni who started to rise from his chair as he stared with hatred at the loudmouth behind them.

"Hold it, man," Loyal muttered. "We don't want to start anything if we can avoid it. This is where we're meant to hook up with Damian. We need to stay calm."

The fellow shook his floppy hair out of his eyes and charged.

From the corner of his eye, Loyal saw the two other men in the bar slowly get to their feet from the bench at their table across the room, their attention pinned to the anticipated action. He didn't know if they intended to join the fight or simply watch, but he dared not wait to find out.

He jumped to his feet. As the first man

approached at a run, he stepped into position, the fighting arts training with his cousin Abe Farmer a decided advantage in this type of situation. But he was too late. As he swiftly threw a kick and nailed their attacker in the chest with the heel of his boot, Adoni was knocked sideways in his chair and ended up on the floor, panting for breath and face florid. The attacker went down like a rock and lay still.

The barkeep stood frozen for a moment, then waving his other customers away he knelt to see if the guy was still breathing. Apparently he was, because he gave a nod, grabbed the body by the heels and dragged it across the grimy floor into the back room. He reappeared shortly. "It looks like he'll live," he said curtly, "But I told you, no roughhousing."

"I didn't start a thing." Loyal grinned, heaving a breath as the adrenaline roared through his body. "Just took care of the problem for you."

The barkeep gave a resigned shake of his head and stepped back behind the bar as Loyal turned to find Adoni struggling to his feet. Offering his hand, he yanked him up. "There you go. Luckily the ale didn't spill."

Adoni gave a grunt and brushed dust off his jacket. "I wanted to give him a good whacking."

"Yeah." Loyal settled onto the bench and took a fortifying swallow of ale. "I know, but you're not ready. Won't be long though. I saw your last training session with Abe's men. You've gained a lot of ground."

His assistant gave him a crooked grin.

Just then the barkeep thumped his fist heavily on the plank in front of him as he stared at the doorway to the bar. "By the dogs of hell, what now?" he demanded hoarsely, his face a dull red.

Chapter Two

Loyal glanced up, expecting Damian Stuke had arrived. Instead, three figures came through the door. They stood in silhouette, the filtering sunlight falling obliquely across their forms. The first was a woman, slender, no more than twenty, with pale skin. Her dark blonde, slightly curly hair lay on her shoulders like a soft shawl. One side was pinned back with a jewelled comb, and an earring of rare amethyst and abalone swung on a gold link from her delicate earlobe. Her robe was old-fashioned, of a style Loyal had often seen around Adar Silva showing the lingering influence of the Old Empire. The stand-up collar was clipped closed at the throat, and embroidery and glitters decorated the sleeves and down the front panels—a very formal and expensive garment.

Emperor Aqatain had his headquarters just south

of here before the Last War sent him into retreat through the northern hills. Empire clothing was distinctive and many still clung to the old styles, robes and belted jackets with the same stand-up collars and wide lapels.

But even more startling, the woman wore trousers beneath the robe. He'd seen women in trousers before, loose three-quarter length garments worn as they toiled in the fields of some farm, but never pants tailored to fit a female shape and paired with a dress robe. Certainly never in public. Loyal stared, then belatedly glanced toward the barkeep whose face had turned a strange shade of puce.

The two young men who accompanied her stopped near the door as if to stand guard. There was a rising murmur of voices as the men at the far table took in the strange sight.

The barkeep blanched. "What are you doing? You can't come in here," he stuttered, waving his hand at her as if to shoo a chicken back through the doorway.

Ignoring him, she raised her head and pasted an imperious, if nervous, smile on her face as she glanced around the room. "I'm looking for Loyal the Hawker," she said.

Adoni gawked openly as Loyal rose slowly from his chair, confusion churning in his chest. *Was this a trick?* He'd never seen the girl before, was sure he would remember that arresting face. He had certainly never seen a woman in clothes like these. In addition, he had no contacts in the village. This place was only a waypoint, a dwelling to stay the night on his travels through the back country. *And how would she know his name?*

He strode forward. "I'm Loyal Hawker," he said, his throat tight. "What can I do for you?"

The colour high in her cheeks, she reached into the pocket of her robe and pulled out a folded onionskin. "My father sends his regards," she said in a low, modulated voice. "And he asks that you meet with him. I am come to take you there."

He smiled as amusement rose in his chest to replace the confusion. "Take me where? I don't even know your father."

She flushed darker as the young men behind her shifted uncomfortably, glowering at him. "He knows of you, sir," she said.

Loyal stared at her a moment, then stepped back, gesturing in the direction of the bench at their table. "Why don't you have a seat and I'll get you a drink." He marched to the bar and took another coin from his pocket. "An ale for the lady," he said.

The barkeep's skin was mottled, his mouth a grim straight line. "By all the gods," he said harshly. "No ladies in here. It's just not done."

Loyal nodded. "I understand. Yet today it has to be done, because I need to find out what this is about."

The fellow sighed mightily and poured a small half-drink in a bowl. "Make it quick," he said. "Do you think she can down that in a hurry?"

Loyal laughed. "Hard to know. I guess we'll soon see."

"If the owner of this place shows up, there'll be hell to pay," the fellow muttered, polishing the plank in slow heavy strokes with a grimy cloth. "Hell to pay. At any rate, he'll certainly hear about it, and then there'll be no end…" His voice trailed off mournfully.

Loyal walked back to the table to find Adoni openly staring at the woman as she nervously gazed at her hands folded around the letter. Her face was now pale as porcelain. He set the bowl in front of her and took a seat on the bench, noting the elusive scent of her perfume. "There you go, Ms. This is my assistant, Adoni," he said. "What is your name?"

"I am Angel Banderos," she said in a soft voice. "I don't have an ident, but my father is Gerwal Banderos. He is unable to travel at the moment and wishes to talk with you." She laid the onionskin envelope on the table in front of him and returned her hands to her lap.

Angel, a good name for a woman who looked like she did. The large eyes were arresting in that heart-shaped face, even when filled with anxiety. He glanced at Adoni who was still gawking.

Loyal picked up the missive, watching her anxious expression. He'd heard of Banderos, there weren't many who hadn't. At the end of the War, society was quick to break down around the remnants of Aqatain's headquarters. Many of the buildings at the edge of Sommerset had burned and the rest were left in shambles. Even this far from the centre of power, Aqatain's control had been destroyed and a cadre of strongmen stepped in to claim what had been abandoned. The far-flung areas had been taken over by a string of local warlords.

Banderos was one of those men. Rumour had it that he had forty sons and a slew of other relatives. Loyal had never heard of a daughter. There were also men tied to Banderos through loyalty or business dealings who strengthened his claim to the land. Although the number of sons seemed unlikely, Loyal knew the man ruled a large area with his strong influence. It was smart to be wary.

Chapter Three

Loyal took a sip of ale and contemplated his next move. The front of the envelope was addressed to him in a smooth almost feminine script that didn't look like anything a man would produce. He studied it a moment. It was highly unlikely Banderos had written this. On the other hand, no doubt he had a scribe to complete such tasks.

"Help yourself," he said to the girl, gesturing to the small bowl he'd set in front of her.

Adoni gently nudged it forward and she blessed him with a shy smile, turning his face bright red. She picked it up and took a sip.

Loyal wrestled with a feeling of irritation as he ripped the onionskin flap open. Adoni had done the courteous thing to encourage the girl, but unreasonably *he* wanted to be the man who eased her way. He shook his head at the unruly thought and extracted a fragile document from within.

Mr Hawker, it read in the same almost feminine script.

I would like to meet with you regarding a certain matter that I feel would be of much interest to us both. I am sending my daughter to escort you to my compound as I am temporarily unable to travel. Your safety is guaranteed by her bodyguards, my sons.

Please do not delay,
Gerwal Banderos

Loyal read it twice, realizing the missive did not add any further enlightenment to what the woman had already said. It didn't explain where Banderos wanted to meet, or for what purpose, and he was left with the puzzle of why he sent his daughter rather than one of his sons to waylay him in Hafford.

"Who is travelling with you, Ms?" he asked. "I'm unclear where we would meet with your father."

"Oh," she said. "My bodyguards are with me. I have enough additional mounts for everyone."

He glanced at the two young men stationed at the door. *Were there more men outside as well?* If so, the proposal to meet with Banderos looked more and more dangerous. The last thing he wanted was to take off into the forest, which is where he'd heard Banderos had his camp, surrounded by a horde of the man's sons.

Damian Stuke still had not arrived. Someone would have to wait for him if Loyal were to go off on this 'visit'. There was something downright fishy about the whole thing.

Leaning forward, he rested his forearms on the table and Angel Banderos immediately shrank back in alarm. He stifled a grin. "Tell me, Ms. Why is your father unable to travel at this time?"

She blinked rapidly then appeared to focus on her clasped fingers. "He's had a fall and is still recovering."

"Hmm." Loyal scrubbed his fingers down a long curly sideburn. "What did he injure?"

"His back," she said, gazing uncertainly into his eyes. He was momentarily distracted by the dark blue irises, but quickly pulled himself back to the issue at hand. She'd been sincere with the first comment and nervous with the second. So, that first comment was probably true and the second one pure fabrication. "How long ago did he fall? Was he badly hurt?"

Adoni gave him a glare for being so persistent with her, which he calmly ignored.

"Uh." She looked at Loyal for a moment as if caught, then glanced away and said, "Some time ago. The medics have all decreed that it will take longer to repair, even though his leg was put in splints after the accident."

"I see. Where are your headquarters?" he probed.

"South west. Not far, we came here in a few

hours." She wasn't looking at him now, but at the table top in front of her where her finger traced the pattern of the wood in a drop of ale. She seized her bowl, swallowing half the contents and was breathing hard when she put it down again. "That ale is quite strong," she murmured.

He laughed and she darted a glance his way. "Perhaps your people serve you watered ale. That would be usual for a woman."

"If they do, they should know better." Her mouth was set in a firm line, but the blush was back in her cheeks, a light pink that enticed him to put a fingertip there and gently stroke the soft-looking skin. He frowned at the thought, and she instantly looked worried. Was he really that frightening to be with?

Adoni downed the rest of his ale and slapped the tankard on the table. Angel watched, then tentatively finished her own, leaving nothing in the bowl. "I need to see your ident, Mr Hawker, and that of your man here."

"Well, let's see what we can do." Loyal stood and Adoni leaped to his feet, extending a hand to Angel to help her from the bench.

Loyal's frown became a scowl. Obviously, he hadn't been around women much due to the shortage of females in the population, because his own manners had all but disappeared.

He walked out through the half door onto the top step, turning to offer assistance to the young woman, but Adoni had gotten there first. He was holding that slender hand in his yellow one, smiling at her fondly with his sharpened teeth as he guided her to the bottom of the stone stairs. Her two guards followed.

Loyal huffed out an exasperated breath. *Adoni better back off if he knew what was good for him.* Then he stifled a laugh. The situation was amusing, if nothing else, and he was out of line to feel jealous because his assistant was being courteous to the woman.

He looked around. There were a dozen horses grazing off to the side of the track. Three young men waited patiently, none of them older than twenty. *This was her bodyguard?* The two who had followed her inside appeared to be even younger. Another man stood alone watching Angel. He was slightly older, tall with dusky skin, and thick through the chest. Perhaps he was the head of her guard.

Why would Banderos send out a posse of boys to protect his daughter? It seemed careless in the extreme, especially given the rumours of unrest that circulated around this area.

Major Dante Regiment of the Khandarken military had informed Loyal at their last meeting that reports of Empire forces organizing in Adar Silva had suddenly been flooding in. It was one of the main reasons Loyal was here in Hafford, on his way to explore the activity near Sommerset.

17

Chapter Four

Angel Banderos turned to leave the tavern, catching a heated glare from the barkeep out of the corner of her eye. It had been nerve-wracking to enter the bar in the first place. Rascal and Runt had both forbidden it. But how would she find Loyal the Hawker if she didn't step up and take those risks? She'd asked Nineteenth to set a watch in the village and when he'd sent word by runner that the Hawker had arrived, she put her plan in motion.

Heading for the door, she stalked past her brothers, chin high. Rascal raised his brows and grinned as he and Runt pivoted to follow down the steps in her wake. Damn him, he never did show respect when it was due, not even to their father. It infuriated Gerwal in the extreme, causing him to issue orders that were not well considered or in good judgement.

She took Adoni's yellow hand to descend the steps, thinking of the circumstances that had brought her to this point. When she'd tried to talk to Father about Mr Hawker, Fourth and Fifth had both been present. They'd just finished dinner, and First had already left for the barns, ostensibly to work with the horses.

But she knew better. The Clone shed was in the same direction and her brothers all took advantage of it. Even though the Clones weren't real women, they 'served the purpose' as First put it. Since the medical experiments during the Last War, fewer females were being born. Simultaneously, new diseases attacked women when they were most vulnerable, at puberty or after childbirth. As a result, the population had become badly skewed, causing a perpetual problem of too few women for the growing number of males. Clones were one answer that seemed to help fill the gap.

Angel had spent weeks formulating her plan regarding Hawker and waited impatiently for the right moment to approach Father. That moment never seemed to arrive. Several of her brothers were always present, dropping in to discuss strategy with Gerwal and his scribe, or staying for a meal before heading out on their rounds.

She didn't know who to seek for support of her proposal. First and Fourth were so full of themselves, she never got a word in before they talked right over her, each lobbying against the other for Father's attention. And their personalities were modelled after Gerwal. That meant no new ideas got past them. Stick to the old ways, that was their motto. As for Fifth, she didn't trust him at all, so would never approach him with anything this sensitive.

Her younger brother Rascal, in spite of his irritating teasing, was smart. She'd finally taken him for a walk above the compound and up the hill into the thin forest near the waterfall. When she told him her thoughts, he'd been speechless. For once. That made her smile, but it didn't last long.

"Are you crazy?" He glared around at the barren landscape, the chimneys of the manorhouse showing from below through a small gap in the trees.

"I'm not crazy. This makes sense," she argued. "You know we can't go on as we have. Father isn't really in control anymore, is he? No one is. And if First grabs the reins from him, we likely won't even survive."

Rascal scuffed his boot through the fir needles in the dirt before glancing back up. "There's more to you than I figured, little sister," he said, eyes narrowed. "I've been thinking along similar lines in terms of what our future looks like. But I didn't get that far with it. You have to assume the others are wrestling with the same questions. Who do you want to take the reins? What would be best for us?"

Her breath caught in her throat. "I don't know. But you're too young and Fourth and Fifth will never take orders from either of us. If someone doesn't step up, there's going to be a civil war in our own family. We have too many brothers, all of them vying for power. You know it's true."

Rascal shrugged, his mouth pursed. "Who else have you told about this?"

She shook her head. "No one. I've tried to bring up the subject with Father, but I'm always interrupted."

"Yah." He nodded. "That's the story of our lives."

They exchanged an ironic look.

"On the other hand, you can't tell him this," Rascal said. "He'll have your head."

She gave a nervous laugh. "I wasn't going to tell him my plan, I was just going to bring up the subject of how we're organized and the best way to manage going forward. I thought I'd talk about Loyal Hawker, his reputation for problem-solving, how he's clever and capable. Everyone knows he's a travelling seller, but there's a lot more to what he does. The rumours are rampant about his connections to people in very high places. He has power that we don't. I'm hoping Father will take heed. Often he'll indulge me when he won't listen to the younger sons."

Rascal grimaced. He was one of the younger sons who couldn't get his father's ear. "How do you know all this about Hawker?"

"From the infolink," she said. "He was interviewed on a program some time ago, and there has been follow-up information if you know where to look."

"Whose infolink? There's no link at the Banderos compound."

"I know that, silly. Why do you think I still go to Hafford for my 'lessons' with my tutor? Wyway lets me watch every week so I keep up to date on what's going on and he's trained me on how to search for information. We can't all live in a cave, even if First thinks that's the best way."

Rascal gave her a piercing look. "So—what's your plan?"

She grinned. "Does this mean you're in this with me?"

He gave a slow nod. "Runt will come along. You know that, it's just who he is. And Nineteenth will work with us. He admires you."

"Yes. But it won't be enough, will it? We need to think this through."

Chapter Five

Angel glanced behind her. Mr Hawker had pulled out a voicelink and was staring intently at the screen. They didn't have links at the Banderos compound, but she knew what they looked like.

Nineteenth caught her eye from where he stood with the others and jerked his head to indicate he needed to talk to her. She'd been pleased by his response to her scheme after she'd worked up the courage to tell him. Nineteenth was much more introspective than his older brothers. But she'd never really had a conversation with him about anything serious, until he'd overheard her talking with Runt about how to contact Loyal the Hawker.

She walked to the line of horses and pretended to pet the long nose of her steed. Nineteenth drew near and whispered in her ear. "Is he coming, or do we need to kidnap him?"

Turning her head, she glared. "We're not here to capture him. There will be no benefit if we bring him to the compound by force. We want his help, therefore we have to earn his trust."

Nineteenth frowned, his dark eyes narrowed. "Okay, I understand. That's strongman tactics and we're trying to carry out a diplomatic operation."

She smiled at his obstinate expression, and leaned to kiss his cheek. "Yes, that's what we're trying to do. Very good, Nineteenth. You're learning."

His cheeks went dusky and he slanted a small grin at her. "I'm not my older brothers, you know."

She patted his shoulder. "I know. Your mother might have been the smartest of all the wives. You're clever, you just keep it hidden most of the time."

When she turned, Loyal Hawker was standing on the bottom stone of the tavern steps, watching her. She lifted her chin, tugged her robe straight and headed toward him.

"We can't get to the Banderos compound today," she offered. "But we can stop at a waystation we have in the hills."

Hawker nodded slowly. "We aren't ready to leave. We've got a meeting scheduled for this village and some business to tend to. Let's walk down the strand and see if there's a place for a meal. We can talk there. I need more information."

She hesitated, looking around for her entourage. Rascal and Runt were engaged in a heated discussion with Nineteenth, and the hands were preparing the horses, tightening saddles and adjusting bridles. They obviously thought the group was about to mount up.

Well, it stood to reason she couldn't just march into some bar, deliver a letter that she'd written in her own script, and expect Loyal the Hawker to come with them to the Banderos compound. She bowed her head graciously, gestured to Rascal and turned toward the path leading into Hafford. She'd known he'd want more information. Her problem was, she didn't have any to give him.

~***~

Loyal followed Angel Banderos down the strand of the tiny village, wondering where this odd encounter would lead. It was strange to receive a contact like this without any notice from the leader of the Banderos stronghold—even stranger that the contact was made by a young woman leading a band of boys. Did Gerwal really operate this way?

It was certainly different from the modus operandi of other border lords he'd dealt with. For instance, DuSatoy of north Khandarken had been rough and ruthless, ruling his men and businesses with an iron fist. There were no women in his band of enforcers. Not that he'd survived. DuSatoy died at the hands of a competing strongman just after the election for Leader of Khandarken last year, an election in which he had taken part.

Angel stopped in front of a modest house and pointed to a picture of a decorative dish and bowl painted on the front plexi. "This place is decent," she said, turning to gaze at him hopefully. "I've eaten here before."

Loyal nodded and stepped forward to hold the door for her, beating Adoni by seconds, to his profound satisfaction.

The interior was steamy, smelling of aromatic baking. Seven or eight tables were placed around the front entry, with a small desk against the back wall, a worn scratchboard tacked above it. An elderly man left his seat behind the desk and lurched toward them, dragging one damaged leg. "How many, sir?" he rasped in a hoarse voice.

"Two tables," Loyal said. "One for the lady and myself. Another for these three gentlemen." He gestured toward Adoni and the two young guards. This way, he realized guiltily, he wouldn't have to compete with Adoni for Angel's attention. His assistant gave a small nod, indicating he would glean what information he could from the boys.

Angel paused, glanced at the guards, and followed the old gent to a table positioned in the front window. Loyal held the chair for her as her cheeks flushed a becoming pink. He took the chair across the narrow table.

"Do you see what you want?" he asked, gesturing to the scratchboard. The daily offerings included Mouldy Sablefish, Fried Olingito and Rarebit. Any of the selections would apparently be served with toasted pané, steamed vegetables and a hearty soup. He didn't know what Mouldy Sablefish might be, but made the quick decision not to find out on this particular occasion.

"The olingito, please," she said, looking up at the old man. "And a fine ale."

"Very good, Ms," he said, bowing low. "It's a pleasure to have you in our establishment. My best to your father, if you will."

She smiled warmly and folded her hands before her on the table.

"I'll have the same," Loyal said. She obviously knew this man, and more importantly he knew who she was. Hafford was probably one of a string of villages that survived solely because of protection from the Banderos organization.

He glanced around for the garderobe and finally spotted a doorway on the far wall with the appropriate symbol on the front. There should be some privacy there.

"Excuse me, Ms," he said. "I'll be right back." He headed for the door, pushing his way inside. Pulling out his infolink, he messaged Frank Maude's office. He needed information on Gerwal Banderos, and fast. He was up to his neck in unknowns here. Yet, it didn't make sense to turn his back on an opportunity to make contact with the man. Loyal might be able to get information that until now hadn't been readily available—about their compound, the size of their organization, and perhaps even take a measure of Gerwal himself. Logic said he should go, yet nothing here seemed logical.

Next he sent a note to Damian to find out where he was, just as a reply from Maude's office arrived indicating information would be sent shortly. He washed his hands and ran his fingers through his hair. A glance in the plexi mirror told him he needed a haircut, and perhaps a shave as well. He stifled a grin and exited the garderobe. It wasn't often on his seller travels that he bothered to notice how he looked. It was usually when he got back to Deep Creek that he took the time to freshen up before stepping out on the town or reporting to the Governor. Things were suddenly different since his encounter with Angel Banderos.

The cook had come from the kitchen with soup for their table and was smiling shyly at Angel while arranging the bowl in front of her. *Were these her relatives?* He would have thought so from the familiarity and fondness with which they welcomed her.

Loyal took his seat. "Mmmm, looks good," he said.

She smiled. "It will be, she's an excellent cook."

"What kind is it?" He leaned forward to sniff and caught a whiff of spice.

"Squash and celeriac," she said, ladling some onto her spoon and taking a sip. "Yes, very good. I love the food here."

He watched her mouth close around the spoon and had to look away a moment. "What's the food like at your house?" he said.

"Oh," she laughed. "It's all made for men. A lot of meat."

He smiled, wondering again if the tales of Gerwal's thirty or forty sons were true. Loyal finished his soup quickly and set his spoon in the empty bowl. He levelled a gaze at her. "Please tell me why your father wishes to meet with me."

The request obviously took her off guard, and her spoon wavered on the way to her mouth. She set it down and glanced at him sideways. "I'm not always taken into my father's confidence when he makes decisions," she tried.

"You wouldn't have been sent to fetch me if you didn't know what this was about."

She looked desperately about the small room. "I think he might like to get your advice."

He waited. "Advice about what?"

"Well, I'm not exactly sure. Perhaps how to handle the growing rumours of upheaval to the south of us."

His heart stopped in his chest, then began to beat again in an irregular rhythm. The upheaval in the south was exactly why he was here. *What did she know?*

"Why me?" he asked, watching her closely. "I'm just a travelling seller. I handle medical equipment and supplies, and talc products from my cousin's mine."

The exasperated look she gave him almost made him smile. She knew more about his activities than he'd imagined. *Where would she get that information way out here in the hinterland, and who would have given it to her?* Perhaps his cover wasn't as secure as he'd thought.

He'd better make contact with Dante Regiment and see what the military could unearth on that issue.

His infolink vibrated against his belt. Good, something back from Maude's office. He just needed a chance to read it. Then his voicelink dinged. Likely Damian Stuke replying to his message. Things were coming together. Now all he had to do was figure out what Banderos was after.

Chapter Six

Seated in the old barn that served as his headquarters, Emperor Carlton pushed his breakfast dishes aside and wiped his mouth with the cloth napkin his server had laid on the table. Smoothing his mustache with his fingers, he contemplated the next move in the campaign to recapture The Empire. His frustration at the lack of progress was rapidly mounting.

He and his men were isolated in a small province in western Legitamia, and every struggle to rebuild his territory had been blocked by opposition forces. He'd tried sending a troop across the border into Khandarken which had resulted in the capture of the village of Discovery. But his men were now surrounded there and immobilized. Any effort to enlarge the holding was met with more loss of life as the Khandarken army fought back.

An invasion of the northern Jirani plains controlled by the Moiselle tribe which abutted his small province had brought about a bomcart attack from the enemy. The resulting carnage had decimated his troops and he was having trouble raising a suitable number of dispossessed out of the hills to rebuild his army. General Elkon's death in the last battle had been a shattering blow to the leadership of his organization.

"Lanser," he shouted. There was a stirring at the back of the barn and footsteps approached.

Judson Lanser was his Advisor and strongest supporter in this frustrating battle to seize back the Empire. If only his Counsellors were as enthusiastic and committed.

Lanser approached his table, adjusted his robe and bowed. "Good morning, Emperor. How can I help you?"

"Have a seat." Satisfaction settled in his gut. He couldn't wait for the world to recognize him as Emperor, as his father had been before him. But even Lanser's small acknowledgement was a comfort. He gestured to a chair on the other side of the table and waved to the server for another bowl of spice caf tea.

Judson Lanser was an older man with iron grey hair brushed straight back from his angular weathered face. His posture was ramrod straight and his expression fierce. He'd had Carlton's back since Emperor Aqatain's death, never faltering in his efforts to restore to the son what had been lost by the father.

Carlton tugged on a sideburn. "We need to get moving on our new plan." This felt right. Certainty and conviction solidified in his chest. Yes, they'd made several attempts to enlarge their holdings, with very limited success. But the new strategy seemed solid from every angle. How could he regain an empire if he fought from the rear? Best to step forward and get out in front.

"I agree, Emperor. Is Major Paynter the man to lead our troops?" Judson set his jaw in a stubborn line.

"Good question." With General Elkon killed in battle, Carlton had been foundering for a replacement, and Paynter stepped up to take control in the midst of the fight. "It isn't his fault we lost the Moiselle territory."

Lanser shrugged. "True. He won the first battles. It was the Khandarken bomcarts that defeated us."

"Yah, but with this new plan, it isn't likely they'll use their bomcarts." He grinned. If they were to be successful, they'd need all the help they could get and support had already been offered from the south. Once the call went out, even more supporters were bound to step forward. Carlton wasn't the only one longing for the restoration of the Empire. There had been a lot of prestige and privilege connected to Aqatain's court. Many would like to see a return to that former glory.

"How do we begin?" he asked. "How to extend the invitation, search out those who will work with us?" He brushed his mustache with a finger again. "We'd better get the Counsellors in here before we make any firm decisions."

"Yes, Emperor. I'll round them up. I think they're out on a hunt but should be back shortly." He tapped the table top with a long yellow fingernail. "On the other hand, it's not always beneficial to give them the opportunity to stall our efforts."

Carlton laughed. The Counsellors were certainly cautious. "Are you prepared to make a trip south to investigate further? Your sister should be pleased to see you." Jessalyn Lanser lived in Sommerset, Adar Silva, where Aqatain had established his headquarters years ago. Many of the elite still resided there.

Judson frowned. "You know she won't support this. I'll certainly not discuss it with her."

He nodded. "I understand. And given her son, Cownden Lanser, is now the Leader of Khandarken, we don't want that information to leak out at this point. But once we succeed, she'll be looking to you to shield her from the repercussions of our occupation. You know that."

Lanser's eyes gleamed. "Yes, no denying she's my sister. And given that, it makes it even more unlikely Cownden would allow the Khandarken bomcarts to be let loose over Sommerset. She might be our main source of protection."

Carlton nodded. He'd already thought of that. It wouldn't be their only protection, but every little bit helped. "Let's get Paynter in here. We have to send out a call for more dispossessed. We need time to recruit and train before putting things into play."

"I'll call him now." Judson rose to his feet, clipping his robe closed.

"One more thing, Advisor." Carlton gritted his teeth in frustration. "I need that woman gone."

When Judson Lanser had been sent to the Penrhy tribe to negotiate a deal, he'd ended up in their prison, along with his scribe and guards. It had been Maa, from the Sanctuary in north Khandarken, who had rescued him. She was the only reason he'd been able to return to Carlton's encampment. Maa had been a major supporter of the Old Empire in Sommerset, a powerful figure with prestige among the leaders.

Lanser sat back down and stared out the open door for a moment as if distracted by the sight of the troops working in formation in the yard. "I see." He turned his head and looked Carlton in the eye. "She single-handedly got me out of that Jirani jail."

"I know, I know." He pressed his lips together. The whole series of events drove him crazy when he thought about it and invaded his sleep with nightmares of betrayal. "Everything went wrong. The Penrhy prince should never have married Chinata. She was to be your bride, Lanser. My sister was not to be used for someone else's gain. I swear to right that wrong as soon as possible." He surged to his feet as anger flooded his chest. Both his siblings had turned their backs on him. His brother Cownden Lanser ignored Carlton's offer to work together for a new empire. Instead he became Leader of the country of Khandarken. His sister Chinata walked past her betrothal to his Advisor Judson Lanser and married into the Penrhy tribe of Jiran instead.

"We can't fix it right now," he muttered. "But Maa has to go. I don't trust her. I know she was close to my father." His neck got hot. Maa had been his father's mistress, causing his mother no end of grief. It still gnawed at him. "But what her intentions are with regard to our plans are unknown. She's a talented mesmerist."

Lanser tried to hide his smile, but Carlton saw it and felt another flare of anger. This was his province, by all the gods, even if it was headquartered in someone else's barn. He'd have the final say in how it was run.

"Send her back to the Sanctuary," he snarled. "It's what she wants, it's where she belongs. When you go south, she leaves too."

Lanser bowed in acknowledgement and strode through the open door.

Chapter Seven

Gerwal Banderos shifted his legs in an attempt to ease the pain. This pallet was new, covered with sheep's wool and stitched up by one of the Clones. It was an improvement over the last one, but didn't stop the agony in his lower back. A fall from his horse had permanently injured his spine. The question of how it happened still plagued his mind.

When had he last tumbled from the saddle? Possibly when he was a boy of five or six. He was raised on a horse, half the time with no saddle at all. Moreover he had no memory of the event, which made it doubly difficult to unravel what had taken place.

He remembered starting out from the compound, his two sons First and Fourth with him and accompanied by four or five soldiers. They'd been heading toward the ruins, where the border station had been built.

It was a routine journey, one he'd made many times over the years to ensure the perimeter of his holding was secure. How could he be sure his orders were being carried out if he didn't see for himself? They had just climbed the last hill above the station when his horse must have reared.

The next thing he knew, he was laid out on a travois being dragged into the courtyard of the compound in front of the manorhouse. First dismounted and bellowed for help. Gerwal didn't remember much else, the pain had overwhelmed him almost instantly. There followed days of blackness with small windows of conscious agony. He realized that Angel was usually there when he woke. Some time later he knew his wife Willa was present, taking care of him. She stuffed phang into his mouth to chew to ease the discomfort. He'd never let his sons bring the stuff into the compound, but obviously someone had a source and he was suddenly damned grateful.

First and Fourth both claimed his horse had reared at the shriek of a mountain lion in the bush and he'd been thrown out of the saddle and straight down the hill onto the rocks below. But Angel had told him, after much hesitation, that she'd seen the injury to his horse. It's leg was broken and First had put the animal out of its misery. But not before his daughter saw the cut to its hindquarters—"like a knife blade, Father," she said. "Rascal looked at it and he agrees with me."

So, although he had a niggling suspicion about what had occurred, there were no real answers to his questions.

Glancing through the wide plexi, he studied the garden that had been cultivated across the front of the manorhouse by his first wife. From where he lay on the rubber plastic lounge, he could see the neglected shrubs and the field beyond where Fifth was organizing a dozen men to conduct target practice. The garden had never looked so forlorn. Some of his wives had taken an interest in it but since Baby's birth and his last wife's death, nothing had been done to it. The flowers had given up, overwhelmed by an avalanche of weeds. All that was left were a few shrubs that struggled to bloom in spring. It was too early yet for the blossoms to appear.

His attention was drawn back to Fifth in the distance as rayguns were distributed to the men and targets set up at the bottom of the field. Fifth had never been the brightest kid and it certainly showed now. The men were in a ragged line and began firing before the service boy had attached the last target to the post. The boy immediately dove for cover as a strong blast of white energy tore perilously close to the spot where he'd been standing a split second before.

Gerwal shook his head in disgust. Where was Fourth, and why wasn't First making sure the practice was properly organized? Ammunition was expensive, his men didn't need to waste it on a badly run exercise. Picking up his horn, he blew a blast. He didn't have long to wait.

First appeared, running from the barns and coming up the front steps. He burst into the house, stopping short when he saw Gerwal sitting upright in his lounge, the sliders locked in position. "By the dogs of hell." His eyes widened and he approached slowly. "How are you feeling, Father? Are you on the mend?." He looked almost disappointed.

Gerwal gritted his teeth. Some of his sons were vying heavily for positions in the organization, which was only natural. It had become more obvious over the last few years, triggered partly by the fact they were getting older and tired of taking orders from him, but mainly because his health was obviously failing. The weaker he got, the more disruptive the competition became.

First was the strongest son, always had been. But ruthless. Ruthless was good in a border warlord—but it needed to be paired with a keen intellect and good judgement. *What to do?* A decision should be made, and soon, to prevent open warfare among his sons.

Fifth was capable enough, but sly. Gerwal watched him like a hawk and mentally questioned everything the man reported. Some of the sons were simply not interested, Fourth included, and the younger ones would never gain the respect needed to take over.

He levelled a look at First. "Where have you been? Fifth is out there wasting ammunition and nearly killed one of the boys setting up the targets."

First backed up a step and glanced toward the plexi. "I was just working on the new map of our holdings, based on the last reports from the border guards."

Gerwal scoffed. "You were in the Clone shed. You think I don't know what goes on? Get out there and find yourself a wife. We need some new blood in this place."

He watched his son's face grow dark. First was touchy about the subject.

"There aren't any women to be had."

He gave a snort. "I got another wife a few years ago, nothing too hard about that." After Baby's mother died, Gerwal had ordered a woman from the far east for his next wife. She'd arrived when the child was one. She'd been more of a caretaker than a consort for him, but he wasn't going to complain. He was old, and his interest had moved on to other things. Like how to organize the Banderos stronghold when his sons couldn't even get along.

He realized that First was going to take over from him if he didn't step in to prevent it, and that was likely the best answer anyway. He may not always do things Gerwal's way, but he was strong and the others would probably follow without too much complaint. That's how the system worked.

"Where is everyone?" he complained.

First gave him a penetrating look, as if he was losing his memory.

He barked a laugh. "I know Ninth is in the office with the scribe. Fifteenth and Sixteenth were just here reporting on their rounds at the border points and left this morning. I mean the rest. Where are they?"

First glanced toward the doorway as the cook came through with a tray of bowls to set the dining table for the midday meal. "Angel has gone to Hafford for her lessons," he said, "and Nineteenth went with her. Rascal and Runt too. Should be back tomorrow. Baby's probably in the schoolroom. Weisner doesn't let him slack off. He's certainly the strictest tutor you've ever hired."

Gerwal shrugged. "Someone needs to get a good education." First had been very tough to discipline as a youth and had little interest in learning to read. "What field are the herds in? Eleventh and Twelfth must have checked in."

First gave him a guarded look as if it were a trick question. It was, in a way. He liked to know what was going on in all corners of the place—were there attacks on the sheep by the mountain lions that roamed the hills, had the horses been shod for the year, how was their supply of grain lasting, what did the border guards find on their rounds? First would never keep a handle on all the workings of the establishment if he didn't look past training the army to the other details that kept the organization going. Even if he delegated it, he needed to pay attention.

"I think they're in the east past the ruins."

Gerwal nodded. This manorhouse had been

constructed on the ruins of a castle built eons ago by some foreign occupant of the area. The foundations were solid and had made it possible to build the manorhouse high to ensure good sightlines in all directions. As Gerwal gained territory after the Last War, he'd found a second structure, at that time surrounded by forest. He and his men had cleared the land, there was a pasture there now that rivalled the one he'd already had. In those days he was away from the manorhouse as often as he was home. It was a wonder he had so many sons because the work…

His thoughts were interrupted by First who was pulling out a chair at the dining table. "The meal is ready, Father. Do you want help to sit up here?"

Gerwal gritted his teeth. There was a sly look on his son's face that only infuriated him further. He waved his arm. "Go and fetch Fifth. I want to talk to him about that botched target practice."

First scowled and marched to the door.

Gerwal pressed the bell and his wife entered to help him from the rubber plastic lounge and into the chair at the head of the table.

Chapter Eight

The old man served two bowls of spice caf tea to Loyal's table and removed the empty dishes. The olinguito had been good, Loyal would seek out this place to have a meal on his journey the next time he came through. Then the cook arrived with plates of fruit compote and baked sweet biscuits. He smiled at the pleased expression on Angel's face. *Perhaps these were her favourites.*

The biscuits were delicious, light and flaky, and went well with the compote. He took a few bites and watched Angel sip her tea. "How many brothers do you have?" he asked idly. Must be quite a few, the rumours were certainly persistent.

She startled. "Do you mean over all?"

He shrugged. "Of course. How many brothers over all." He smiled to himself at the question.

"Well, some have died," she replied.

"Oh, I see. I'm sorry."

She counted on her fingers. "There were twenty-seven."

He paused. That was a lot, counting her that would make twenty-eight children, although she'd said some of them were dead. *What kind of a man was Gerwal Banderos?*

"How many have died, Angel?" he asked gently.

She stared into his eyes. "There was Second. He died after a fall from the top of the wall in the west pasture when he was seven."

He paused to think about that. "Second? His name was Second?"

She nodded, the gesture gracious. "First is the oldest, of course. Third died as an infant. I think he was only a few days old. His mother died giving birth to Fourth. I didn't know any of them, of course. It was well before my time. Sixteenth died in a fight." She hesitated as if it was difficult to talk about.

"I see." Perhaps he shouldn't pursue this. It seemed to upset her, which wasn't surprising. Just then his voicelink beeped and he pulled it from the halter on his belt. Damian Stuke had arrived in the village.

"I must leave for a moment. Take your time finishing your meal. Adoni can bring you when you are ready." He took another biscuit from the plate and stopped to deal with the old man at the desk. The meal was surprisingly inexpensive and he paid with a chit. The old fellow stared at it for a long time before

45

putting it in the desk drawer.

"Do you know how to cash it?" Loyal asked. "I'm sorry I don't have enough coin on me to pay you."

"This is fine. We get to the bank every few months and can trade it in then."

Every few months? Strange way to conduct business. Why not use an infolink? He didn't have time to contemplate it further as he stepped out the door onto the strand.

Damián Stuke stood by their transport, clad in civilian clothing, his aerial scooter parked behind the trailer. He was looking up and down the line of small buildings. When he spotted Loyal, he grinned and gave a nod, setting off in his direction.

"Loyal," he called. "There you are. Adoni here too?"

"Yah, in the eatery. How was the trip."

Stuke shook his hand in a strong grip. "The trip was fine, no serious encounters. You know things might be a bit unruly because of the battle with Carlton in north Jiran. But it seems pretty calm around here."

"Huh." Loyal glanced back at the restaurant plexi. "There's been a complication. I'll explain." He pulled Damian aside and told him about the missive from Gerwal Banderos.

Damian blinked a few times and glanced sideways at the young men guarding the horses as they grazed at the side of the strand. "There are quite a few animals here. How many in their party?"

"It looks like seven, with the girl. But there's no telling who's waiting to attack once we enter the forest."

"Yah." Stuke rubbed his chin. "That's my thought. How many are concealed in the trees? Have we got arms? I just have an old-fashioned pistol with me at the moment, not much ammunition."

Loyal laughed. He'd always liked Stuke, right from the moment he met him, and the man had just reinforced it. Damian was supposed to be here to work with him in Adar Silva. This wasn't his fight, but Stuke was committed to the expedition as soon as he heard what was going on.

"We have some weapons in the transport, and with Adoni, we're three."

"That should do it," Stuke declared. "If Banderos was planning to capture you, he would have stopped your transport in a lonely spot and done it there, surely?"

Loyal nodded. "That's my opinion. It's just an odd way to do it, sending his young daughter and a group of boys."

"Seems inexperienced." Stuke stroked a sideburn as he thought about it. "Unusual, from what I've heard about him. Never met the man."

"No, nor I." He glanced down to pry his infolink out of the clip. "Let's see what Maude's office has been able to scrape together." The men bent their heads over the funnel as Loyal slowly fed the information through.

"He's been out here a long time, since before the end of the Last War," observed Stuke as he read.

Loyal grunted. "Looks like he has quite a force at his disposal. Are these numbers accurate? A hundred men, forty dispossessed as backup." He glanced up. "The daughter says there were twenty-seven sons. A few have died."

Stuke stared. "Seriously? That's a lot of children. How many wives at a time, do you think? And where did he get them, given the shortage of women?"

Loyal laughed. "Well, you found yourself a wife, no problem. And from what I hear, you weren't even looking to get married at the time."

Stuke's cheeks flushed a dark red as he grinned. "Sometimes these things take you by surprise."

He chuckled. "So I hear. Hasn't happened to me, though." He glanced back at the infolink. "These holographs show the Banderos compound isn't in a forest at all. It looks cleared and some of it is being farmed."

"Yah, pretty organized. The village of Hafford is probably part of it, as is the next one along here." Stuke gestured ahead of them to where the strand petered out to become a cart path leading south through the forest. "So, is it decided? We let ourselves be escorted into the Banderos compound? It kind of fits with why we're here."

"Yah." Loyal acknowledged Adoni with a nod, as he walked toward them. His assistant was followed by Angel Banderos and her two guards.

"I see what you mean," Stuke said out of the corner of his mouth. "Her guards are pretty young. But then, so is she." He stared. "I'd follow her if she asked me. Look at those trousers," he muttered.

"Yah. You're married, you hound."

Stuke took a deep breath and gave a grin. "But I'm not dead."

Chapter Nine

Angel took Mr Stuke's hand as he bowed low over her wrist. "Pleased to meet you, Mr Stuke," she said. She gestured to the others. "This is my brother Nineteenth, and these are Rascal and Runt."

Stuke exchange a surprised look with Loyal the Hawker, who seemed to wear an amused expression whenever he looked her way. Well, she would just ignore it for now. She had a plan and the Hawker was part of it. She hoped something positive would come out of all this effort. If not, she'd have to work up a different scheme, because someone had to step in to help make a change in the family enterprise. Rascal gave her a wink and she took comfort from that small token of support.

"Nineteenth, which of these animals are for our

guests?"

Her brother stepped forward and began to organize the group. Angel mounted her horse and Runt and Rascal followed suit, ranging themselves on either side of her. She grimaced. They'd talked about how best to do this. Their job was to act as her guards but they didn't have to go overboard. On the other hand, she had no knowledge of Adoni, the Hawker's assistant, and Mr Stuke was an unexpected complication. Perhaps it was wise to keep her guard close, even if Runt was only thirteen.

"I think we should take the northern route," she said to Nineteenth. "We can't reach the compound tonight but we'll stay at the border station there and get home tomorrow."

Her brother nodded. "I'll send Scamp ahead with word that we've got people coming. They'll at least prepare a meal for us." He mounted his steed and rode over to speak to the small boys at the rear. Soon one of them dug his heels into his horse's ribs and raced down the track through the trees and up the hill on the far side.

Loyal sent Adoni back to the bar with instructions for them to secure his cart and supplies, then watched Angel's activity with interest before coming up alongside her. "Sending messages home?" he asked.

"Yes," she smiled. "We won't reach Banderos manorhouse tonight, so we're making sure there will be a meal waiting for us at the border camp." And there was no way she was sending a warning message to Father, not if it meant alerting First to what she was up to.

"I see." He gazed long at the now empty trail. "Okay, I guess we had better get started. Is Nineteenth the leader?"

Nineteenth gave a short nod and urged his horse out in front, taking the wide trail into the thin forest ahead of them. Angel and her guard followed, then Loyal and Stuke. Adoni came next and the two young service boys rode at the rear, leading the spare horses.

~***~

The trees soon gave way to an open plain undulating ahead of them as far as the eye could see. Loyal noticed Angel sat the saddle well, as if she did a lot of riding. Perhaps they didn't have a transport or wagon or any other method of travel. It was unusual for a woman to be so practiced on a steed. Even the Jiranis used wagons for their women and children. It was the men who rode horse.

"What do you think Nineteenth means?" muttered Damian beside him. "Could he be number nineteen in twenty of a half troop in the Banderos organization?"

They both grinned in disbelief as Loyal shook his head. "It's possible, but the girl just told me she has brothers named First and Second, so perhaps he's related to her. He doesn't look like Angel, with his dusky skin and dark eyes. Is he from the west?"

Stuke nodded. "From my experience, I'd say so. Might be where Banderos gets a lot of his men, there and among the dispossessed. Let's face it, unlike some countries, Adar Silva has had no use for the men damaged by the War. I was one of those men." He grimaced. "I'm sure any of them would be glad of a chance at a job, food and clothing."

"Yah. And living with a strongman, you don't have to follow society's rules, all the little niceties you've forgotten and everyone else expects you to observe."

Stuke nodded. "I remember feeling that way," he said after a moment. "It was Cownden who saved me, he and Frank Maude."

Loyal remained silent. He'd never belonged to Khandarken society, himself. Raised on the edge of the Western Territory in a tiny village, by a mother embittered by life and a father who deserted them, he hadn't had time to figure out those social rules that others came by naturally. It was his cousins, Abe and Beth Farmer, who had extended the welcoming hand after Jade Hawker, his father, died. He owed them everything, even the introduction to Governor Maude for his current 'second' job.

"Do we know where we're going?" Stuke said. "I don't like heading off into the wilderness without a map."

Loyal laughed. "I think so. I had a look at the chart earlier." He pulled out his infolink and tapped the funnel as he nudged his horse closer to his friend. "This is what we know about the Banderos territory."

Stuke studied it a moment. "Bigger than I thought," he muttered. "Runs north nearly to the border of the Shafoneur tribe in Jiran—and further west than Adar Silva territory. Kind of a no-man's-land between the two countries."

"Seems so. We'll know more when we get there. I estimate we'll be stopping here." Loyal pointed to a spot on the chart. "There seems to be a camp of some kind." He spurred his horse forward. "Angel," he said. "Have a look at this map and tell me if I'm right."

The girl halted and her two guards followed suit. She took the infolink and stared at it a moment. Loyal pointed, and she squinted her eyes to focus. "You tap the funnel," he said. "That way the map will open up."

She tapped. "Oh, my. Look at that. Why, that's a map of our holdings! Rascal, come and see." The two boys shifted closer and soon three heads were hanging over the tiny screen trying to decipher what they were seeing.

Nineteenth halted and looked back. "What's wrong?" he called.

"Nothing," Angel replied sweetly. "Come and see this, Nineteenth. You'll be ever so surprised."

Loyal gave Stuke a quick glance and pressed his mount into the mix. "I just want to know where we're stopping for the night. I figure it's this spot, where the buildings are grouped at the edge of the river." He indicated it with the tip of his finger and Angel glanced up at him.

"I'm not sure," she said. "Let me look, I've just never seen it shown quite like this before. We have our own maps, of course, but they are somewhat different…" Her voice trailed off as she shifted the holograph up and down. "My goodness. Where did you get this?"

Loyal felt a smile hovering on his mouth and tried to repress it. "The Governor of the Southern Territory of Khandarken sent it to me," he said. "His office has a lot of data on our whole country and surrounding areas. For protection, you understand. We need to know what our neighbours are doing."

Nineteenth gave him a glare and glanced at Angel. "It looks good, right enough," he muttered. "We'll be halfway to the compound by nightfall, should reach the river and the border station in good time tonight."

"Yes, I know," Angel said. "It's just so exciting to see it laid out like this. First draws most of our maps and they're –well they don't have as much detail." She and Nineteenth exchanged a meaningful look.

"Great. Thanks for the information." Loyal closed the infolink and hooked it on his harness. "So we're going straight west, a bit to the south perhaps."

"Straight west, yah," Nineteenth grunted. "Then north. Tomorrow it's south west to reach the compound. Let's get moving." He urged his horse around and started again down the meandering trail, the others falling into line.

"Did you hear that?" Stuke muttered in his ear. "First draws the maps. Does no one have a name in this organization?"

Loyal pursed his lips to hide a smile. Angel had a

name, and it suited her rather well. He'd see about the others when they finally arrived.

Chapter Ten

Angel was relieved when Nineteenth finally called a halt. She was used to riding to Hafford and back for her lessons but usually took a shorter, less strenuous route. They dismounted in the shade on a wide stretch of trail. Pulling a bottle of water and a drinking bowl from her saddle bag, she stood with her back to the group until she caught her breath. No point in showing any weakness, nothing these men could use against her.

The water was cool, tasting of lemon, and she drank her fill. Nineteenth approached and she glanced at her older brother. "Where's First today?" she asked.

Nineteenth nodded his understanding of the question. "He's at the manorhouse. You were wise to suggest a longer route and delay our arrival. This way if we stay at the border camp, we can get to know these men a bit before we introduce the Hawker to Father. First is scheduled to leave for the South Station first thing tomorrow morning. He's making contact with Olaf Nazur. There are rumours among the men that he wants to make some kind of deal with them."

The Nazur land lay to the west of the Banderos holdings and the two families had been unreliable allies as the armies shifted back and forth during the final stages of the Last War. Since peace had been declared more than ten years ago, they'd co-existed in an informal, yet uneasy arrangement.

Alarm sent a shot of adrenaline to her limbs at this news. "Father already has an arrangement with him. Why would First be trying to change it?"

"Don't know. 'Course he's getting on in years, like Father. Maybe he's changed his mind about their deal."

She nodded. "All the more reason to make something happen before First cements a different deal and it's taken out of our hands entirely."

Nineteenth's expression was grim. "First isn't going to like it."

"I know. But if he's off making nice with Olaf Nazur, he isn't going to know about it until we've had a chance to meet with Father and hopefully get him onside."

Her brother shrugged. "Not likely."

She knew that. This was a risky move on her part, and Father was one stubborn man.

They were soon back in the saddle and the sun was low in the sky as the border station came into view. The patrol was in the yard, five men on horseback arriving from the west. Nineteenth went forward to greet them.

The station had been built on the ruins of a structure from a different age, the rock work still solid. The Banderos men constructed their camp atop the mortared stone, allowing a view for a great distance in every direction. As they drew to a halt, one of the men was herding the grazing horses into a corral for the night.

Angel gathered the reins in one hand and was startled to find the Hawker standing beside her horse, his hand outstretched to assist her.

"Oh," she said, flustered. "I'm fine, I can manage to dismount without…"

He gave a slow smile. "It's my job as a gentleman to help a lady when I can."

"I see." She hesitated, then took his hand and swung out of the saddle. "Thank you." Her face grew hot and it was made worse when she spotted Rascal and Runt exchanging a sly grin.

Darn them, anyway. Just for that she handed her reins to Runt to take care of her horse for her and stalked into the station.

Fourteenth was seated at a table in the middle of the great room, filling out his daily report. He waved and rose from his bench. "There you are, little sister. I was expecting you any time now. Sup is ready when you are."

"Perfect," she said. "I'm hungry and I'm sure the others are, too."

Fourteenth narrowed his eyes. "How many are with you?"

She glanced behind and stepped forward to lower her voice. "Three strangers. Loyal the Hawker and his assistant, plus a friend of his named Stuke."

"I've heard of the Hawker. Why is he here?"

Angel hesitated. There were only a few who knew the whole story of her machinations and with every step she took it seemed she was forced to tell someone else. Soon it would become common knowledge. It was difficult to predict which side some of her brothers might take.

He frowned before she could speak. "Is this group here to meet with First at the manorhouse? Are you a messenger for our eldest brother? That would mean you're trying to form an alliance to support First's bid…." His mouth turned down. "I'm not going to back that, Angel."

She stared into his eyes. Fourteenth was a number of years older than her and had gone out on border patrol at an early age. She'd never formed a solid bond with him, or the other brothers who worked guarding the perimeters of their land.

She took a breath and made a quick decision. "I can't talk about it right now, but I will tell you." she said. "I promise."

He backed up a step, his gaze fixed on her face.

"Then what is it? Spit it out, Angel. You may be the favoured child, but you can't pull a fast one on me."

"Keep your voice down! I'm not the favoured child. Father doesn't hear a thing I say on any topic, because I'm female." She glanced behind her as the others strode through the door.

Fourteenth gave her a penetrating stare, then turned to greet the men. "Welcome to the northern border station," he said. "Sup is ready whenever you are. Have a seat at the table." He gathered his papers together and tucked them into a cubby in the far wall.

"Nineteenth, how are you? Rascal, Runt." He nodded to his brothers then openly stared at the strangers.

Angel performed the introductions and encouraged everyone to sit as the camp cook appeared with large bowls of elk stew, roasted vegetables and brown gravy. "Fourteenth has been captain of the border stations for a few years now," she teased. "He's used to taking control."

Fourteenth gave her an exasperated look and turned to the Hawker. "Loyal Hawker, I've heard your name. You come through the area once or twice a year."

Hawker nodded and shovelled in a mouthful of meat. "I do," he mumbled. "Been to Hafford a few times."

"What do you hawk?" he asked.

Loyal swallowed. "Chiefly medical supplies and equipment. Talc products from my cousin's mines in the Hawker Hills." He gave Fourteenth a keen look. "If you're the one in charge of the stations, you'd be the one to ask. We've heard rumours of unrest in north Adar Silva and around these parts. Are they true? I'm concerned about our safety as we travel." He shot a quick glance at Stuke, then concentrated on his dinner.

Fourteenth shrugged. "There are always rumours."

"I know. These just seem more persistent."

Nineteenth spoke up. "We've seen signs of activity in the south, coming from the other side of the Adar Silva border. Not sure what it means or how many are involved." He ignored Fourteenth's glare. "It's common knowledge around these parts," he said. "But whether these men intend to take action or are just another threat to our stability is another matter. We won't know until the fighting starts."

Hawker nodded.

"Meanwhile," he added, "some of our workers, mostly dispossessed, tell us they are being recruited by border patrols. They've been offered food and clothing, perhaps weapons, in exchange for their commitment to work."

Fourteenth nodded in defeat. "We've lost a few men from the stations, but not many. First runs the military and we haven't heard yet what it's like out there. Fifteenth left this morning with a small troop to take a reckoning around the perimeter. The last thing we need is to find a herd of sheep untended somewhere because the workers ran off without letting us know."

Angel felt the blood leave her head. *Another war?* If so, her plan might have come too late to make a difference. First would seize control, no matter Father's opinion, and there wouldn't be much any of them could do to stop him.

Chapter Eleven

The guests were settled for the night in the loft upstairs where the border guards slept on pallets laid out on the floor. Angel locked the door to the garderobe and stripped off her clothes. She was sticky with perspiration from the day's hard ride. Shuffling out of her pants, she threw them on the hook beside the robe. Then she filled the basin and began to wash. The water was cool as she sluiced it over her face and down her arms. So much better.

The evening had gone well. Hawker had definitely been trying to pry information out of them, but it was knowledge that perhaps would help their cause when they finally got him to sit down with Gerwal Banderos. If others knew there was unrest in the south and a possible uprising in the near future, would Hawker take their talk more seriously? Would Father? She added the thought to her slowly building mental arsenal of issues to deal with. One way or another, they had to sort out the leadership of the Banderos organization before First sorted it for them.

When she emerged dressed in a fresh house robe, Fourteenth was waiting. "Join me in the office," he gritted. "I'm going to fetch Nineteenth, because I need to know what's going on."

"Fine," she said and flounced off down the hall. Fourteenth had always been such a tyrant, ordering her around. She stifled a laugh. Nothing annoyed him more than her immediate compliance with his demands.

Soon the three of them were seated around the old carved wooden desk, a remnant they'd found when building the station. The wood was engraved in intricate patterns around the edge of the smooth top and down the front panel of each drawer. It had become warped with time, but Fourteenth added a support to one of the legs to keep it from wobbling.

"Okay." Fourteenth laid his hands flat on the desktop. "What's going on?"

Nineteenth nodded at Angel and sat back to watch.

Angel pursed her lips. "You don't have to be so demanding. I told you I'd explain."

His frown grew darker. "So explain."

"Well, Father's health is not good."

They all exchanged a knowing look and then Fourteenth stared at her. "Yah, so?"

"First wants to lead the family. He's made that

very clear. Not everyone feels he's the best candidate. But if we don't come up with a different solution, we could have a war within our ranks. Fourth and Fifth will side with him, perhaps some of the others will too. It'll rip the family apart."

Fourteenth thought about that for less than a minute. "That's not new information," he said. "First has been working solely with that in mind for years."

"Yes, but I think he's ramping up. Father is nervous and physically weaker. Fourth and Fifth jump when First calls them. Something's changed within that group."

Fourteenth pursed his lips and rose to pace across the room. Then he sat back in his chair. "I've known for some time that First can't be trusted."

Angel felt a clenching in her stomach. "Not trusted how? He does everything Father asks of him."

Her brother flexed his shoulders, gazing out the window at the darkness beyond. "I was there when Sixteenth died."

Nineteenth leaned forward, his eyes pinned to Fourteenth's face, but didn't speak.

Angel stared at him. "I know what happened. He and First were having a fight. Sixteenth swung at him and missed. He fell against the stone pillar by the front door and broke his skull. It was so sad."

Fourteenth gave her a stern look. "Sixteenth didn't swing and miss. He shouted something at First. I was too far away to hear what it was. Then he turned to walk away. First hit him on the back of the head with a club, and he fell against the stone pillar. At least that much was true. There was blood on the pillar."

She put her hand over her mouth, but even so a small helpless cry escaped. "No, no, no." It was a whispered entreaty. She gazed at him through her tears. "He wouldn't."

Fourteenth raised his hands in a helpless gesture and let them fall. "He would. And he did."

Nineteenth released a deep breath that he'd been holding. "I thought something like that, but didn't have any proof. It's what it looked like—his head bashed from behind."

There was silence in the room.

"Does Father know?" she asked cautiously.

Both men shrugged. "Doubtful," Nineteenth said. "He was away at the time, remember, negotiating an agreement with Nazur. Sixteenth had been challenging everyone at that point, questioning decisions. Father left First in charge while he was off on his trip and Sixteenth got belligerent and demanding."

Angel waited.

"I think First saw him as a threat to his authority," Fourteenth said. "He couldn't put up with that."

She glanced at Nineteenth, who was watching her.

"He'll see you as the next threat, Angel, when you bring in some guy to talk about who's going to run the organization."

Fourteenth slowly turned his head toward her. "Is that what this is about?"

Angel gave a hesitant nod. "I wanted to ask for help from someone with important connections outside our family, who's knowledgeable and educated. He can talk to Father, maybe help organize the change of command."

He gave a slow nod as he stared at her. "You've got nerve."

Nineteenth snorted. "No news there," he muttered.

"But it just might work."

Angel looked back at him. "Will you support this?"

"Yah, you bet I will. I don't want the job, Fourth is an idiot and Fifth is a puppet . Are you in, Nineteenth?"

His brother nodded. "Yah, I support her. I've already bought in, and First is due to leave the compound early tomorrow morning. Gives us time to work with Father before he returns. Are you coming with us to the compound?"

Fourteenth grinned and gave a decisive nod.

Chapter Twelve

Now they were prisoners. The Emperor's men had captured five of the rebels, including the captain. Loyal squatted in the dirt beside the others, wondering what would happen next. One eye was swollen shut and his knee ached where he'd been kicked when he resisted in the fight to capture him. Some of the others weren't so lucky. The captain was bleeding badly from a wound in his side, which they'd bound tightly with a sash, using a wad of leaves for a compress to try to slow the loss of blood.

Would they all be shot? That's what he'd heard from the rumours that passed through the freedom fighters at the front. The Emperor's troops had orders to execute anyone they caught.

He tugged at the rope wrapped around his wrist and tied to the arm of the man on his left. Maybe his life was already over at fourteen. It had happened to many boys his age in this never-ending battle called the Last War, no reason his life would be any different.

He tensed when one of the soldiers came down the hill and stopped, dropping something heavy on the ground. It landed with a muffled thump. The man barely slowed, just marched on past, heading for the campfire around which the Empire troops had gathered for the night. Loyal was already certain of what he would see before he even turned his head. A young girl lay amid the leaves and dead grass, her arms flung wide from her body. He heard her above the erratic beat of his heart, just a sigh of breath in and out.

He shuffled forward on his haunches, tugging the others with him as he moved until he could finally reach her. She was still breathing. He felt for the thready pulse at her slender throat, the sound of her panting faint but steady. She was alive...

Loyal woke with a start, sweat standing out on his forehead. He used the cover to wipe his brow and down the sides of his face. He hadn't had that nightmare in a long time. Why now?

He rolled to his side and waited for his heart to

slow to a regular beat. Perhaps meeting Angel had triggered the memory. She was guarded by a group of boys in an area of roaming dispossessed amid the threat of military action. Could that have been what brought back the memory?

The girl was so young, sweet and innocent. He couldn't just leave her there …

~***~

Early next morning, Loyal heard a bell clanging below stairs. He turned his head to find Adoni already sitting up, pulling on his trousers. "Is that the breakfast bell, then?" he muttered, pushing his fingers back through snarled curls. He had been weeks on the trail and his hair was getting unruly.

His assistant grinned, his sharpened teeth glinting strangely in the low light. "Sounds like it," he said. "The men are stirring."

They glanced across the floor of the loft to where the station workers were flipping pallets against a stand in the middle of the room and lining up at the water basins against the far wall. Loyal shifted to his feet. Today was going to be interesting. He was anxious to meet the Banderos chief and get a measure of the man.

Descending the outside staircase, he took a deep breath of the fresh air and stepped off the path to relieve himself against a tree. Flowers bloomed in patches across the meadow below, in colours of ivory and purple, with small smudges of blue where bushes offered a spot of shade. Those would be the larksden that he'd picked for his mother when he was a young boy. She'd often seemed morose, and he'd done his best to cheer her up. Now he knew it was because his father was seldom home. Being a hawker was a tough job, the constant travelling was hard on families. He was determined that if he ever had a wife and children he'd treat them a lot better than Jade did. He took a breath to take his mind off the past and turned to watch the action in the yard.

Already the station men were working in the corral, cutting out mounts, strapping on feedbags and saddles in preparation for the day's rounds. The place looked organized—Angel had explained that every day a crew rode the perimeter of the Banderos land going from one border station to the next, looking for signs of encroachment or any suspicious activity.

One of the men in the corral stopped work and stared down the field for a moment. He called to the others and pointed to two men who had emerged from a copse of trees on the far side. One ran to ring a bell at the door of the station, while the others watched them approach. The strangers stopped at the entrance to the compound and waited uncertainly.

At the sound of the gong, Fourteenth stepped through the station doorway. "What is it?" he called. The workers pointed to the gate and they all stared. *This must be an unusual event,* Loyal thought. *Else the workers would have simply greeted the men to see what they wanted.*

Fourteenth glanced around, motioned for his men

to follow him, and walked across the yard. He stopped some feet from the strangers, where a discussion ensued. Finally he called, "They're ours." His man rushed to unlatch the gate and push it open.

When Loyal entered the station, the men were seated at the long table in the hall having a bite of pané and smoked pork amid much talk with the station guards.

Angel was already seated at the head table, her rich golden hair curling on her shoulders. She was speaking with Nineteenth, a serious expression on her face. Her brother nodded, then shrugged and rose to exit through the back. When she turned to take a sip of her tea, there was moisture on her cheek. He wanted to wipe it away, to wrap his arms around her and offer comfort for whatever was wrong. Adoni gave him a nudge with his elbow as he passed, heading for the workers' table.

He fought his annoyance, knowing his thoughts must have been mirrored on his face and his assistant had read it right. This was no time to become enamoured with someone from the Banderos family, even if she was lovely enough to catch his attention every time he looked at her.

He bowed before her. "Good morning, Ms. May I join you?" Watching her mouth curl upward in a shy smile, he felt something tighten in his chest and had to look away.

Bowls of spice cat tea and platters of toasted pané and smoked pork were laid out on the table. Loyal helped himself, knowing it might be many hours of riding before they ate again. Just then Nineteenth emerged from the back and resumed his breakfast. It was a few minutes before Fourteenth joined them, taking a seat beside his sister on the bench.

Fourteenth nodded toward the workers' table. "Those men are from the herders who look after our sheep and llamas," he said. "Second group to call by this week. They've had problems with a mountain lion attacking the lambs. We've got to work out a better system so the men are safe as well as the animals. Something's amiss in the hills, disturbing the lions."

Loyal's ears perked up. "What do they say about that?"

Fourteenth gazed at him a moment as if assessing his interest. "Not much. Something about numerous dispossessed passing through the lions' normal hunting grounds. The men coming through say they hear there is work available. I haven't put out word for workers, but obviously someone has."

"Will you hire them if they come here?" Loyal gave him an easy smile and dipped a piece of pané in herb oil, taking a bite.

Fourteenth shrugged. "I can probably use a few. We had two men leave this month, so there are jobs to be done. I might shift some over to the west station—it's harder to keep men there, more isolated than this place."

Angel had been listening to the conversation and

glanced at Nineteenth. She motioned with her hand. "Tell us what you learned," she said.

Nineteenth pursed his lips and shifted his gaze to the workers' table. "It's just a rumour," he said.

"I know." She folded her hands together. "But it's important to pay attention, don't you think?"

He gave a nod under her searching gaze. Leaning forward, he lowered his voice. "One of the riders who arrived from West Station last night heard something regarding the Nazur tribe."

His brother and sister stopped eating to listen. "You can't repeat this," he said, glaring at Loyal. "It's unconfirmed."

Loyal nodded and grinned. "No problem."

"He heard from a couple of men on the road to Sommerset," he continued. "Olaf Nazur is sick. Didn't say how he knew, just that he's sick. Probably the high temp virus. Everyone is afraid to get near him. It's contagious and deadly."

There was silence for a moment as this news was digested. Then Angel placed her hand flat on the table. "Isn't that where First is travelling this morning?" She stared anxiously at Nineteenth. "He might be in danger. He could catch the virus, even bring it home with him."

Nineteenth shrugged and gave his brother an eloquent look. "Don't know," he said, glancing back at her. "Just something to keep an eye on, I guess."

"You think he'll be safe?" she asked.

"I imagine so."

Nodding, Angel rose from the table. "When do we leave?" she asked.

"Soon." Nineteenth stood and stretched. "About a half hour. I'll look to the horses."

She nodded at Loyal. "As you will see, Mr Hawker, it is a complicated life we live." He grinned as she patted Fourteenth on the shoulder and headed to the rooms at the back.

Loyal leaned forward, smiling into the other man's eyes. "Is she in danger? Does she not need a bodyguard, with the dispossessed wandering closer and rumours of illness circling?"

Nineteenth nodded. "She has a bodyguard, don't ever think different." He gave him a gimlet-eyed stare and stalked from the hall through the front door.

He glanced at Fourteenth who let a small smile escape. "She always has a couple of her brothers travelling with her when she leaves the compound, Loyal. And all the workers in the territory are on the lookout for where she is and what she's doing. She might not always know it, but it's there. Everyone takes care with her."

Loyal leaned back and nodded. *Yes, that was probably true, with so many men and so few women.* "Are there no women at all?" he asked.

Fourteenth laughed. "Yes, some. A few of my brothers are married, several of them have children already. There is family housing in the compound for the married men. We even have a school, there are enough kids to fill a classroom. We aren't completely uncivilized."

Loyal's face grew warm, but he forced a laugh. "Not quite what I meant," he said. "Just the scarcity of women that I encounter through Khandarken and Adar Silva seems prevalent. I didn't know if it had reached these parts or not."

Fourteenth smile was rueful. "Yes and no. Most of the children in the school are boys, although there are more girls than you might think. And some of the wives come from the west, as you can imagine. Our father was fond of getting his women there, too. You will have noticed the darker skin of Nineteenth and myself. A lot of my brothers are similar in appearance."

Loyal nodded. "Very handsome look. Lucky guy." He gave a rueful grin and ran his fingers through the thick blond curls on his head, wondering how many wives Gerwal Banderos had.

Chapter Thirteen

Gerwal eased to his side on the pallet, stretching his back. His legs ached badly today, but the pain seemed to centre in his spine and shoot down the muscles and ligaments. He couldn't remember what it felt like to be pain free—to just rise in the morning and head out in the saddle on a trip to inspect the Northern Station, or go into Hafford for a meeting or a meal.

The Great Hall was silent, everyone off attending to different tasks. He sighed and shifted again, stuffing a cushion into the small of his back. First had left this morning for a trip to the far border station and perhaps a visit with the Nazurs. Gerwal had written a note and given it to him for the attention of Chief Olaf Nazur, but had little confidence it would be delivered. Something had changed with his eldest son—it showed in the expressions on his face when he was unguarded, and was voiced in his body language—a feeling of disrespect for his father.

He gazed out the wide plexi window. The field was empty today, other than the small herd of llamas grazing at the far end. Fourth and Fifth had gone with First, the three of them always working together. They had each other's backs, First claimed. And perhaps it was so.

He heard the play of the pipe signalling class was out for the day. A gaggle of schoolchildren crossed the path and headed around the side of the compound to the family housing. Strange that so few of his own sons had married. He'd already been producing children by the time he was twenty-one, and steadily ever since. But not a lot of his boys.

Ninth was the scholar. He worked with Gerwal's elderly scribe and was married with three children, another on the way. Gerwal was glad to have this son's agile brain focussed on the documents and contract issues that arose in the day-to-day workings of their territory. Ninth had even taken over transcribing the agreements he'd negotiated with his neighbours. Nazur held a lot of land to the west, and between the two of them, they'd worked out a system that benefited both, but Ninth had put it all down on parchment.

Thirteenth was less scholarly and more oriented to production. He ran the bakery for the compound. The manorhouse and quarters housed more than a hundred people. Thirteenth handled it well, with his wife's help and some other workers. Their two children had been walking with the stream of youngsters leaving the school house.

He had hopes for his other sons, but nothing had come of it yet. Perhaps he should just order in some women from the west and see where that led.

He spotted riders at the bottom of the field. Ah, there they were. He'd been expecting Angel with her crew late last night, but a young runner had arrived yesterday with word they were spending the night at the north border station. He'd recognize his daughter in the saddle no matter what she was wearing, her small back straight, relaxed hands holding the reins.

His sight was still keen, and he picked out Nineteenth riding in the lead and several unknown men in their midst. His gaze sharpened. That was Fourteenth with them. He wasn't scheduled for a trip home till next week. Something must have happened.

Soon he heard the tramp of feet and Angel entered the Great Hall, Nineteenth on her heels. "Father," she cried. "I've missed you." She bent to wrap her arms around his shoulders. He grunted. Too much emotion for a man to stomach, he always thought, but couldn't help a small smile that curled one side of his mouth.

He patted her back. "There, there, that's enough," he muttered. "Nineteenth, what's going on? I saw Fourteenth out there. And who are the strangers?"

Angel tugged off her outer robe and laid it on the back of a chair. Then she pulled a stool up close to his rubber plastic lounge and sat. "There are three men who've come with us today, Father." She glanced toward Nineteenth who remained silent but waved her to continue. This son was not a talker, but paid keen attention to everything that was going on. Today he was focussed on Angel.

"Who?" he demanded. "Guests? Sellers?" He made a motion with his hand to encourage more information.

"Actually, one is a hawker," she said. "His name is Loyal, and he has an assistant with him. The third man is his friend, Damian Stuke. We encountered them in Hafford, and they accompanied us here."

Her face was pale and he wondered what that signified. Angel liked to sit and talk with him when he had the time to listen, but now she seemed nervous. Something was amiss.

He glanced back at his son, then gave a slow nod. "So, what does Loyal the Hawker want?"

"He wants to talk to you, Father. I'll invite him in and order up refreshments from the kitchen." Grabbing her robe, she hustled out of the Great Hall, leaving Nineteenth staring after her.

"What's happened, son? I can tell when things go awry."

"Nothing awry, Father." Nineteenth took the stool Angel had just vacated. "This fellow Loyal is well connected—cousin of the Farmers at Farmer Holdings in the south Khandarken mountains. Works with Governor Maude of their Southern Territory. I don't know if you knew Loyal's father, Jade?" He squinted the question at him.

Gerwal waved his hand. "I met Jade the Hawker a few times. Never trusted the man."

"Well," he replied, "Loyal is not his father. He's different. And the other man Stuke is a solid guy as well—his father was a medic during the Last War, Stuke fought in the final battles along the Helmcken Trail with the rebellion, and his sister is married to Cownden Lanser, the new Leader of Khandarken. They're people with connections who are smart and knowledgeable, and interested in what we do here."

Gerwal felt a jolt in his chest. *Interested? How interested? And for what purpose?* This might not be a good encounter. "Why?" he demanded. "Are they going to try to tell us what to do? Or are they going to take over?"

Nineteenth gazed down the hall as if seeing something Gerwal could not. "No, Father," he said. "I think they want to help."

Chapter Fourteen

Fourteenth led the visitors to some rooms in the barracks behind the manorhouse and showed them where the garderobe was located at the end of the hall. Loyal took the opportunity to get cleaned up. He had a quick wash, managed to subdue the curls on his head and found shears to conduct a rough trim of his long sideburns. By the time he was in clean clothes, Adoni and Damian were waiting and Nineteenth appeared to take them up to the house.

Nineteenth pulled the bell pull to announce their arrival and opened the tall carved wooden door. They stepped directly into the Great Hall. Several people were already there. A large older man occupied a rubber plastic chair, the scaled slides fixed to allow it to recline. His body was lean and muscled, long legs propped on a padded stand. His straight iron grey hair was combed back from a broad heavily lined forehead. This must be Gerwal Banderos.

Angel was seated on a stool by his side, looking nervous but hopeful. He took in her beautiful heart-shaped face, wondering what she expected to accomplish with this meeting. A middle-aged woman was setting out bowls and carafes on a table to the side.

"Father," Nineteenth intoned. "This is Loyal the Hawker, his assistant Adoni, and Damian Stuke."

Loyal stepped forward, a broad grin on his face and hand outstretched. "Good to meet you, Mr Banderos. I've heard so many good things about you and the establishment here, it's a pleasure to finally see you face to face." He took the proffered hand in a firm grip and received one back. Gerwal may be injured but he was certainly no weakling.

"What have you heard?" Banderos wore a distinctly suspicious expression.

"Great things," Loyal replied, maintaining an easy smile. "For one, I heard you have forty sons."

Banderos gave in to a wry grin. "Yah, that rumour grows bigger as the years go by."

Loyal laughed. "Perhaps. Still, forty is a lot of boys, so you must be proud."

"Not forty, not yet," the older man muttered. "Twenty-six at last count."

Loyal nodded. "Well done, I say. May I sit?"

The woman stepped forward with a carafe of lemon water, pouring for each of them. Banderos sipped and eyed him over the rim of his bowl. "To what do I owe the honour of your visit?"

Loyal grinned. This was going to be fun, and he'd learned from the best how to engage and disarm the most suspicious of customers. Jade had been very good at it, one positive thing that could be said for his father. "I was on my route through the country. I work in Khandarken, and have done circuits through Adar Silva before. But it seemed to me there might be a market in your area. What do you call this? The land hasn't been claimed by either Jiran or Adar Silva."

He pulled his infolink off the belt clip and tapped the screen. The funnel opened but wouldn't connect. "My map calls it 'no-man's-land', but that can't be true." He raised his brows in an admiring look. "I've been very impressed by what we've seen so far. The border station was a masterpiece of construction, giving your men a view of the country on all sides. And it was organized down to the last man."

Banderos relaxed a little in his chair. "Yah, we found an old installation and built on that. The rock work was still in good shape."

Loyal nodded. "Well done. I could see that. From the people who were here long ago, I imagine."

Banderos shrugged. "The nomads, that's what they were called. Except they weren't, of course. Nomads don't build permanent installations of stone."

"Right." Loyal measured him with his gaze as he

took in the rest of the room. This manorhouse might be somewhat isolated, but still contained the comforts of most such establishments. The dining table was made of hand carved wood with matching padded chairs. Yet the cupboards against the wall behind were constructed of modern plexi and contained a myriad of old-fashioned books. He'd noticed his links were somewhat scrambled the closer they got to the centre of the Banderos territory. There must be no power station anywhere nearby.

The older man gave him a measured look. "What have you brought to sell?"

He laughed. "My usual stuff, nothing special I'm afraid. Medic equipment and supplies. Do you have an aid room that you keep provided? I can probably help with that. My other main product is talc from my cousins' mines—paints, colourants, body powder. The talc has also been shown to prove a strong deterrent to the high temp virus, if you're interested."

Banderos waved the serving woman over. "Do you need anything for the medicine room, Willa?" he said. "This is the man to talk to. Maybe get some of that talc in case we have a threat of high temp virus around here."

Loyal pointed to Adoni who pulled a list from his sleeve and spread it on the table for the woman to peruse. Then he turned back to Banderos. "My assistant is from Legitamia, as you can see. His father is a sookie, and Adoni worked in the clinic with his parents for years while growing up. He's not a trained sookie himself, but he knows a great deal. It's obvious you're in some pain, Mr Banderos. Why don't you let him have a look at your back?"

Chapter Fifteen

First arrived at the Nazur compound late in the afternoon. It was a long ride to this western region, and he never came alone. Fourth and Fifth had accompanied him, along with twenty of his men from the guard. Gerwal had entered into agreements with Olaf, the senior Nazur, in the past, but First knew there was little trust involved between the two men. Even less when it came to negotiations with the son. Orde was tough and ruthless, but First felt he was a match for him. If Olaf was sick, as the rumours suggested, then it would have to be the son that he dealt with initially.

They were challenged by a watchman at the compound gate, and waited while word was sent for permission to enter. Orde appeared in the doorway of the manorhouse a few minutes later, a frown on his face. It cleared when he recognized his visitors.

"First," he called. "Sorry about that, we're very cautious of who we let in. Pass your mount to your men there. The guard will see them to the barracks."

First wasn't best pleased to leave his men behind as he entered the manorhouse, but it was something he would have demanded of Nazur had he arrived in similar circumstances. He waved to his brothers and dismounted, handing the reins to a guard.

"This way," Orde declared. "I was just taking a bite in the hall." The Nazur manorhouse was small, but well positioned on a hill overlooking the river valley below. First had been here before when Gerwal came to meet with Olaf. This time would likely be different, given Father was not present.

Orde waved him to a chair at the table in the entry and shouted for drinks, then took a seat and resumed his meal. "What can I do for you?" he said around a mouthful of soup. "I'm surprised to see you here. Where's your father?"

First 's face got hot. With Orde rudely failing to offer him food while demanding information about Father, he'd been thrown off balance. "Gerwal is out of the picture these days, weren't you aware?" He didn't like this man, and hated to be challenged. "He had a bad fall a few weeks back. Mostly bed-ridden now."

A young boy entered carrying a tray, and set out a plate of salted nuts and bowls for tea. First poured himself some Chilean and pulled the bowl across the table in front of him.

Orde sat up at the news, focussing on his face. "When was that?"

"Ten days ago, maybe twelve. I'm in charge now. I'd like to talk to your father."

Orde stirred his soup with the spoon. "I see. Well, Father is dead. I thought you might have heard." His expression was stern, the lines around his mouth prominent.

First caught a thump in his chest. *Nazur was dead? Since when?* "No," he said cautiously, glancing around. "There was a rumour he was taken ill, but…"

"No rumour," Orde declared. "He fell sick and died that night. High temp virus, we thought. No time to find a medic."

He gazed toward the stairs then back to Orde's face. "I'm sorry to hear that. Quite a loss for the Nazur tribe. No one else caught the illness?"

The question was simple, but Orde's reaction seemed extreme. He bristled, sitting back in his chair, his eyes hard. "No one else. Just Father. Lucky, I guess. Why do you ask?"

He shrugged. "Don't want to get it myself, is all."

"Right. So what did you need to see Father about?"

This was the tipping point. First was finally where he needed to be and perhaps this was an omen. It might be easier to come to an agreement with the son, after all. "It's like this," he said, leaning forward. "Now that Father has backed out of the way and I'm in charge, I need to take steps that he's been avoiding for some time. Unrest is growing in the hills and forests to the south, and it seems to start with the New Emperor and his ambitions. The dispossessed are starting to get organized, and who knows which side they will end up supporting. Perhaps there are some ideas that we could work on together."

Orde's face lit up. "Really. This is good timing. I've been having the same thoughts myself."

~***~

Sup consisted of corned bread and oil, eggs poached in broth, a leg of pheasant and fried lentils. Then the serving boy brought Bishop's cake and allspice biscuits. They were on their third round of clouded ale and First was feeling pretty relaxed. They'd moved into Orde's office, a spacious room off the entry that had been his father's just weeks before.

"We need a map," Orde said, and rose to shuffle through the stack of parchment on a shelf at the back of the blackened desk. He pulled out a document from the middle of the pile and unfolded it on the desktop. It was a hand drawn plan, with the rivers and roads meandering in vague detail across the land. "Here we go." He pointed to the outlines of Adar Silva and Khandarken. "This is what we're talking about. Jiran is to the north but they don't have a firm border, and no one has claimed your land or mine. Your western border runs along this valley."

First blinked to clear his vision from the effects of the ale. "It does not. We control all the way to the river." He pointed out a spot further west. "Don't try and pull a quick trick on me. I know exactly where our land reaches, and we conduct boundary rides weekly covering the entire area."

Orde grinned and wiped ale from his chin. "Good one, First. Thought I could catch you off guard. So, what you're proposing is that we combine our resources and our land. We control it with an amalgamated force of your men and mine. And this way we keep the Empire troops from taking over."

First sat down suddenly in his chair as his balance gave out. "You wouldn't believe it. The number of dispossessed who wander out of the forest, or ride close to the compound, and when we challenge them they back off as if they are there by accident. It's no accident. They're searching for new territory and think they'll have a try at taking ours."

Orde nodded. "We've had a few groups come through, don't think we haven't. We've run them off. But a combined force—that would be what, two hundred men?"

First glanced at him. "How many do you have?"

"About eighty."

"Just eighty, huh?" He stroked a sideburn thoughtfully. "I thought it might be more."

Orde bristled. "Why? How many have you got?"

First shrugged. "There are seventeen brothers. Then we have the guards at the border stations, about forty-five in number. The troop is a hundred strong." He was exaggerating, of course. Many of his brothers had taken up functions in the office or other areas, and Rascal and Runt, along with Baby, were still kids, but it didn't hurt to bump up the numbers. And why give it away? If Nazur had fewer men and a smaller area, maybe he had been hasty to suggest an equal share of the combined territory.

He sipped at his bowl of ale. "You know, it sounds like we are about twice as big as you in numbers and in land. Perhaps this wasn't well thought out."

Orde's face grew dark and his eyes looked like small nuggets in his face. "Are you backing out now?"

"No, just thinking out loud. We each get a share the size of what we bring to the table. If we have a hundred and seventy men and you have eighty, that means we have two-thirds. If the land is similar in distribution, it just makes sense that the Banderos family controls two thirds of the combined organization."

Orde stood and strode across the room to gaze out the plexi at the dark sky. "And what about your sister?" he said after a moment.

First looked up in surprise. "Angel?" he asked.

"Yah, Angel. How does she fit into this proposal?"

He rolled his eyes. "She doesn't. Angel isn't part of this."

"Why not?" Orde walked slowly back to his chair. "If I get Angel as my wife, I'll agree to one third of the combined organization, and you get two thirds."

His throat tightened so fast, First thought his head might explode. He had never considered something like this. He would do a deal with Nazur where he had control of the major portion of the territory, and get rid of Angel at the same time. She was a thorn in his side, always questioning what he said, giving Father ideas about how to handle the issues that arose. He'd be free of her.

Elation rose and swelled. He lowered his head to hide his reaction and fumbled for the ale bowl in front of him. *Don't let him see, don't give him a clue as to how much I want this.*

"Yah, I understand your reasoning," he muttered, "but I'm not sure. I'd have to really think about this, Orde. She's my only sister and very precious to us all."

Chapter Sixteen

Angel sighed and stared at herself in the plexi mirror. She picked up a brush and pulled it through her hair. The evening had gone well. Father had been somewhat suspicious at first, but Loyal Hawker seemed to have a way of disarming people. Soon they were deeply engrossed in a conversation about the shifting of the dispossessed out of the hills and onto the plains, and the rumours of Emperor Carlton's ambitions and possible military action.

Damian Stuke had added his views and Fourteenth and Nineteenth asked enough questions that Father had finally opened up to speculation about the best way to manage the Banderos territory in the face of an uprising. The goal was to protect them against being overtaken by hostile forces.

Now the Legitamian assistant Adoni was giving Father a second treatment for his back. It was surprising Father was even letting him do it. Gerwal Banderos had always held very vocal negative opinions about 'foreigners', especially Legitamians, even though several of his wives had been from the west with their dusky skin. Adoni's first treatment before sup had caused him some pain but also a bit of relief. Perhaps this second one would work out better.

She dropped the brush on the counter and pulled a shawl from the hanger on the back of her door. It had been days since she'd spent a moment in the gardens. The sun had just set, and a near full moon shone in the clear sky. Enough light to take a turn in the rows of plants. Lavender perfume hung heavy in the air as she opened the gate and stepped inside the garden. Seventeenth was in charge of the vegetable crops, but he would look in and take care of her patch when she was away. Everything appeared neat and tidy.

She heard the latch jiggle on the gate and glanced behind her. Loyal Hawker stood there, holding it open with one hand. "Do you mind if I join you, Ms?"

She gave a light laugh, heat blooming in her cheeks. Thank heaven for the darkness. "No, not at all," she said. "There isn't much to see, I'm afraid, just an herb patch that I've cultivated over the years."

He walked through and pulled the gate closed behind him. "It smells good," he observed. "What do you have here?"

"That's lavender. And the sagium is in bloom, it always perfumes the air nicely."

"Wonderful." He gazed about. "Tell me what I'm looking at. I don't know much about herb gardens, or any gardens for that matter."

She laughed. A little thrill ran down her spine at his interest. "Well, this part is all herbs." She led him to the first row, pointing out plants as they walked. "I grow flowers for my own pleasure in this section." She gestured to the next rows. "It means we can have cut flowers in the entry most of the spring and summer season. My mother loved that."

He glanced at her. "Is the woman who brought us refreshments your mother?"

"No, that was Willa, Gerwal's current wife." She looked across to the small graveyard beyond the fence. "My mother died. Of loss, I sometimes think."

"How so?"

His gaze felt tender on her face.

"I was her oldest child," she said. "Twenty came next, but he died as an infant. I don't remember him. Then she had triplets, but they came early and were undersized. They all died within days of each other. I remember a very lonely woman. She was loving, but preoccupied. She had Rascal and Runt. Baby was the last child, and she passed away when he was a few weeks old."

"How old were you?" He took her hands in his and just held them.

"Nine," she said.

"That's sad." He leaned to press a kiss in each palm. "I'm very sorry."

"Oh, my." There was a strange feeling in her belly, like a shimmer of joy that took her by surprise.

Loyal lifted his head. "I know we leave tomorrow. But I hope to see you again. May I call on you when I come through?"

She gazed into his pale blue eyes and forgot the question. "Yes?" she asked in a fluster. "Pardon?"

"May I?" he said and leaned toward her. His mouth pressed briefly against her temple, just a flutter of sensation. "I want to see you again."

"I see." But she really didn't, too confused to focus on what he said. She looked up as Nineteenth called from the gate.

"Come, sister," he said. "Father wants another talk with the Hawker."

Loyal pressed her hands between his, then dropped them and turned. "Of course," he said. "We're coming."

Angel followed slowly. This seemed like progress. They would also have time to meet again in the morning, before their guests had to take their leave. They needed to be gone from the compound well before First returned with his men.

She was excited and confused by their talks with Father, and mourned already the loss of Loyal's presence.

~***~

Since becoming Leader of Khandarken, Cownden Lanser had found himself in the centre of a storm of pressure. His position was a political one, something he didn't feel totally comfortable with as he was a very private man. But with his assistant Anatoliy at his side, he'd managed to cobble together a working Board of Representatives and begun the task of dealing with the myriad issues left half unfinished by the assassination of Harold Master, former Leader of Khandarken.

Not that all the Representatives were on his side. The news that he was half-brother to Emperor Carlton had hit hard in some areas, and the trust level had been left sadly wanting. FitzGibbon, who had been former Assistant Leader and simply assumed he'd move up to top position when Master was killed, was especially critical.

Plus Cownden had gotten married days before the election was held, and still had no place to call a permanent home. His wife was a patient woman, but the pressure was mounting to sort out their own place to live.

Cownden was slowly getting round these issues. The fact he'd been the former Chief Constable and dealt with crime and corruption in the police counted for something. Having Major Dante Regiment of the military on his side also helped. Now, if he could only find a decent house in the City to move into…

In the middle of a Board meeting in the downtown administration buildings, he was interrupted by his assistant. Anatoliy had been fiddling with his link and now slid his tomo across the surface of the boardroom table to Cownden's elbow. "Have a look,

Sir," he whispered. "Probably best to read it now."

He glanced at the device and saw Emperor Carlton's emblem slowly unroll in the centre of the document. A message from his brother? Highly unlikely. They had last parted on very unfriendly terms. He raised his brows at his assistant.

Toll pursed his lips. "Important," he muttered.

"Okay." Cownden sat back and glanced the length of the table. Some of the men were taking notes or looking at their own links, but most were focussed on him, stark curiosity marking their expressions. "Gentlemen, we'll take a break. Back here in half an hour. I think we can get through a good part of the agenda this afternoon."

He slapped his hand on the table and stood, heading for his office, Toll on his heels. Walking behind his chrome and plexi desk, he collapsed into his chair. "What is it, that couldn't wait, Toll?"

Anatoliy laid the tomo before him and tapped the screen. The emblem faded and a formal looking document appeared. He leaned closer as he caught the words *meeting* and *ceasefire*. "What?" He began reading from the top.

This was an offer from Carlton to hold a meeting between himself, Cownden, and Prince Shandro of the Jiranis. The purpose was to negotiate a ceasefire between the three leaders and allow them all to move forward.

He glanced at his assistant. "Have you read this?"

At his nod, Cownden laughed. "What is he

thinking? And what does he see we have to gain with such a meeting? He's grabbed some of our land, along with some Jirani territory. Should we just give it up so he can have a ceasefire?"

Toll shrugged. "Perhaps there's an opportunity here, nonetheless."

Cownden nodded slowly. "And I'd better run it by the Board of Representatives. This isn't a dictatorship, after all. Unlike Carlton's organization."

"Should others be involved?" Anatoliy was toying with the wand he used on the tomo, tapping it thoughtfully against his chin.

He glanced at his assistant. "You mean like the conference held in Gilsigg. General Barrington could be affected by such an offer. Plus True-May in Adar Silva. After all, Sommerset is probably where Carlton is hoping to end up."

He pondered a moment. "All right. Let's write up an invitation but don't send it out yet. We'll wait till we run this by the Board and see where it goes. I can't believe it. After that last invasion through the Moiselle tribal grounds in Jiran, he has the nerve to issue such a notice. Well, no one has ever accused Carlton of running out of nerve."

Chapter Seventeen

"He'll see you now," Ms Balsom said.

Loyal stopped pacing the length of the office, tucked his ident in his pocket and took the stairs two at a time. He'd flown back to Deep Creek, Southern Territory of Khandarken, once they reached Sommerset, leaving Adoni with his sales gear and a list of stops to make on the route. This information was too important to keep to himself.

Governor Maude was seated behind his desk folding an old parchment document. "Loyal! Come in." He rose and extended his hand. "There's no one here but me," he said. "I didn't have time to call on Dante Regiment or Cownden Lanser for this, but obviously it's important. Have a seat, let me get you a drink." He turned to the side counter and poured out a shot of brandy in two bowls, offering him one.

Frank Maude was a tall, slightly stooped older man, with a patch over one eye. He'd been injured in the Last War, once in the leg and the second time losing an eye. Like many his age, he was now in a position of responsibility in a brand-new country recently risen from the ashes of the Old Empire. He and Dante Regiment ran a team of men who went about their legitimate tasks around the country and at the same time did undercover work. Loyal had become one of those agents.

Loyal took a swallow of the brandy and waited for the heat to track down to his stomach. Good stuff, must be a Learmonth product, considered the best spirits in the country. "Ah." He set the bowl on the edge of the desk.

Maude grinned and downed his in one gulp. "Okay, son. Tell me what you've got."

"No real proof of what I'm about to say," Loyal said.

Maude nodded in understanding. "There never is."

"True." He propped his ankle on the other knee and leaned back. "I've just been through the no man's land between Jiran and Adar Silva to the west of our boundary. As we all know, a number of strongmen control that area, mostly small time. But there are two or three bigger organizations, one of them led by a man named Gerwal Banderos."

"Yah." Maude played with his bowl a minute, then set it aside. "I've heard of him, has about forty sons, runs a big operation. Because no country has claimed the land, he's grown in size and control since the Last War ended."

Loyal laughed. "He told me it's twenty-seven sons, but who's counting?"

Maude raised his brows. "Twenty-seven? Really? That's something. I figured forty was doubtful, but still…"

"The thing is, Banderos has been injured, so he's physically weak now," Loyal said. "And his sons are engaged in a running battle to sort out who will succeed him. Meanwhile, rumours abound all around them—about the New Empire, Carlton taking over, Sommerset the eventual target, and so on. The dispossessed are pouring out of the hills, being recruited by someone. The Banderos organization says they have used dispossessed in the past for their operations, but have never seen so many turning up. Someone has put out a call."

"That's not good news." Maude shifted in his chair and grabbed a military facelink from the sideboard. "Let's get hold of Dante and see what he knows about this."

Loyal waited as the Governor tapped in the particulars for the contact. "There's something else," he added. "They have no links. It's like it must have been when the nomads roamed the land. Even our boosted military devices were fuzzy and non-functional out there."

Maude focussed on the facelink as he listened.

"I think we should build a military installation," Loyal said. "Near the Farmer talc mines in the hills to the south. It would allow the Banderos people to communicate with each other, and we could monitor the messages. We'd know what was going on.

Maude broke into a grin and gave him an approving nod just as Malahide appeared on the screen of the facelink. Dante was out of the office but should return shortly.

~***~

When Loyal left Maude's offices, evening was setting in and the downtown of Deep Creek was quiet. It had been a long meeting, but he'd gotten what he was after. Military towers would be installed in the Hawker Hills behind Abe Farmer's talc mines. Dante Regiment had jumped on the idea. With the dispossessed pouring out of the hills and rumours abounding of an uprising, he couldn't get it done fast enough. Monitoring by Regiment's men would be heavy until they figured out who was using the link connections and what their purpose might be.

Loyal's goal was reached. Gerwal Banderos had invited him to return for further discussions of the political and military activity arising near his compound and what steps he needed to take to contain it. He would head back to the Banderos territory and see Angel again. His chest tightened at the thought.

He hadn't slept well the last few nights. Visions of her pretty face and soft hair rose in his mind's eye as soon as he lay down. If he wasn't busy, he was plagued by thoughts of how to create an opportunity to speak to her, how to find out if she was already betrothed, how to express his interest without scaring her off. Her and her twenty-six brothers. Although Banderos had indicated some had died so there wouldn't be that many now.

He walked down to the transit yards at the foot of Main Street where the night-time activity was just getting into high gear. His cousin Abe Farmer had his fighting arts training centre here and Loyal was booked in for a session. Abe was a skilled fight combatant and had transformed that interest into a facility rivalling any in the country. Many dispossessed, too damaged after the atrocities of the Last War to comfortably fit back into society, had managed to get through the training sessions and come out not just healed, but skilled and ready for work.

Loyal knew it was a gift to have this training available, and he took advantage of it every chance he could. Then he'd return to Mother's for dinner before heading west again—to see Angel.

Chapter Eighteen

Upon arriving with his men in Sommerset, First took off his jacket and shook it out. The dust of the trail had settled like a second cloak over him as they travelled south. This was an important opportunity, one he'd thought of constantly for almost a year. He wanted to appear prepared and businesslike.

He'd brought Fourth and Fifth, along with ten of his troop as bodyguards. The precautions weren't really needed as Adar Silva was a civilized place, but it made him look good—gave him an air of authority to have his men around him. For now they were all billeted in the barracks at the edge of town.

Sommerset was the capital of Adar Silva and a very formal place, with a lot of the upper crust established here, a remnant of the Old Empire. He'd do his best not to stick out like a dispossessed in the midst of all the finery. Stopping at the nearest inn, he booked a small room and a bath. The concierge took his hat and coat and promised to have them cleaned and returned forthwith.

The bath was small but he managed to fold his long body into the cramped compartment. As he scrubbed, he mulled his options. His talk with Orde Nazur the week before had gone much better than expected. The fact Orde's father was dead still seemed surprising, but First was under no illusion that negotiating with Olaf in the absence of Gerwal would have been as productive. Now he had a deal with the Nazurs, not in writing, but worked out in general terms nonetheless. Orde wouldn't likely back out if he was going to have better security with the Banderos organization at his side in such times of upheaval.

On top of that, First would be rid of Angel. He chuckled as he scrubbed his feet. Two birds with one stone, as it said in the Old Book. Or was that where he'd seen it? He wasn't strong on book learning, much preferring armed combat and hard riding.

When he'd returned home after his encounter with Orde Nazur, Fourteenth had been there, a startling situation. His younger brother was a steady man who stuck to the rules and schedules. He hadn't been due for a home visit for another week.

But even more alarming, Father appeared to be much better. He was moving around, walking with a stick for support. He'd also seemed to be in charge again, asking questions about where First had been and what he'd accomplished. It had taken him by surprise. He'd been set back on his heels until he managed to cobble together a story that moved Father off the scent of his real mission and sent him in a different direction—something about the llama herds travelling onto Nazur land and settling a dispute with Orde. If Father continued to improve, it would put a real clog in the wheels of First's plans for the future. But that was an issue for another day.

The rumours continued in abundance from the dispossessed and travellers that passed through Banderos land. Talk of uprisings, of small bands of men pledging to take the side of the Emperor, or wanderers looking to fight on any side in the Next War. Also talk of others passing through—luckily he'd heard Mr Judson Lanser was in Sommerset. Lanser had a sister who lived here and he was likely visiting her.

Now, how was First going to get his chance to talk with the man who was Advisor to Emperor Carlton? He gave himself one last rinse and stood, water sloshing over the rim of the tub as he reached for the drying sheet. He'd find a way, that was his strength. He set a goal for himself and then found a road to achieve it.

~***~

In the City, Major Dante Regiment stalked across the Great Entry of Regiment House to where his father, Paulo, kept an office. Father was not at his desk, but Scribe was tidying the parchments on the shelves against the back wall.

"Where is the General?" he asked.

Scribe gave a shallow bow of greeting and straightened. "Your father is out," he intoned. "I believe he has an engagement with Ms Hart." Mildred Hart was a widow who had taken a particular liking to Paulo, and they spent a lot of time together. Her son, Puntledge, had been a close friend of Dante's in training school and was now the Chief Justice of the Court of Appeal of Khandarken.

Dante felt a twinge of annoyance. *Did Father think the military ran itself?* There were too many issues up in the air to neglect his duties like this. They needed a different arrangement to make things work. He looked at the stack of onionskin documents on the desktop. "What do you have on Emperor Carlton and the proposal to meet?"

Scribe twitched into action, seizing the stack and sorting quickly. "Not much, Sir. The original invitation"—he held up the familiar looking onionskin—"and your note that accompanied it."

He shifted his shoulders impatiently. "He hasn't taken any action on it?"

"I don't believe so."

Time to make some changes in the hierarchy of the military, as this simply didn't work. Irritated, Dante turned to go. Scribe called after him. "I do believe he is seeing Mr Puntledge Hart today as well, to discuss the legal ramifications of any meeting."

"Great," he muttered. "That'll be useful if we ever get a plan in place."

His own office was just down the hall in one wing of the house, and he returned to his desk to gaze unseeing at the pile of documents spread across the surface. He needed to take action on this issue, and fast. *Who should attend?* Father and himself, plus Leader Cownden Lanser. That took care of Khandarken. He'd issued an invitation to General Goodnight Barrington in Gilsigg, Legitamia. He didn't have good interpreters but hoped the message he'd dispatched would be intelligible enough for Barrington's advisors to transcribe for him. Then there were the Jiranis. He'd talked to Prince Shandro Penrhy, not knowing if each of the main tribes should be invited, or just the dominant group. Penrhy had promised to spread the word. Perhaps there would be a dozen tribal leaders from that region.

He grimaced. It wasn't really within his control, but nor were they planning to go into this alone. Emperor Carlton would have to face down the whole crowd if he was serious about an attempt at peacemaking, which Dante doubted. On the other hand, anything was possible.

Carlton wanted the encounter set up near the north Khandarken border. It sounded like he wasn't too comfortable traveling further inside the country, which made sense. After all, he'd invaded them not more than a year ago, and still held a small village to the north. So they would meet in Collaros Territory.

Martonosha was the territory capital, but Carlton's Counsellors had decreed it was too heavily populated and had suggested a spot near Krimen to the west.

At least the meeting place had been agreed upon. Now to arrange security. "Malahide," he called, and soon heard the heavy tread of his right-hand man coming down the hall. "Let's get this thing on the road."

Chapter Nineteen

Loyal returned to the tiny village of Hafford in a military aircart, the sight of which seemed to alarm the citizens. At first glimpse of the vehicle they ran, leaving their places of business and streaming down the track away from town. When the cart silently landed and pulled to the side of the road, however, the residents returned, approaching slowly, their eyes wide with curiosity.

Loyal exited the craft, lugging his bags, and spotted his dusty transport and trailer parked behind the local bar. Adoni was already here, good man.

As the aircart took off again to excited shouts from the children gathered on the track, he entered the bar and glanced around. His assistant sat at the same table as before, nursing a bowl of ale while the barkeep nervously polished the plank in front of him, his gaze darting toward the glowering customer at the back of the bar. Loyal tried not to laugh. *Surely they weren't going to play the same scenario over again?*

Adoni gave him a grin as he took a seat on the bench facing him.

"How did it go?" Loyal asked. "Make any sales?"

"Good. Managed to unload about half of the medic supplies, and on the way back my links suddenly started to work a whole lot better."

Loyal laughed and waved at the barkeep for an ale. "Yah, there's a good reason for that. We got the installations set up in the Hawker Hills by the talc mine. Should cover this whole area." He pointed to one of his packs. "I've brought links for the Banderos tribe."

Adoni's gaze travelled from the pack to Loyal's face, but he remained silent.

Heat climbed his neck. Yes, he was doing this to aid the network of contacts he was building in the area, but his primary goal was being in touch with Angel. Adoni was no idiot. He'd seen his instant attraction to the girl. He clenched his teeth. Lowering his voice, he leaned across the table. "There have been developments, Adoni. Things are heating up."

His assistant nodded and took a swig of ale. "You mean here or in Khandarken? I haven't heard anything new on the infolink."

"No, it hasn't reached that yet." Loyal leaned back allowing the barkeep to place the ale on the table in front of him, then waited till the man was out of earshot. "The meeting with Emperor Carlton has been set. It's to take place in Collaros Territory near Krimen. The Emperor wasn't comfortable coming any further inside the country. I can't say as I blame him. He travels by horse, after all. His brother, Leader Cownden Lanser will be there, also Leader True-May from Adar Silva. Prince Shandro Penrhy is coming from Jiran with his wife. Princess Chinata is actually Carlton's sister, so that will be even more awkward for him, I imagine. General Goodnight Barrington turned it down—obviously Legitamia isn't that worried about having Carlton occupying a small corner of their province."

Adoni grinned. Loyal was slowly getting used to the sight of his sharpened teeth, but at first it had been somewhat alarming. "Barrington doesn't worry overmuch," Adoni said. "From what I saw, he's got a pretty firm grip on that country, and with Zhang as head of police, he's aware of damned well everything that goes on."

Loyal sipped his ale. "I think once the news is out about this meeting, the unrest will increase. Already the dispossessed are streaming out of the hills looking for action. Let's hope we're ready for whatever happens."

~***~

His assistant had hired two nags from the local barn and they headed through the trees toward the trail leading to the north border station, hoping to connect with Fourteenth if he was still there. As luck would have it, they arrived at the same time he did.

As they approached, their horses sweating and lathered, Fourteenth rode into the station compound. His sandy hair was covered by a broad brimmed hat. One of the corral workers tied a feedbag on his animal as he stripped a sac from the back of the saddle and walked toward them. "Didn't expect you back so soon," he said. "This is good news. Come in." He escorted them across the yard and into the empty station hall, calling for refreshments from the tiny kitchen at the back. Bowls of tea and a large plate of biscuits were placed in front of the group as they took seats at a table.

Fourteenth gestured for the men to help themselves. "I didn't realize you could get home and return again so quickly."

Loyal took a swallow of tea. "I went by aircart," he said. "Adoni didn't get home, he did my sales rounds without me. Got some big orders, so that's welcome news."

Fourteenth glanced at Adoni. "I can see by the colour of your skin you're from the north. How are you received this far from your homeland?"

Adoni grinned, and the man shrank back slightly at the sight of his sharpened teeth. "Remarkably well. There was a small encounter in Hafford the first go round, but that got settled fairly quickly."

Fourteenth nodded. "In Hafford, eh? I'll bet I know who it was—cranky elderly fellow."

Adoni shrugged dismissively. "Old news."

"I have something for you," Loyal said, reaching into his bag. "This is a voicelink, and we've had an energy tower installed in south Khandarken that can give you good coverage. Why don't you try it?"

Fourteenth gazed at the object a moment before reaching out to take it from his hand. "I don't know much about these. Can't say as I understand how—"

"Here, let me show you." They spent the next hour going over the various features of the link, how to recognize the caller, initiate a call, enter particulars and receive messages, until Fourteenth seemed fairly comfortable with it. Adoni went outside and contacted him with his own link. Fourteenth's pale skin went red and he grinned broadly as he tapped the screen to answer. "This is good," he muttered. "I can learn this quick enough." Then his face clouded. "Who would I call, besides you?"

Loyal pointed at his bag. "I have a few more. I think Nineteenth should have one, Angel for sure, probably Rascal."

"Yah," he said eagerly. "And Father. I sometimes worry when I'm not…" He glanced down, then thumbed the 'on' button. "Just so I can reach him if needed, you understand." He looked thoughtful. "Are you here to meet with Father again? Because First is away and it's a good time to talk."

"I was hoping to see your father," Loyal replied. That wasn't all he hoped and his heart beat a little faster at the thought. He narrowed his eyes consideringly. Everyone seemed to be anxious to have First away from the compound when they brought him in for these 'talks'. It was something to be aware of. "What do you expect to get out of these meetings, Fourteenth?"

It had been confusing until Loyal realized Gerwal's sons were pumping him for information. The voicelinks should help with the need for knowledge. "Are you trying to form a connection with Khandarken for support in these uncertain times? I'm not sure I'm the best man…"

Fourteenth shook his head. "Not quite. More to gather facts and make a plan. Angel can fill you in on the goals, but Father is key, so we have to work with him."

He nodded. "I see. Well, we should get going, then."

Fourteenth stood. "I'll go with you. Let's do what we can while the coast is clear. First is away on a trip to Sommerset."

Loyal felt a jolt in his chest. *Sommerset? Why would he go there?*

Chapter Twenty

Judson Lanser descended the steps of the Sommerset Learmonth Hotel and adjusted the folds of his robe as he paused on the street. His honour guard quickly caught up and ranged themselves on either side. The men obviously were not well trained, or he never would have been able to leave them behind just walking out of the hotel. *Where was the leader?* He glanced around and spotted the man standing beside the entrance to the garden, his arm around the narrow waist of an attractive girl who'd been serving him earlier in the dining room. *Ignorant bumpkin.* He clicked his fingers and the fellow's head snapped up. Dropping his arm, the guard marched over and awkwardly stepped into place with his men.

Just then a fellow approached, holding out his hand in greeting. He might have been a dispossessed if not for the fact his clothes were relatively clean.

"Mr Judson Lanser?" he asked.

Did he really expect him to shake that hand? Lanser kept his arms at his sides and raised an eyebrow as his guard crowded closer. "And who are you?"

The man's face went red, then suddenly pale. "My name is First Banderos. I'm the eldest son in the Banderos tribe and have taken over from my father Gerwal. We hold a lot of land north of here. I wondered if I could talk to you for a moment?" He took a nervous breath and ploughed on. "What I have to offer should be of utmost interest to Emperor Carlton."

Lanser looked up the strand and back, pondering the possibilities. Ideas and helpful suggestions had come from some surprising places and people during the last years since Emperor Aqatain died. Why not from this man? On the other hand, he'd never heard of the Banderos tribe and wondered exactly what 'a lot of land' might mean. Not to dismiss the idea out of hand—Carlton's whole focus at this point was gaining territory.

"I can give you five minutes," he said, gesturing toward the hotel steps. "We'll find a cubby inside where we can talk." He turned his back and stalked toward the entrance with his guard in tow, not knowing or caring if the man followed.

~***~

Loyal couldn't believe how much the Banderos landscape had changed in the time he'd been away. The longer days and warmer weather had prompted the locust trees to bloom, with their tall upright purple flowers standing like candles at the ends of the branches. The grass had shot up, turning a darker colour and the herds of sheep in the distance seemed lost in the dense greenery.

"We've had some problems with the sheep," Fourteenth remarked, frowning into the distance. "The mountain lions. We've lost several lambs, only found the carcass of one of them. You can tell—they rip the guts out and eat the belly first."

"Huh." As they got closer, Loyal saw the sheep herder send his dog to round up a couple of stragglers as he moved off into the next field. "Does that happen often?"

"No, pretty unusual." Fourteenth glanced at him. "The lions stay in the hills, we don't see them as a rule. I think the migration of the dispossessed is causing a disturbance."

"Are your herders in danger?"

The man grinned. "They know enough to keep an eye out, and their dogs stay close."

It was late when they finally reached the Banderos compound. Gerwal and his daughter waited for their arrival in the Great Hall. Angel looked bewitching in an evening robe of red and gold, glitters sewn to the lapels and along the narrow sleeves. Her long tawny hair was down, gathered like a shawl over one shoulder. When her gaze met his, he felt a shiver pass over him. He had a goal now and that goal was Angel.

"You must be tired after your travels," Gerwal

said, as Loyal managed to drag his attention back to the others in the room. "I know we will have time to talk in the morning, Loyal, but I hoped Adoni might…" He looked uneasy as he glanced at his assistant. "I wondered if…"

Adoni stepped forward. "I could do a treatment on your back tonight," he offered. "Then the one tomorrow will be that much more effective. Is that all right, Mr Banderos?"

Gerwal's expression turned to mused chagrin. "I would be most grateful," he muttered. Rising to his feet with the help of his stick, he lead Adoni from the room.

Loyal turned as Angel gestured to the lounge beside her. "I've sent for refreshments," she said, her cheeks turning a becoming pink. "Will you join me?"

He crossed the floor in swift strides, unable to stop the grin. "Gladly. How have you been, Ms Banderos?"

She gazed up into his face, lips curled in a smile. "I'm fine, Mr Hawker. I'm glad you are here. Perhaps we don't need to be quite so formal."

Loyal laughed. Just then the cook from the house kitchen appeared, setting a tray on the table at Angel's elbow. There was a pot of spice caf tea, a carafe of liquor and bowls for serving.

"What will you have?" she murmured. "I know most men prefer the brandy."

"Yah, I'll have that. Maybe tea later."

She poured and passed him the bowl. "Are you

here long? I know First will…" She looked uncertain.

"Just overnight, Fourteenth told me. We will leave before noon tomorrow."

"Yes, that's good. Still, long enough to spend time with Father." Her serious expression pulled at his heartstrings. "He needs your guidance, Loyal."

"I understand, and I will do everything I can to help." He took her hand in his, anticipation burning in his belly. "Have you ever been to Sommerset?"

"Why, yes." She brushed a strand of hair back from her cheek. "I went there once when I was small. Father took all of us with him. He had some business to attend to, and Mother showed me the sights—the Emperor's Headquarters and the Sparkling Wheel."

Loyal suppressed a chuckle in the face of her excitement. "Would you like to go again? The Sommerset Fair is on this week. There will be lots to see and do."

She gazed at him in astonishment. "Go to Sommerset? How would we get there? And I certainly couldn't go alone with you." She put her palm against a suddenly red cheek.

"No, I don't expect you to. Listen. Bring Rascal as a companion. I'll have Adoni with me. We would be four, which is a respectable-sized party. What do you think?"

"That would be so exciting." Her voice rose, bubbling up. "What would I wear? And when do you want to leave? I'm not sure that Father…" She stalled, gazing around the entry as if in consideration.

"I think I will take a trip into Hafford to see my tutor. I could join you from there. Would that work?"

Loyal put back his head and laughed. "Are you avoiding giving your father the news? I imagine you're old enough to make those decisions on your own. We could certainly meet you in Hafford. We'd go to Sommerset in our transport, it seats four quite comfortably. I'm thinking of staying two nights in Sommerset. We can see all the sights, then back to Hafford."

"No," she said, looking disappointed. "I only ever stay one night. Father would be worried."

"And you won't tell him where you're going?"

Her mouth firmed. "He's very protective of me."

"Yes, I can understand that. How about one night then? If we leave here by noon, we get to Sommerset in plenty of time to see the night's highlights, spend the next morning at the fair and return to Hafford in time for your ride home."

Her eyes sparkled up at him. "I'll just run to tell Nineteenth, as he will stay with the horses in Hafford while we are away."

Chapter Twenty One

Nineteenth came the next morning to the barracks with an invitation for Loyal and Adoni to break their fast in the manorhouse with the family. Gerwal was already seated at the dining table when they arrived. The deep lines around his wide mouth had relaxed somewhat and his eyes were bright. Angel sat beside him, the wavy strands of her hair held back with glittering combs. His chest grew tight at the sight—it seemed he'd waited forever for this woman and their conversation last night just reinforced that feeling. He barely managed to pull his gaze away to greet his host.

"Loyal," Gerwal said, "pull up a chair. We can get down to business." He indicated the place across from him. "I'm looking forward to another opportunity to talk with you."

Angel rose and poured them each a bowl of tea before returning to the table. She gave him a small smile. "Mr Hawker," she said in greeting. "Adoni. Please help yourselves."

Loyal smiled and followed Adoni to the sideboard,

where a delectable array of dishes were warming over a funnel from the fireheat below. He selected points of toasted pané, lentil porridge and fried sablefish. He was starving after the long day yesterday, and knew today was going to be stressful—not sure even now what was expected of him in these 'talks' with Banderos and his sons.

He was just glad someone here wanted to see him for whatever reason, otherwise how would he have met Angel? How he was to continue seeing her was the bigger question, one he was driven to answer. Hopefully the links would aid in that endeavour and the trip to Sommerset would add to his opportunities to get close to her.

"Gerwal," he said, taking his seat at the table. "You're looking better. Perhaps more comfortable?" He gave an easy grin. "What's changed?"

His host's face grew dark as he glanced toward Adoni. Gerwal had seemed to be put off by Adoni's appearance the first time they had arrived at the Banderos compound. "Your assistant is an aide in more areas than one," he muttered. "My back is getting better. I've been able to move around more comfortably. Something's shifted. Not sure..." He frowned into his tea bowl then gave a grudging nod at Adoni. "Perhaps another treatment before you leave today."

Adoni grinned and took a big bite of his porridge. "Be glad to," he mumbled. "I'm not as skilled as my father, but I did learn quite a bit while helping in his clinic."

Angel favoured him with a grateful smile. "We can't thank you enough, Adoni. Father has been in great pain for a long time, and this relief is most welcome."

His assistant flushed a dark red and Loyal frowned into his sablefish. He snorted. He was acting like he did when he was six and Mother complimented the boy who lived next door. Jealousy was a waste of time and he was too old to sink into sulks.

Raising his head, he gave Adoni an affectionate pat on the shoulder. "He's a very valuable member of my team," he said, looking into Angel's eyes. "I couldn't manage all I do without his assistance."

Loyal took another bite of his meal. "I've brought some links with me. Already gave one to Fourteenth."

This news was greeted with complete silence. Glancing up, he caught an alarmed look pass between Gerwal and his daughter. "What?" he said. "You don't want a voicelink? It'll help in all kinds of ways."

Angel spoke first. "We don't know how to use them, or what they do, for that matter. And we've been told there is no connection in our area to make them work. We also learned if we get a link it means our enemies can spy on us and hear what we talk about. Is that true?"

Loyal choked back a laugh, knowing that's exactly what the Khandarken military wanted to do with their new installation. "I know there's been no decent connection here. Adoni and I both noticed our links got scrambled and finally lost contact when we were travelling through the last time. But that has been resolved. A new tower was installed in Hawker Hills, just inside the Khandarken border."

Angel's delicate brows rose in surprise. "Hawker Hills? Are they so named after your family, Loyal?"

"Yah, after my father's father." He grew warm under her interested gaze. "He was a miner. They've had talc mines there for generations, now owned by the Farmer family, my cousins."

"So these towers will make links work in our area?" Gerwal asked.

Loyal unclipped his infolink and tapped it on. "Here's the map of Banderos land. I showed it to your daughter on our journey here last time." He adjusted the funnel and passed it to Gerwal. "That link wasn't working the first time we came here, but it's performing very well now."

"I see." The father frowned at the screen. "This is our map? It looks different from the one we have."

Angel laid a hand on his arm. "First draws those, Father. The actual perimeter is not the same as the one he's laid out."

Gerwal shrugged. "And what about our enemies knowing where we are and what we're talking about?"

"Who are your enemies?" Loyal asked. He felt Adoni lean in at his shoulder to hear the answer.

"The Nazurs for a start. And all the dispossessed in the hills who collaborate with Emperor Carlton."

"Hmm." Loyal took a sip of tea. "Not likely the

dispossessed have links. And who are the Nazurs? Never heard of them."

"Well, you will if you hang around here for long," Gerwal muttered.

Angel put her hand on her father's shoulder in comfort. "They're the family to the west of us," she said. "Olaf Nazur is the head, and his eldest son Orde runs things for him. They don't have as much land as we do, but they've been known to claim some of our territory in the past. There have been a few battles, haven't there, Father?" She gave Gerwal a worried look. "It's just best if we stay on top of the situation before it gets out of hand."

"I see. It sounds complicated." The more Loyal learned, the more he wondered what they wanted from him. "Well, these links might help in that regard. I think one for you, Gerwal, one for you daughter, also Nineteenth. Then I'm not sure. Would Rascal be the one who is in contact with you most often?" He was looking at Angel now, hoping she would tell him what worked best.

She blushed bright pink. "I don't know how to use it."

Heat bloomed in his chest. "It will be my pleasure to show you," he said.

Chapter Twenty Two

Gerwal Banderos rose to end the talks and Loyal eyed his host as he left the room with Adoni for a final sookie treatment before they departed the compound. He was getting somewhere with the tribal leader, if only to lay out the concerns of the Khandarken government regarding Carlton's plans for expansion. But Mr Banderos seemed to have a different agenda than just defending his land, and Loyal hadn't been able to figure out exactly what it was. Angel must know, as she'd recruited him in the first place.

He found her in the garden at the side of the manorhouse, a basket of flowers on the ground at her feet. "Your garden's beautiful," he said.

She straightened, cheeks turning pink at his comment. "Thank you." Her work robe was shorter, ending just below the knee, and leggings peeped out from beneath the hem. It was a delightful reminder of how she'd looked the first day he met her in Hafford, with her form-fitting trousers under that formal robe. Her hair had fallen out of the comb on one side, and he wanted to lift the silky strands and rub them between his fingertips to feel the texture.

His gaze must have been intense because she put a hand to her hair, watching him guardedly.

He smiled and gestured to the basket. "Are you gathering your daily bouquet?"

She relaxed, nodding. "Yes. These are all flowering well and the scent is lovely. They fill the Great Hall with their perfume." She set her shears in the basket. "Have you come to show me how to work the link?"

"Yah. But there's something else." He looked down the field a moment to gather his thoughts. "I get the feeling you aren't comfortable with your safety, or that of your family."

"Oh." Seemingly speechless, she gazed up at him. Finally she pointed to a bench in the shade at the side of the flower garden. "Would you sit with me a moment?"

He followed and took a seat after she did. Perhaps now he'd learn some of what he needed to know.

She clasped her hands tightly as the colour came and went in her cheeks. "First is the leader among my brothers," she stated. "Father arranged that early on and as the years went by the sons grew accustomed to the idea. Most of them are fine with it, Fourth and Fifth more so than the others. But there are further considerations. With Father's failing health and First taking more and more control, it has become obvious he will be a tyrant over the family. My brothers are not all amenable to that situation."

Loyal nodded. "The matter of succession has finally raised its head."

She gave him a grateful smile. "Exactly." Then she frowned. "But there are other issues to consider."

"Okay." He smiled into her eyes. "Tell me."

She hesitated. "It's confidential," she said at last. "You can't reveal this to anyone."

He took her hand in his and stroked the backs of her slender fingers. "I promise," he said solemnly. "You have my word."

Angel stared at her hand where it lay clasped in his then glanced away. "Several of my brothers have died under strange circumstances."

"I see." He didn't, but it obviously bothered her and he squeezed her fingers in sympathy. "I'm very sorry, Angel."

"So am I," she murmured. "First has been involved each time."

He stalled. "First involved? How do you mean?"

"I think First killed them."

There was a thud in his chest as his heart leaped in alarm. He hadn't met the oldest brother, but this information was more than surprising. "You might be in danger," he said savagely. "I won't allow that to happen."

"Pardon?" She squinted up at him.

"I can't leave you here without protection." He stood abruptly. "You'll have to come with me."

She stared, then a gentle smile spread across her lips. "That's so kind. I don't think anyone has ever…" She gazed across her garden and her expression changed. "That isn't what is worrying. First is no threat to me, as I will never be in line for succession. I am not the one who will challenge him for control. I think Father is in danger, because his health has been failing and my eldest brother can't wait to take up the reins of the establishment. Now, with the treatments Adoni has given him, Father is getting stronger rather than failing. It will make First angry. It's possible Father was injured to begin with because First arranged it. I think he was supposed to die from that accident, but he survived. My brother is getting more and more directive, as if he can't wait for Father to go."

Loyal took a seat, his gaze pinned to her face. "Are you sure you're not in any danger? If First is that desperate, it's possible there's no limit to what he might do."

"I know." She looked sadly back at him. "But I believe it will be Father who is next to die from an accident."

Loyal nodded. "That's how your brothers died?"

"Yes. Second was only seven when he fell from the wall of the compound." She pointed to the high barrier in the distance that encircled the manorhouse and extensive grounds. "I heard from my mother what a clever and kind boy he was, learning much faster than First did in the classroom. One of the grooms said he saw First up on the wall with Second and they were wrestling, but no one actually saw Second fall. It was very sad. Their mother died of a broken heart, it was said. Fifth was only a baby then."

Loyal thought a moment. "Was there a boy called Third?"

"Yes, he died an infant, a few days old."

"I see. What a tragic story."

"I think it's why Fourth and Fifth follow First so closely and do exactly what he tells them. They're devoted, but also afraid. They understand what he's capable of."

Loyal rubbed a hand over his face. This was more complicated than he could have imagined. With that many men struggling for control, it was hard to tell what would happen or which way it might go.

Angel wrung her hands. "That isn't all."

He placed a hand over hers. "I'll help any way I can, Angel. I care very much for you. I hope you know that."

She looked longingly into his eyes. "There's more," she said.

"Tell me." He raised her hands to kiss the backs of her fingers.

"Sixth died in his bed one night when he was twelve years old. There was nothing wrong—that is, he wasn't ill. He was dead in the morning. My mother heard his face was flushed beet red when they found him, as if he couldn't breathe. I think First smothered him."

Loyal took a breath. "Why do you believe that?"

"Our tutor. He said Sixth excelled at riding and hunting. He was better than First at target practice, beat everyone at the races they used to have. Father was pleased with him, would talk at the dinner table about how clever he was with the horses. First would get angry, leaving the table in a huff. Then Sixth died, and First calmed down. It just looks like a pattern. Father wouldn't hear it, of course. He defends all of his sons, no matter their actions."

Loyal looked at her. "This is mostly speculation, you realize. First may be dangerous, but you don't know for sure if he did these things, other than kill Second. That sounds pretty compelling. But they were just boys."

"Sixteenth died two years ago," she said. "He was twenty-five."

Loyal got an ominous feeling in his gut. "How did he die?"

"He fell and struck his head against one of the pillars at the side of the house. First killed him."

"You have proof?" he asked doubtfully.

"Not till recently. At the time, Nineteenth saw him fall. But Fourteenth told us just a few days ago he saw First club him on the back of the head. They'd been arguing. Sixteenth hit his head when he fell, but his skull was already bashed in."

Loyal blew out a breath and gazed to the

compound wall in the distance, imagining two young boys fighting on the top of the structure. It would be easy enough to shove your competitor off without losing your balance. Especially if you were the older, bigger brother.

Chapter Twenty Three

The sun was now high in the sky, and Loyal knew they would be leaving the Banderos compound shortly.

"Angel." Leaning forward, he carefully brushed a kiss against her temple where the warm golden hair waved back from her fair face as his heart thundered in his chest. "I'm very fond of you. I want to see you, which is difficult when you live so far away from where I work." It was a desperate situation, in his view, made worse by the yearning in his heart.

"Oh." She put a hand to her red cheek, then awkwardly rearranged her robe. "I was hoping you would visit us again."

"I will if I'm invited." Hopefully, he smiled into her eyes.

She nodded eagerly. "Your talks with Father are finished for today. But I think there will be other opportunities. And we are going to Sommerset." Her eyes glowed.

He rubbed his thumb carefully across her full lower lip. "I don't know what you hope to gain from these meetings."

She searched his face with her gaze. "I hope you will help Father form a plan to manage the Banderos organization, especially for the time when he grows too weak or ill to do it himself. The way we are organized now doesn't work, the dispossessed are coming onto our land searching for something. Emperor Carlton is making noises about returning to this area and we sit right in the middle."

"You're a clever woman," he said. "I can see all the chaos around you, can your father?"

She smiled. "I've been working on that," she said.

"Good." He reached into his pocket. "Listen, before you run off to get ready for our travels—I brought two beltlinks with me. These are links for short distances, and they're silent. That means you can communicate with someone nearby and no one else will hear or be aware that you've sent a message. I want you to take one."

She looked confused. "I already have a link, you just gave me one."

He smiled. "I know. That one is a voicelink, to talk to your brothers, your father, or me." He raised his brows playfully and, to his delight, she blushed. "It's a public device, makes noise when you use it. But the beltlink is different. Who is near all the time, someone you trust who could come to your aid if needed, or call for help if he couldn't rescue you himself?"

She laughed. "That would be Rascal. He's only thirteen, but he's always here. He travels with me to Hafford, and stays to ride home with me. I trust him."

He watched the lovely smile spread across her face, as his gut clenched in reaction. He was in so much trouble with his attraction to her. He felt a violent need to keep her safe. "So, you keep one beltlink and we give the other to Rascal. Don't tell anyone else. It may be you can't trust some of the others right now, but this link gives you a little insurance. I just hope you never have the need to use it."

~***~

The trip to Hafford was quickly arranged, and the party left the Banderos compound at noon, as planned. Fourteenth branched off toward the north border station, while Nineteenth led the rest through the shortcut, quickly arriving at the small village. Loyal decided to leave his trailer in the storage shed behind the bar and drove the transport to the side of the Hafford track, shutting down the engine.

"Nineteenth, we will be back tomorrow afternoon, never fear." Angel patted his arm reassuringly. "I'll have so many stories to tell you about what we've seen."

Her brother gazed fondly into her face, a small smile curling his lip. "Be careful, that's all I ask." He narrowed his eyes at Loyal. "Take care. I don't want anything to happen to her."

Loyal nodded and shook the man's hand. "I'll protect her, don't worry. Is First still in Sommerset, do you think?"

Nineteenth shook his head. "He left there this morning, heading to the south station to do an inspection, according to his men. I imagine he'll be back at the compound tomorrow." His gaze landed on the transport and he raised his brows. "Is that contraption what you're travelling in?"

"Yah." Loyal laughed at his expression and helped Angel behind the frontboard, loading her bag in the compartment at the back. Adoni and Rascal crammed themselves into the rear seats and they were off.

Chapter Twenty Four

Angel couldn't contain her excitement. It had been years since she'd travelled anywhere outside the Banderos compound just for the pleasure of seeing something new. The city of Sommerset had always held a huge attraction for her, given Emperor Aqatain had his headquarters there. The schools set up for the upper class and military sons, with jousting, hard fought games and deadly battles had a reputation for separating the leaders from the rest of the students. Some of her older brothers had attended the school, although that all fell apart when the Emperor was forced to flee Sommerset, only to be defeated in the hinterland to the north.

But the beautiful buildings and courtyards were still there. The stories of the Sommerset Fair were legendary—the Sparkling Wheel sat at the centre of expansive grounds that hosted the event. There were barns and fenced fields where competitions of all types took place. Horse and llama races, pig races, even goat carts. She'd heard there were hundreds of different types of animals from tiny hens laying eggs the size of a coin, to giant birds with eggs that fed ten men. She was sure it couldn't all be true, but it was so terrifying to think about.

Just to ride in Loyal's transport was exhilarating. The engine seemed to be silent, but the body was armoured, so perhaps it was a military vehicle. The frontboard held a holograph map that showed their route—she followed the path with her finger along a winding rural track that widened into a road, then through outbuildings at the edge of Sommerset. The street layout seemed quite intricate, but she found the spot on the map where the Wheel was located. They were travelling at an alarming speed, because according to the numbers at the bottom of the display, they would arrive shortly. She was astounded, knowing how long it had taken her family to get there when travelling by horse.

She wiggled in her seat and Loyal leaned to speak in her ear above the whistle of the wind. "Are you comfortable? I think there is a seat cushion in the cubby at the back." He started to slow the vehicle, but she laid her hand on his arm.

"I'm fine," she said. "Just excited."

His expression changed from the sober concentration of handling the transport to amusement and heat as he glanced at her, his pale blue eyes focussing on her face for a long moment. She felt the warmth in her lower limbs, as if a slow fire had started in her belly and spread downward. He had a compelling presence, and she was having trouble deciding how to handle it. Thank heaven Rascal was with her, protection against a misstep on her part triggered by this powerful attraction.

Father hadn't even raised an eyebrow at her decision to make an unscheduled trip to Hafford at the same time Loyal was leaving the compound. He probably thought it made sense to travel in a larger group. She pursed her lips to keep from laughing. This was an adventure, and she was determined to enjoy it. After all, she wasn't a prisoner of the family compound, and had been in charge of her own travels for years, although she always had an escort. In the early days, several of her older brothers had gone with her and collected her again for the journey home. But things had been stable for some time in the territory around them, and Rascal became her companion. He would have a good time on this trip.

Before she knew it, they had entered the city streets and pulled to a stop in front of a formal looking building, the façade built in stacked layers almost like a birthday cake. "The Sommerset Learmonth Hotel," Loyal said. "It's the best place to stay." He handed the keys for the transport to Adoni, passed the luggage to Rascal to carry and stood by the transport door to help her out. His hand was warm and firm on hers, and a little flutter took up room in her stomach at his touch.

He gave her an enigmatic smile. "This way." He tucked her hand in the crook of his arm and lead her between the gates of a flower garden and up the wide, slightly blue granite steps to the dark carved double doors of the establishment. An attendant immediately stepped forward and opened the door, bowing low. "Welcome back, Mr Hawker," the fellow said.

Loyal gave a nod of acknowledgement. He must stay here often to be recognized by the staff like that. She studied his tanned face, the curly white-blond sideburns along his jaw. She'd thought he was a hawker of goods, but knew deep down he was much more than that.

The walls of the hotel entry were panelled in gleaming gold cloth above wainscoting of carved reddish-coloured wood. The floor was scattered with rugs decorated with figures of wild animals and birds against a dark background. She'd never seen carpets so thick. Her feet sank in the pillowy fabric as they approached the desk situated against the far wall.

"Loyal Hawker," he said, and the clerk promptly turned to grab a handful of heavy brass keys from a cubby on the wall behind him. "Here you go, sir," he said. "Your usual rooms and an extra one for your guest." He smiled at Angel, the light of curiosity in his gaze as he seemed to take her measure. Her cheeks got hot, but the clerk gave an approving nod and wink at Loyal. He frowned, grasping her elbow and steering her toward the curved staircase.

"We have three rooms," he said, his gaze intent on her face. "I usually take two, one for me, one for Adoni. I thought Rascal could bunk in with Adoni and you would have your own room. Does that work?" He lifted his brows.

"Yes," she smiled. "That's fine, isn't it, Rascal?"

At Rascal's nod, Loyal relaxed. "I'm thinking about security. Angel takes the middle room, and we are on either side of her." He gestured to his assistant. "Let's go. We've got a lot to see tonight."

Angel's stomach fluttered with excitement. Yes, they did.

Chapter Twenty Five

Angel was so excited, she thought it would be impossible to fall asleep in the strange bed. She'd not stayed in a hotel room before, certainly not on her own without family present. Having Rascal next door was some comfort, but with Loyal on the other side, her excitement mounted. She glanced at the door connecting her room to his, knowing it was locked on her side and he would never presume to knock.

They'd had dinner in the hotel dining room where a huge banquet had been laid out for the guests. She'd never seen so many different kinds of dishes—llama roasted, baked and stewed, game birds on a spit, numerous vegetables with a rose wine sauce, hundreds of desserts. Rascal was totally overwhelmed and ate too much, ending up with a stomach-ache.

She giggled as she moved around the room. He was still just a boy, after all. She often saw hints of the man he would become, but not yet it seemed. He'd recovered in time to ride the Sparkling Wheel in the fairgrounds, though. That had been equally thrilling and alarming.

Two by two, they were strapped into seats as the wheel slowly turned, so they finally ended up at the top of the giant structure looking down on all the lights and movement far below. It was breathtaking. She'd never been that high in the air. Once the seats were full, the wheel began to move at a swiftly progressing pace until her hair flew out behind her from the force of the wind, and the sights below blended together in a whirl of flashing lights and sound. She felt like she was flying.

Her hands clung fiercely to the handle in front of her and she was grateful when Loyal reached to wrap his arm around her shoulders. She leaned against the solid wall of his chest, glad of the comfort offered when he pulled her close.

As the wheel gradually began to slow, he lifted her chin with a tender finger and placed his lips over hers. The effect was electrifying. She sank into the kiss with abandon, feeling the weightlessness in her belly as the ride slackened in the air. She fought for breath, her lungs labouring. His eyes gazed into hers with such desire and determination, she couldn't look away and was taken by surprise when Rascal shouted at her from where he stood on the ground.

She realized he and Adoni had already been released from their seat and she would be next. Hurriedly, she glanced down and shifted away from Loyal, tugging her robe into place as the wheel attendant reached to unhook the bar. She took his proffered hand and stood on unsteady legs.

She gazed at the connecting door to Loyal

Hawker's room. She was alone here, and he was alone there. His kiss had been captivating. What more would she experience, if she just unlocked the portal and walked through? *Would he be shocked?*

She smiled to herself. Not shocked, that wasn't the reaction she was certain she'd see if she took that step. She was a grown woman, not some child who had to do her father's bidding at every turn. She could make her own decisions.

She stepped forward and grabbed the handle.

~***~

Major-General Dante Regiment arrived at Krimen in a rainstorm. The aircart's bumpy landing caused his teeth to click together before the pilot brought it to a lurching halt. He glanced across at his aide. Malahide was a burly military man who bellowed his way to achieve whatever was needed in the way of cooperation from those around him. Dante's scribe was there for more mundane matters such as recording notes and agreements.

He'd arrived in the north before the others. This conference with the so-called Emperor was going to be a challenge to organize, and he wondered what, if anything, the country of Khandarken would get out of it in the way of benefit. In his view, Carlton was tricky and untrustworthy. Even if an agreement was reached, what guarantee would they have it would be adhered to? Yet, almost everyone had agreed it was worth a try.

Goodnight Barrington of Legitamia had turned down the invitation. Too bad, because it would have been an opportunity to pull him onside, rather than having him stand independently. He supported Carlton in a way that rankled with Dante, allowing him freedom of movement in his Legitamian province. In spite of the meetings held last year in Gilsigg, and the decisions hammered out and agreed upon by all in attendance, General Barrington continued on his own course, undeterred.

Collier True-May, Leader of Adar Silva, would arrive tomorrow with the others. He didn't seem to have much interest in the proceedings, given Carlton's current physical location north of Khandarken. But with the rumours of his goal to reclaim Sommerset in the south, Dante figured True-May should be worried. He wouldn't want to be in a position of handling it without support from surrounding countries if the Emperor showed up, troops in tow, demanding his old headquarters back.

Dante grinned and climbed out of the aircart. A military transport waited to take them to the Krimen Learmonth Hotel, the only place big enough in such a remote location to comfortably accommodate a group this size. The Learmonth Hotel chain had establishments in many business centres across the country, although this particular one was rundown and well used, given the small size and remoteness of the location. Once the core group was organized, they'd move off to Krimenreh, an even smaller village where he'd located a large barn to house the meetings.

He expected Leader Cownden Lanser this

afternoon, along with his assistant Anatoliy. Several of the territory representatives would attend, especially Norcross, Governor of the Collaros Territory which had suffered an invasion from Carlton's troops. They still occupied some land near the border. Governor Phelong of the Foothills was also coming. Foothills Territory was south of Collaros, and Phelong was antsy about the many rumours of sightings of the Emperor's troops in the adjacent hills.

Dante planned to send troops of his own into the surrounding land, hoping to keep the populace calm and head off any action that might ensue as a consequence of the conference members being here. The dispossessed were always a problem, and this kind of unrest was bad for everyone in the area. His job was to organize, and back it up with more organization.

He glanced at Malahide. They were going to be very busy during the next few days. The pressure was on.

Chapter Twenty Six

In the hotel room, Loyal relaxed against the bolster on his pallet, one arm propped behind his head. It had been fun taking Angel and her brother around the Sommerset Fair. She was just as thrilled as Rascal to see the sights. Like two little kids, they ran from one pen to the next to view the different animals. He would have thought living on a huge farm, they'd be used to all the creatures, but had to acknowledge a lot of the strange species came from elsewhere. Even he had been interested to examine the ungainly and ferocious-looking mammal from the far west. The sight of its crossed eyes, long hairy neck and huge hooves made Loyal grab Angel around the waist and haul her out of danger.

He rolled to his side. The ride on the Sparkling

Wheel had been worth it. Angel had been thrilled, her eyes as bright as the lights on the turning machine as they spun through the night. He ached to kiss her, had wanted to forever, and that was his first opportunity. The kiss was perfect, better than perfect, so much so he forgot where they were, or that her brother waited below. Except it ended too soon. If only….

He turned his head at the sound of a click, watching in frozen anticipation as the handle slowly twisted on the door leading to Angel's room. He held his breath, afraid to move as it opened and Angel appeared as if he'd conjured her up in his mind. She was wearing a nightdress of some gauzy fabric that reached her ankles, and her hair shone like a dark golden shawl on her shoulders. His cock sprang to attention with painful intensity. Was he imagining this?

"Angel?" He leaned up on one elbow and pushed the cover down, then remembered he was naked and hastily pulled it back up. "What's wrong? Do you need something?"

She smiled and he was won over instantly. Whatever she wanted, it was hers. He didn't care— did she want to leave right away, this instant? Fine, he'd get dressed. Did she need some money? She could have everything he owned.

"I wanted to see you," she said as she advanced toward the bed.

He gawked. *See him?* "Sure." He sat up and looked

around but realized his clothes were on the bench across the room. As she drew closer, he noticed the fabric of her nightdress was almost transparent. He saw the shadow of her waist, the rise of her breasts and the small peaks where her nipples pushed against the cloth. Surely she didn't expect him to ignore that, but as a gentleman he should at least try…

Before he could decide what a gentleman should do, she pressed her knee on the cover and eased up onto the pallet beside him. He took a deep breath, reached out and pulled her close, holding her for a moment. Then he shifted to press her head to his shoulder and kiss her temple.

"What are you doing to me, Angel?" he muttered. "I can't stand much more of this. Do you need my help? if so, you'll have to go back to your room while I dress."

She giggled and he felt a smile form on his mouth, which promptly disappeared when she replied, "I want another kiss like the one on the Sparkling Wheel."

"By all the gods of heaven," he breathed. He wanted that too. "You test me."

"Yes," she said. "I test myself. Please kiss me again."

She didn't have to ask twice. He was already turning her in his arms and laying her back on the pallet as he leaned to press his mouth over hers. The comfort and connection were instantaneous—the heat and excitement, her soft sigh and tender breath against his cheek. He ran a hand down her nightdress, feeling the seductive shape beneath and was suddenly lightheaded. He pulled in a ragged breath.

"Angel, I love kissing you." He placed his mouth on hers, plunging his tongue into the hidden depths between those beautiful rosy lips. His temperature went up another couple of notches and his erection became more urgent.

She wrapped her slender arms around his neck and pulled him in. He was panting against her cheek and then the side of her neck as he began to explore new terrain. The nightdress slipped easily to the side to allow his mouth access to her throat. He tugged with a finger and felt the snaps give. Then he was gazing at her breasts, beautiful pale mounds of flesh, skin so soft as to appear translucent, rosy peaks begging for his attention. When he placed his mouth over her nipple, she gave a gasp, a light flutter that reverberated beneath her breastbone.

He paused. "Did I hurt you?"

Her eyes were like midnight blue fire, gazing back at him. "No," she said low. "I was just surprised."

"Did you like it?"

She gave a hesitant nod and he kissed her till her eyes slowly closed, then moved to suckle one peak, then the other. Her body jolted, hips pressing persistently against his.

His heart pounded to escape his chest, lurching with every move she made. He knew this could be a mistake, she was too innocent. There might be a better way to handle the situation, but he couldn't seem to pull back.

A loud thump sounded in the hall outside his room and they both jumped. His arms tightened protectively around her as he waited and listened, but everything had fallen silent again.

He glanced down to where her head lay across his arm almost in surrender, one pearl earring glowing dimly in the low light. Her nightdress was in shambles, gaping open to reveal her beautiful breasts. He gazed long, then reached to tug the dress closed, protecting her from his gaze.

"Angel."

Slowly her head turned toward him, eyes opening to show that riveting dark blue gaze.

"We shouldn't do this now." He took a shallow breath and sank back against the bolster, covering his eyes with his forearm. "It isn't right. Your father doesn't know where you are or who you're with. It would be a mistake to take it any further…" He felt beleaguered, as if he were signing his own death warrant.

"Yes," she whispered.

"What?" He dropped his arm and leaned over her, trying to hear over the rush of blood in his ears. "Yes, what?"

"Father doesn't know where I am. I'm a woman grown, I can make my own decisions." She looked hesitantly up at him. "Don't you want to make love with me?"

"By the dogs of hell," he hissed. "I'm dying to make love with you. I'm just having a hard time…"

She nudged him with her hip and giggled lightly. "I can tell you're having a hard time."

"Very funny," he muttered, pressing himself against her. "It's useless to deny I want you."

She kissed his neck and a shudder rippled down his spine. His glare was ferocious as his fingers fumbled with the snaps on her nightdress, opening it again for his eager gaze. "I hope you're sure, because I won't be able to stop…"

"Loyal," she whispered. "I'm sure."

Pausing, he glanced back at her face, entranced by the soft voice that seemed to flow over his skin like liquid honey. "Say that again," he said. "Just for me."

Chapter Twenty Seven

Angel heard the jingle of harness and neighing of horses. Looking out the plexi to the barns at the back of the manorhouse, she saw a string of men coming through the gate. It seemed First had arrived home. Fourth and Fifth were with him, as always, and he'd taken a guard of ten men as well. What had he been doing at the Nazurs? He'd just travelled to Sommerset and hardly stopped at the Banderos compound long enough to change his clothes and saddle new mounts before leaving again. Next they heard, he had headed out to supervise the patrol of the perimeter lands.

Luckily, she was in Sommerset after First made his journey. Her stomach jumped as she thought about his reaction if he'd discovered her there in the company of Loyal Hawker and Adoni, even though she had Rascal as companion.

Father was doing remarkably well. After Adoni's treatments, his back and legs were better and the pain somewhat alleviated. In the past, he'd used a lot of phang for the acute discomfort, chewing chunks of the stuff as he lay in his rubber plastic lounge mulling different problems, and she'd been worried about his increasingly fuzzy thinking. The phang oil especially seemed to muddle his speech to the point where she left him to sleep it off because his words didn't make sense.

But the more Adoni worked on him, the faster he seemed to mend. And it was all due to Loyal the Hawker. She warmed at the thought. Loyal had suggested the treatments in the first place, then made his assistant available to work on Father's back.

Her fingers tingled where he'd pressed his mouth to them in the garden. She couldn't believe she'd divulged so much information about her family, but he appeared totally trustworthy. He was concerned and wanted to help her, help all of them.

She placed her palm against her temple, where he'd kissed her. It had been startling. No one treated her in such a way. Living where she did, with all these brothers, there wasn't a man in the whole guard who dared approach her. She placed her fingers over her lips as the effect of his kiss tumbled her heart in her breast. *What did it mean?* He'd had such an intent expression, it was hard to look in those fierce pale blue eyes that said so much…

Everything had changed from the moment they made love together in his Sommerset hotel room. She thrilled whenever she thought of what it had been like—the push and pull, the plunging and withdrawal, how he'd seduced her with his tender ministrations until she was mindless with need, then pulled her along with him toward her own surrender. She pressed her hand to her belly as the ripples of remembered tension and release played in her memory.

When would she see him again? There was a message on her voicelink from him the minute she and her brothers left Hafford for home. She giggled. There had been quite a few since. She'd replied to each one, and last night he'd called her to talk. His voice was warm like honey, settling her nerves and soothing her tummy. At the same time she was in such turmoil she couldn't get to sleep once they said goodnight. He mentioned he had plans for them. *What plans?* Her whole body tingled when she thought about it. *When would she find out?*

His talks with Father had progressed at a surprising speed. Gerwal began to divulge his worries about the future of the Banderos tribe. He discussed the dispossessed, all the guards and border attendants he'd recruited and trained. He even went so far as to express apprehension about how First handled the men, and whether he was paying attention to all the details that kept them strong and safe. Angel was astounded, never having heard a word said against her eldest brother.

Loyal had some good suggestions, speaking about his experience with the Governor of some territory in Khandarken whom he worked for. He wasn't just a seller of goods. She hugged herself, hoping they were making progress. Things were still up in the air at the Banderos compound, but it looked like progress with Father to her inexperienced eyes.

She hurried down the stairs and arrived in the Great Hall just as First burst through the door. In a foul mood, First's face was like a thundercloud, deep furrows dug in his brow.

"What's going on here?" he roared.

Angel paused on the bottom step, alarm racing along her limbs. "What do you mean, First?" she said, trying for a calm voice.

"I hear from the staff that hawkers have been here, a couple of times now. But never when I'm around."

"Don't be silly," she said, feigning indifference as she descended the last step and walked across to stand beside Father's lounge. "How would we know when you'll be here? You certainly don't tell us."

His frown lessened. "Father," he said in rough greeting. "How is the pain today?"

"Good." Gerwal rose from the rubber plastic chair. "I seem to be on the mend." He walked across to the scroll-top desk against the far wall.

First stared, his mouth open. "You're well?" His voice had risen half an octave. "When did you begin to walk again?"

"I could always walk," Father stated irritably. "It was just very painful. But the pain is largely gone, and I'm healing."

First's face became shuttered. "Well, that's…" There was a long pause. "That's surprising."

Angel scrutinized his face, taking in the disgruntled expression. "How did things go in Sommerset?" she asked. "Did you get what you wanted?"

He turned on her. "How do you know what I wanted?" he snarled. "Little sisters should learn to keep their mouths shut."

Gerwal frowned. "First, watch your tongue."

She backed up a step. "Then how did it go at the Nazur compound?"

He gave her a slow grin. "Olaf is dead. Did you know?"

Father turned at the news, astonishment written on his face. "Dead? Since when?"

"Since a few weeks ago. High temp virus. He went fast, according to his son."

"That's awful." Angel covered her mouth with her fingers. "I've not heard that the high temp virus is travelling through. We'd better be prepared. How many others caught it?"

"No one, according to Orde."

She frowned. "That seems odd. It always attacks at least a few people before it moves on."

"That's what I've heard," First grunted.

Gerwal frowned. "That means we'll have to negotiate a different agreement with Orde Nazur, the son."

"Already started on it," First sneered.

"Is that going well?" Angel wondered if things would become more difficult dealing with the Nazurs without Olaf as the steadying hand.

"Better than you might think, little sister," First said, grinning. "Better than you might think."

Father reached for something in the desk. "I've got a link, son," he said. "And there's one here for you. That way we can keep in touch and you can let me know where you are and what you're working on. I need to be involved in negotiations with Orde."

First gaped. "A link? I told you those were a bad idea. They don't work here, anyway."

"They do work," said Angel. She pulled hers out of her pocket, leaving the beltlink where it was hidden clipped to her waistband. She clicked on Father's particulars. The device chirped in his hand, prompting him to chuckle and tap the button in reply.

"Where did you get those?" Her brother strode across the floor and snatched the gadget out of Father's hand. "Who gave them to you?"

Gerwal took it back with a measured grasp. "We got them from Hawker." He gave his son a gimlet-eyed stare. "There's one here for you if you want it. We have a link at each border station now, and Fourteenth and Nineteenth are able to keep in touch. It's called progress."

First turned and stalked from the room. Angel watched him leave and wondered what the repercussions would be when he found out everything that had happened while he was away.

Chapter Twenty Eight

First walked into the men's barracks and slammed the door to his rooms on the main floor. He shuffled his dusty clothes off and threw them at a chair. Someone would fetch and wash them—he didn't have to deal with it. He stepped into the garderobe and stood under the shower, sluicing water over his head.

The trip to Sommerset had been a huge disappointment. Who did Judson Lanser think he was to dismiss First Banderos out of hand? He scooped soap from the dish beside him, ran it over his head and began to scrub. He wasn't a nobody Lanser could flick off like ridding himself of a bothersome fly. First had land, a lot of land, and even more once this deal with Orde was hammered into place. There were tribal claims in Jiran smaller than the territory the Banderos family would soon control. However, on this trip, he'd discovered the Advisor had left Sommerset for meetings with the Emperor. There had been no one to negotiate with. He scrubbed harder.

Once the deal with Orde was solidified, Angel would be out of his hair, literally. He laughed and rinsed his head, smoothing the soapy water down his body. No one challenged him like she did. The brothers didn't bother, although some, like Fourteenth and Nineteenth worked around him more than with him. But he still held the control.

He grabbed a bath sheet from the drying rack and towelled himself dry. He was hungry, it had been an early start this morning. The cook would have something to get him through till it was time for sup.

He dragged on some clean clothes from the chest of drawers in his rooms and walked through to the cookhouse, settling alone on one of the benches. Soon there was a large tankard of clouded ale in front of him. A bowl of llama and leek stew quickly followed, the aromatic steam rising to his appreciative nostrils.

What was Father up to anyway? Links, suddenly everyone had a link? It put a different light on things. The family could communicate without relying on the old method of sending a boy to deliver a message. This couldn't be good—unless he learned how to manipulate that, too. If he had his own link, and sent misleading information to the others, it would send them off track long enough to get his plans into motion.

He took another bite and stirred the bowl thoughtfully. Was there a way to speed things up? He hadn't yet succeeded in negotiating the arrangement with the Emperor that was needed to put his strategy in place. What else could he do? *Approach Carlton directly?* It wasn't likely the Emperor would even give him the time of day. But if Lanser didn't see his way clear to cooperate, who else was there to negotiate with?

He'd find a way. He was determined and no one was going to stop him.

~***~

Angel checked her voicelink. There hadn't been a message from Loyal since earlier this morning. *I miss you*, it read. *I can't wait to get back to Banderos to see you again.* She smiled to herself as butterflies took up residence in her stomach. She replied, *I miss you too. When are you coming?* But there was no answer.

He told her he was flying today with Adoni to Krimen, a town in northern Khandarken. *Flying?* It sounded so exciting. She'd never considered doing such a thing. There were meetings to be held with Emperor Carlton and leaders from the surrounding countries. Loyal would be there to assist his boss, as some of the Governors would attend as well.

She hoped he would be safe. Somehow the idea that he might be in danger sent her heart scurrying in a faster beat and her stomach twisting in knots. *Please be all right, please be all right.* She deleted the message. It sounded childish and he treated her more like an adult than anyone here, including Father. She felt she'd become a woman during their time together in

Sommerset.

Maybe Nineteenth and Rascal were the exceptions to that. Nineteenth carried his link with him wherever he went, and checked in with her daily, reporting where he was working and when he would be back. It was a real comfort. But Rascal had undergone the biggest change.

When she gave him the extra beltlink and told him why Loyal had given her two, he'd blinked in surprise and focussed tightly on her face. "I see," he said as he listened to the story, "I see. This is like an insurance policy for you." He frowned down at it. "Show me how to use it. I'm still getting to know this voicelink thing."

They'd spent some time figuring out how to work it effectively and Rascal clipped it to his belt under his shirt. "It's secret, right?" He gave a nod. "I won't even tell Runt. This is too serious."

Since then, he'd checked in with her several times a day, always letting her know where he was going and when he'd be back, and asking her own plans. He seemed to have grown an inch in the meantime, not just in stature but maturity.

Runt complained he was no fun any more, but Rascal just smiled and said he had business to tend to.

Chapter Twenty Nine

When Loyal arrived in Krimenreh in northern Khandarken, he was astounded to discover the meetings with Emperor Carlton would be held in this tiny village in a barn at the end of the track. "Nowhere else would work," Governor Maude muttered. "Can you see a bigger building around here?"

Loyal gazed up and down the short row of houses and shook his head. The place was remarkably similar to Hafford near the Banderos territory. There were two or three shops, a stable for travellers, a few houses built along the trail that wandered past, and this barn attached to a farmer's shed. They had managed, with some persuasion, to move the farmer and his family out of the place so they could prepare for the meetings. The structure had been cleaned and washed down, furniture flown in and tables arranged in an approximate pattern of a boardroom, with extra chairs lined up like a gallery deeper in the space.

Loyal wasn't sure how it would work. Leader

Cownden Lanser and his assistant were already setting up their files at the end table. Major-General Dante Regiment had arrived with his man, Malahide, and was working with a scribe to lay out what they would need. True-May, Leader of Adar Silva, had just flown in and his huge entourage was taking up a lot of space at the other end of the room.

Emperor Carlton was scheduled to arrive this evening. No one had confirmed how many would be in his party, but the guesses swung wildly between three and twenty. No doubt there would also be a large guard.

"I heard Prince Shandro Penrhy and his wife Princess Chinata have just arrived at the landing strip," Maude declared. "They've sent a transport to fetch them."

"Yah," Loyal replied. "And how many governors are on the attendance list?"

Maude shrugged. "Norcross, for sure. This is his territory, and it was his land that was seized by Carlton at the beginning of the recent battles. Phelong is coming from Foothills. He's got hordes of dispossessed in the mountains to the west, all marching toward Carlton's recruitment tent, it seems. I hear Jukes will be here, after that attempted invasion at Eight Mile in the Northern Territory last year."

"So, where do we set up?" Loyal scanned the jumble of furniture at the rear of the barn. "Not at the main table, I imagine."

"No." Amused, Frank Maude gestured toward the

back of the building, where extra tables had been lined up with a row of chairs behind them. "We're over here. Let's take these." He waved to the end row. "We can get in and out without disturbing the others, and it's easier to hear the discussion."

They moved off and began unpacking just as a group arrived at the barn door. Prince Shandro and his henchmen entered carrying their gear. Dante Regiment greeted them and introduced the others. Loyal was surprised to see Princess Chinata with him, a charming-looking woman with very pale skin and deep black curly hair, remarkably similar to Cownden Lanser. No one else had brought a woman, but then he remembered that she was not only Shandro's wife but carried authority in her own right as Aqatain's daughter. She would be able to reinforce any stance the Prince might take to protect their land.

Maude watched the Penrhys mill in the entrance. "Must be from Jiran," he murmured. "They have that look about them with the dusky skin."

"Yah," Loyal slung another pack on the table. "Prince Shandro and his wife Princess Chinata."

"Do you know them?" Maude's head swung around in surprise.

Loyal grinned. "I've met him. We did some negotiations over a rather large delivery of medic supplies. I'm guessing that's his wife."

"I'd say so," Maude said. "She has the same appearance about her as Emperor Carlton."

"Huh." Loyal took another look. "Aqatain must

have had some strong genes." He wondered what his own children would look like. *Would they take after him with the white blond curls and tanned skin, or would they look like the mother who bore them?* That thought lead him straight to memories of the night he'd spent with Angel Banderos in Sommerset and he felt his face flush.

Maude laughed at his expression, obviously taking it to mean something else. "Yah, he said. "I've known for a long time that Cownden Lanser was Aqatain's son, and just found out recently about the daughter. But I've often wondered how many others are still out there."

~***~

First fingered the piece of parchment in his pocket. It was the second message he'd received from Orde Nazur, demanding another meeting to sign an agreement about everything they'd discussed during his last visit to the Nazur compound. He was ready to set out the timelines that would bring it to completion.

He must be pretty anxious to get his hands on Angel, First thought with a grin. However, First wasn't ready to sign an agreement. Nor was he interested in putting the plan in writing. The last thing he wanted was the existence of proof of what he hoped to accomplish. That kind of information in the wrong hands might prove fatal for the whole scheme. And the wrong hands included Father's. Nor was First totally committed to the arrangement he'd discussed with

Nazur.

He was doing his best to set up another meeting of some kind with one of Carlton's men, but so far without result. Just who that might be was still unknown. No one knew when Judson Lanser would return from the northern meetings. But if First could get an arrangement in place with Emperor Carlton, it would significantly impact the plan he'd laid out for the Banderos and Nazur lands. Things were still up in the air.

He finished his breakfast and rose from the table in the Great Hall.

"What are you up to today, First?" Father's voice was no more than a growl. He paused to clear his throat. "What are you working on, son?"

First reined in his temper with difficulty. He was well past wanting to report to anyone, least of all his father. But he wasn't there yet, still had some steps to take in advance of that. He turned toward Gerwal, noting Father was standing straight, not leaning on the table or the back of his chair for support as in the past. He gritted his teeth in frustration. Father had been wasting away the last weeks. What had spurred this sudden surge of renewed health?

"Just working on a new map. Now that I've seen the link version of the layout of our land, I can see I've left out the valley in the southern corner."

Father grunted. "What's happening with the dispossessed down there? Wasn't there a camp that had increased in size over the last months?"

"Yah." First gazed at his fingers, trying to keep from shouting his frustration. "We rousted them out with the guard from the southern border station as backup. They've all moved on."

"I see."

First didn't wait for more, leaving the dining room for the entry with long strides. He had to figure out how to handle Orde before things blew up in his face.

As he reached the door, he heard a commotion in the yard out front. Flinging the door open, he strode onto the landing, catching a glimpse in the distance of a string of riders fast approaching the gate to the compound. One of the horses was dragging a travois behind with a figure strapped to it. It swayed as the horse slowed for the turn. They were his men, he recognized the sashes on their shirts. Something had happened.

He heard rather than saw Father arrive at the doorway behind him just as he left the landing, jogging down the steps and across the yard. The horses had passed through the gates and slowed, milling about as the riders dismounted in the field below. One of the guards approached.

"A firefight at the southern station," the guard reported. "We've got your brother, he's in a bad way. Rayguns and all."

First stared blankly at him, then stepped forward to stare at the figure on the travois. It was Fifteenth, who appeared to be unconscious. His face seemed fine, but there was a burned smell rising from his clothing and First looked closer to see the side of his tunic was still smoking where it had melted to his skin.

"Quick! Take him to the medic—in the barracks behind the manorhouse." Two men bent to the task and lifted the pallet to head down the path, just as he heard a low cry and turned to find Angel running down the path on bare feet, her hand clamped over her mouth. Father was right behind her, his stride firm and strong. *By the dogs of hell. Could nothing go right?*

"Who is it?" she whispered as she stopped beside the still figure. "Fifteenth! What happened?" She whirled to gaze up at First, wanting some answers. And he didn't have any.

He waved at the men. "Get him to the medic," he shouted, then turned back to the troop. "Who did this?" he gritted.

"Not sure," one of the men said. "No insignia on their shirts, but too organized and well equipped to just be the dispossessed. They attacked the station without warning at dawn, and before we got fully organized, they retreated and were gone."

"Huh." First stared at him, running the scenario through his mind. "What about their mounts, any information to be had from them?"

"Well, we wounded a few men and one of the horses was killed. He had a Nazur brand on his rump, but not sure what that means. The horse could have escaped and been captured by someone else."

"Yah, that's true." First felt a thump in his chest. It

172

was true but unlikely. "Any more of our men injured?"

"A couple. They stayed at the station, minor injuries so we patched them up."

This was an attack out of the blue, with no provocation. *Did that sound like Orde?* Unfortunately, yes. He fingered the parchment in his pocket as his heart thumped heavily in his chest. *What had he started?*

Later that day, as Fifteenth lay unconscious in the medic's room, his burns soaking in salve and herb oil, a young boy from the day school brought First a note. It was wrapped and sealed, with his name inscribed on the front. "Someone called me to the compound gate," the boy said. "Just as we were leaving class today. He wasn't a dispossessed, there was an insignia on the sleeve of his shirt but I didn't recognize it. He said to give this to you, that you would know what to do."

First nodded and took the missive, watching the boy walk back down the path. *What now?* But he already knew. This parchment was the same quality as the other notes from Orde Nazur. He opened it with a feeling of fatality in the pit of his stomach.

Hand over Angel, or there will be more of the same, it read.

.

Chapter Thirty

Collier True-May, Leader of Adar Silva, arrived in Krimen with an entourage of three aircarts weighed down by mountains of paraphernalia, including his own bed, Loyal had heard, and a guard of forty men. Given the meetings were being held in Khandarken, a strong and committed ally of Adar Silva, it was a surprising show of strength. However once the talks began, True-May sat back and barely participated, seeming to take the view that it was Jiran and Khandarken that needed to deal with the issue of Emperor Carlton, his country being too far to the south to worry about threats of invasion.

Maude didn't have much to say about True-May that was complimentary, but Loyal took that with a pinch of salt. He'd make up his own mind. He was impressed with the Jiranis, however. The Prince and Princess seemed to work well together, and Carlton's face got redder every time his half-sister Chinata spoke. At one point, his Advisor Judson Lanser had to lay a hand on his arm to restrain him from jumping to his feet in protest as Princess Chinata set out the charges of Carlton's invasion in the Moiselle lands.

Regiment declared a break at that point and sent the parties to opposite ends of the barn to cool off over spice caf or Chilean tea and biscuits. Not an ounce of alcohol in sight, he noted, although there was no telling what the attendants might carry on their person. The only prohibition had been weapons and the scanner at the door had hummed full throttle as everyone entered earlier in the morning. Lunch was soon brought in from a recently landed aircart in the nearby field and served from a counter inside the building doorway.

Loyal walked outside to take a break, and noticed True-May in a heated discussion with Carlton's Advisor. "You were there," True-May swore. "You stayed at the Sommerset Learmonth Hotel. I have a hundred eyewitnesses. How did you get into the country in the first place?"

The Advisor raised an imperious brow. "If you're so sure I was there, you must be able to figure that out, too," he said and walked away.

True-May stared after him, his mouth a tight line. He gestured angrily at his assistant who was standing nearby and issued a long string of commands. The man immediately hustled into the barn for his case and waved the nearest transport forward to take him to the field of aircarts. Loyal wondered if the Advisor had been in Sommerset during his own visit there with Angel. Now that he'd seen him, he would recognize him if ever they were to meet. These talks were beneficial in all kinds of ways.

The atmosphere had calmed by the time everyone was assembled again around the tables for the afternoon discussions. Cownden Lanser began with a concise list of conditions he would need to see in any agreement before he would consider taking it before his Board of Representatives for discussion and ratification. When he had finished speaking, Judson Lanser conducted a lengthy private consultation with Carlton. Then he stood and responded to each of Cownden's points, one by one, with numerous reasons why it wouldn't be possible to comply.

Maude had his scribe taking notes while Loyal watched the other governors for their reactions. The red faces and violently shifting bodies spoke of the controlled rage in the room. Regiment called a halt later in the afternoon. The four governors who were present rode together in a military transport back to Krimen and Loyal was seated in the vehicle behind with some of the other guards. "A right mess," one of them commented. "Lots of talk and no action at all."

He had to agree. *What would the next two days produce?* From his view, they had made no progress whatsoever. Perhaps everyone had to blow off their frustrations upfront before they actually got down to business.

~***~

Loyal gratefully retreated to his bed when the next shift of guards came on duty, and rolled uncomfortably on the pallet, wondering what Angel was doing. He hadn't had a moment alone to respond to her messages, and now was not a good time to call her particulars. It was too late in the evening. She would be sleeping the sleep of the innocent. That thought got him even more excited and it was a long time before he dozed off. When he slept it was to dream of The Last War.

The bandage over the captain's wound was tight and the bleeding had slowed to a dull pink seepage around the edges of the binding. The young girl was still alive. Loyal used his free hand to tug her dress down covering her legs for privacy where she lay in sight of all the men. He patted her shoulder gently. "You'll be all right," he murmured. "We'll look after you. Don't worry."

The other men gazed on with disinterested eyes, but he wasn't going to give up on her. She seemed so fragile lying there unmoving in the dead grass and dried leaves. As night fell, the Emperor's troops broke out urns of whiskey and the noise grew louder around the fire

Loyal ducked his head and thrust fingers in the side of his boot, pulling out a knife blade. The men around him immediately grew alert as he sawed at the rope tied around his wrist. The strands slowly parted and he was free. He passed the knife to the next eager hand and soon all had cut their bindings. They turned as one to stare at the blind man. He was tall and lean, wearing a long grey robe, and had joined their ranks a few days ago. Loyal didn't know where he came from, the man simply appeared in their midst.

"Captain," the blind man murmured. "Can you walk?"

The captain got unsteadily to his feet and the blind man took his arm, silently leading him into the forest as the others followed. Loyal turned back. The girl was still alive, he couldn't leave her. He wasn't like Jade, his father; he was an honourable man. Grabbing her up in his arms, he lumbered after the others into the safety of the trees.

Chapter Thirty One

Loyal woke in the middle of the night to the sound of an uproar in the corridor outside his room in the Krimen Learmonth Hotel. Quickly donning pants and clipping boots on, he slung a shirt over his shoulders and ran to check on Governor Maude in the room across the hall. Maude was already awake and up, standing with a group of soldiers, Major-General Dante Regiment in the middle of the pack.

"No," Regiment was saying, "we've just heard. Four aircarts stolen from the Sommerset airstrip. Two pilots killed and a guard wounded. But as the aircarts are silent, no one heard them take off or leave the airstrip. We don't even know which way they might have gone."

"Carlton," Maude muttered loudly enough for all to hear. "Got to be his men."

Regiment lifted one shoulder. "We don't know

that. No proof. Could be a band of dispossessed, although most would not know how to fly one. The vehicles weren't around when the Last War was still raging. I'm trying to decide whether to wake Carlton to see what he might have to say."

"By all means," Maude said, running fingers through his grey hair and adjusting his eye patch. "I'd like to hear his response."

Dante nodded. "I agree. No reason for him to get a good night's sleep if the rest of us are awake." He motioned to his men and sent a couple of soldiers to the other end of the hall. They banged on the door, then waited a moment and hammered again. When they returned empty-handed, Dante sent a guard to the front desk on the main floor. The hotel manager arrived, officiously led the way to Carlton's door and knocked politely several times before inserting the key in the big lock.

The room was empty and the bed hadn't been slept in. The same was true for the adjoining rooms. Carlton and his entourage were gone.

The upheaval soon affected most of the people in the hotel as True May woke to the news, and Cownden Lanser appeared with Toll at his side. The discussion dragged on, till Maude finally retired near dawn, at which point Loyal also returned to his room.

The next morning, he woke groggily to the sound of his voicelink rumbling on the bedside table. His pallet was a tangled mess of twisted sheets. Grabbing the device, he clicked it on. Three messages. The first was from Fourteenth. *Had an attack on the southern station,* it read. *Two men injured. Came out of nowhere. Fifteenth was there.*

Loyal sat up as alarm tingled along his nerves. He read the message again. Perhaps the dispossessed were getting too aggressive. The Banderos clan would have to take measured steps to guard their area more carefully if that were the case. And who knew if Carlton was involved with instigating an uprising in that area or not? It wasn't even certain he'd been behind the theft of the aircarts.

The second message was from Gerwal. *How are the meetings going? Any progress?* This was the first time the older man had reached out to him showing an interest in the wider landscape rather than just the Banderos compound. Loyal quickly replied. *No progress so far. Will keep you posted.* He would tell Gerwal about the latest developments when it seemed appropriate.

The next was from Angel. *I miss you,* it said. His chest contracted. He missed her too, bone deep. This set of meetings had obviously gone off course, so perhaps he'd get a chance to see her sooner than he'd imagined. He continued reading. *Fifteenth has been injured and I've got my hands full nursing him.*

Fifteenth injured? Was this the same event Fourteenth had referred to? This was one of the brothers whom Loyal had not met and he didn't know where he worked or how he fit into the organization. The unsettled feeling in his stomach churned again. He had to get out of here and back to see Angel. It was a driving need that rode his shoulder with every step he took, yet seemed further away then ever after the news of the aircart raid.

He entered Angel's particulars but she didn't answer. He had to be satisfied with sending a message. *Please be careful*, he wrote. *Don't leave the compound, and stick close to your brothers.* He paused in mid-thought. He didn't want to say how he felt about her in a voicelink message. It was too personal, too private. He longed to tell her his heart was breaking for her situation, but what if her father read it? Or First?

I'll get there as soon as I can, he finally added. *Listen to Fourteenth and Nineteenth, they care about you.* He closed the link in frustration and went out to see if Governor Maude had a new plan for the day.

~***~

Carlton tugged the wig from his head and threw it on the seat beside him. Brown hair? That wasn't him. His hair was black as a raven's wing, just like his father before him. He shrugged out of the frayed coat he'd worn as he waited in the airfield this morning and laid it on top of the wig. It was an old garment no emperor should be caught wearing. The disguise had been his Advisor's idea.

He relaxed in the seat of the aircart and turned to look out the plexi at the scenery passing below. Major Paynter was a talented man and he was piloting the aircraft. Carlton didn't know if there were many others among his men who had those skills, but

Paynter assured him there likely were quite a few. And if there weren't, he'd promised to train them.

Six of his Counsellors sat in the seats behind. The scenery was stunning. He'd longed to see his land again, after being stuck in that Legitamian province for so many years. His father had lost the land, but the son was going to gain it back. After this, he'd have the right to travel across his territory, to see the rivers and streams pouring off the high mountains, making their way to the lowlands and eventually to the Catastrophic Ocean. It would all be his.

Those must be the Coal Lick Mountains, he thought, leaning forward to get a better view. Paynter was careful not to fly directly over Khandarken or Jiran but somewhere along the border between the two countries. He'd heard from his men that the city of Sommerset was taken this morning, as planned. There were some casualties, but it left him free upon arrival to proceed to his Empire Headquarters without delay

He figured with True-May away and the huge guard travelling with the Leader in the north, no one had been paying much attention to the homeland. This too had been Judson's idea, by the gods. All his Counsellors advised against such a bold move, but Carlton had grabbed the opportunity, and it was about to pay off handsomely.

When they landed in the airfield outside Sommerset, his men would be waiting, along with the corps of dispossessed they'd recruited and trained in the unclaimed land to the west. Amazing that activity hadn't drawn anyone's attention, but people saw what they expected to see, and no one anticipated finding Carlton's men right outside the Adar Silva border. It was too well known he was safely contained in the corner province of Legitamia.

His excitement mounted. The silent engine of the aircart vibrated lightly as they continued on over the Hawker Hills. He almost couldn't believe it was happening, couldn't take it in. After all these years of struggling to establish a foothold somewhere, to gain the recognition he deserved, he was about to walk with his men into the headquarters his father had lost during the final battles of the Last War.

He, Carlton, the son Aqatain barely acknowledged, would right the wrong done to the father and take his due place at the head of the New Empire.

Chapter Thirty Two

Through the day, the meetings in the Krimenreh barn were interrupted constantly with requests for more information. The attendants had devolved into small camps of offended and worried participants. Dante Regiment received the news that Sommerset had been destroyed by fire, and the information took everyone by storm. True-May flew into a towering rage that consumed the attentions of the other leaders around him. Cownden Lanser tried to pull him aside, managing to get him sequestered in one corner of the building, huddled with Prince Shandro and his wife. Now and then a burst of angry dialog floated on the air toward the other tables.

Maude gathered the Governors together and took them to the back of the building to form their own plans for response and defensive action in the coming days. Loyal was kept busy taking messages and half-written documents back and forth between the tables. Each bit of news arriving from the Khandarken military surveillance—the fall of the city, the burning of the buildings, the bands of dispossessed as part of Carlton's new army— inflamed things further and changed the direction of the talks.

Meanwhile Loyal had no chance to find out what the impact had been on the Banderos organization. *Were they attacked as well? Is that how Fifteenth had been injured?* It was galling, but there was no break in the activity until well into the evening, when the meetings finally broke up and the aircarts and transports all returned to the Krimen hotel.

Heart racing, Loyal finally got through to Angel just after midnight. He'd lost count of how many messages he'd sent in the last hour asking her to call. Even using voicelink to contact her brothers hadn't been successful as no one seemed to be attending to their devices, which was alarming. It probably meant there was a great deal going on at the Banderos compound.

The news from the south was even more alarming. Carlton's troops had overcome the Adar Silva military to take control of Sommerset and the surrounding area. He had now returned to the Old Empire headquarters. The Banderos land was frighteningly close to those borders, and although Loyal had heard the Adar Silvan military had retreated southward, it made sense that their defeat would not have been an orderly procession but an undisciplined route. There had to be bodies of military men wandering in all directions away from the site of the battles.

"Loyal." Angel's soft voice sounded breathless over the voicelink. "I'm sorry I didn't call you earlier, but it's been very busy here." A laugh seemed to catch in her throat.

"Are you all right?" He felt like he was demanding information, and was in no position to do that. Yet he needed to know. "Has the battle spread to your lands?"

"No," she sobbed. "But we have all our troops gathered along the eastern line, waiting to see what will happen. It's frightening."

"Yah. I'm sorry." Impatiently, he ran a rough hand through his hair. "I wish I could be there. The reserves have been called up and I'm on standby. We'll be travelling south again tomorrow but Governor Frank Maude has issued orders for us to stay on alert in case of activity along Khandarken borders. I don't know when…" He clamped his lips shut in frustration.

"It's all right here," she said, her tone forlorn. "We are as safe as can be. First says he has an arrangement with the Nazurs and they will send more men as reinforcements if needed."

"Huh." Loyal digested that bit of news. When he'd been there last, Gerwal had expressed concern about the Nazur tribe, especially with the father's death. "Do you think you could come here? I'll be in Deep Creek, it's close to the border just north of you. I could find you a place to stay and you'd be safe until all this calms down. And I'd be able to see you." His voice dropped lower as he thought of that enticing possibility. It was what he longed for.

"I'd like to, but I don't know," she said hesitantly. "I never leave the compound without a guard and with all the upheaval I'd need more men than normal to accompany me. Everyone is vital here right now. First has the troops roaming in half-strength with more to spell them off during the night. It's tense, but Father says…" Her voice seemed to fade.

"What does Father say?" He raised his voice, hoping he hadn't lost the connection.

She sighed. "Oh, Loyal, Father is still not well, but he's much improved with the treatments. I wanted to say thank you for that."

"It was the least we could do." His voice had turned gruff now. "I'd do more if I could. You know that, don't you?"

"Yes," she said, breathless again. "I know. Father says we've faced times like this in the past and we were fine. And we'll be fine this time."

There was a pause as he thought about that. Loyal cleared his throat. "I love you, Angel. I love you and I'm worried about you."

"Oh." There was a short silence. "You do?" Her voice sounded excited over the connection and he had to grin.

"I do. I've never said that to anyone before." There weren't enough women for him to have ever gotten close to one like he had with her. But even so, he knew in his heart that he'd fallen for her. At their first meeting as she strode into that bar in Hafford, head high and cheeks blushing, he'd been caught. She was on a mission, and he was that mission. He still wasn't entirely sure if he'd given her what she expected from those meetings with her father, but he'd damned sure tried. And he'd keep trying.

"I want to marry with you," he whispered. "Just think about it, Angel. Don't say no, not yet. You aren't betrothed to another man, are you?"

"No." Her voice was so soft he could hardly hear it. "No betrothal. I think perhaps a mother might look after things like that, but Father has never mentioned it. With my brothers, he's left it up to them to find wives. With me, I'm not sure what he expects…" Her voice trailed off again.

"I don't think anyone is looking after you," he replied, a sudden determination burning in his chest. He would be the one to do that. "I want to marry with you. Can you consider that?"

"Oh, yes!" She was almost choking on the words, her voice wobbling. "Loyal, I never considered… But if you feel for me…"

"Oh, I feel for you, sweetheart. I can hardly bear to be apart from you. This callup of the reserves couldn't have come at a worse time and I don't know how long it will last. It's breaking my heart to be away from you. Promise you'll be careful. Promise me. Don't take any risks, don't leave the compound. Stay with your brothers." He didn't know what else to say to caution her. "Please be careful."

"I will, Loyal," she whispered.

~***~

Back in Deep Creek after the Conference had been wound up, Loyal lay down on his pallet in the fighting arts barracks in a long line of sleeping men and fell into his dream.

They had been walking most of the night and finally reached the banks of the Violetta River. He was amazed the captain had been able to keep going, he looked so weak, but the blind man was at his side the whole way. His own arms were numb and his back ached from carrying the girl.

"Our men are on the other side of the river," the captain said low. "We just have to find a way across before the Empire forces discover we're gone."

One of the men gave a low laugh. "That shouldn't be too hard. They had quite a supply of whiskey in those urns. Wonder where they got it?"

Loyal sank to his haunches and laid the girl on the ground beside him. Her eyes were closed but he was sure he saw her breast move in a shallow breath. His heart contracted painfully in his chest.

"We need something to eat," said the captain, pressing a hand against the bandage on his side. "Just a few mouthfuls would do to keep us going until we

reach help."

"I've got something here," the blind man said. He opened his pocket and began to pass out handfuls of bush nuts. "Been saving them," he muttered. "Knew we'd need something eventually."

"Good man." The captain leaned back against a tree with a sigh and began to munch steadily on the nuts in his palm. "We'll take an hour, have a rest. Everyone settle down. I'll wake you when it's time to go."

Loyal lay beside the girl as the other men stretched out on the ground to rest. He held her hand in his and sank into a kind of stupor, his limbs twitching with fatigue. He was determined to save her. How could he possibly abandon a young girl who had been so abused by the Emperor's troops? He simply couldn't leave her at the side of the trail to die alone.

All too soon, he heard the captain calling softly to rouse the men. "Time to move, he said. "We can't chance it to stay longer." Loyal scrambled to his feet.

Chapter Thirty Three

Sommerset was burning. As the aircart landed on the air field just outside the city walls, Carlton caught the heavy smell of smoke and glanced out the window. Flames shot from the roof of the nearest building, smoke billowing into the air in clouds tinged a combination of angry red and dark grey. Not quite what he'd imagined for the triumphal return of the New Emperor.

Captain Paynter brought the vehicle to a standstill and walked back from the pilot's cage, bowing before he leaned to open the door of the aircraft. There were men on the ground wearing empire insignia on their shirts who immediately formed a welcoming guard. Carlton smiled. That was better, he was on his way now.

Grabbing his bag, he handed it to Paynter and descended the steps as the men saluted. Excellent. The thrill of arrival filled him with excitement, and he straightened to return the acknowledgement before walking toward the hut at the far side of the field where a pair of transports waited, engines idling. They were not quite what he expected for an Emperor's vehicle—no insignia on the side panel, no elk-head flag of the Empire attached to a back post. But that would all come in good time. He reined in his impatience.

Clambering aboard the first vehicle, he waited while his guards took up positions behind the frontboard. The Counsellors struggled to climb into the escort transport behind.

"To Headquarters," he instructed, and sat back, anticipation rising in his chest. Judson Lanser should be there waiting to greet him. He wanted to laugh, to lean back and roar with merriment, but it would be unseemly in front of his men. He smirked. There would be time for that, too. Once he was ensconced in his quarters, and the nobility were waiting for his attention in the Great Hall before the Big Chair his father had once occupied, then he'd laugh. Oh how he'd laugh.

As they progressed along the streets, the smoke grew thicker. Many buildings were still burning, some totally destroyed by the blaze that must have swept through in the midst of the battle to take the city.

Bodies lay scattered here and there. The dead were arranged in piles at the side of the street or dragged to the curb to allow transports to pass. Some were mere civilians, but even more wore the military uniform of the Adar Silva guard, their gear still attached to the harnesses on their chests. This would all have to be cleaned up, as there was no way for an Emperor's parade to be held in the midst of this disastrous display.

Lanser reported that the Adar Silva army had been in disarray shortly after the invasion began. Perhaps having True-May out of the country disrupted their routine, because it seemed unusual for the military not to be ready to defend the capital.

Carlton's troops of dispossessed came out of the forests to the west and struck without warning. Their sudden success took everyone off guard, but then the fires started. Raging panic ensued, the populace fled the city gates and the place was almost abandoned. Perhaps the fires were a fortuitous event, they seemed to cement the quick takeover. If he'd known it would be this easy, he wouldn't have waited for years to make the attempt.

Leaning forward, he realized they were approaching the centre of Sommerset. This is where the Emperor's Headquarters were located, along with the schools and training facilities, the barracks for the boys who were sent here to be moulded into soldiers.

There it was now. Carlton's eyes widened in dismay. The building was so badly damaged he hardly recognized it. Smoke still drifted from the scorched ruins of the Great Hall and entry. All that was left of the establishment were the additions at the back that had been used to house the service staff.

There was no Headquarters left to return to. By all the dogs of hell, who had started the fire?

~***~

Dante Regiment stalked through the Great Hall of Regiment House and into to his father's office. Paulo was bent over his blackened desk, writing orders on a parchment.

"Father, have you heard?"

Paulo glanced up, then back down to finish what he was doing. He dotted a final period on his missive, and set his nib to the side, picking up his blotter to tamp the wet ink. "Did I hear what?" he asked, raising his head.

"Sommerset has been taken." Dante felt determination solidify in his gut as he watched Paulo's eyes widen in surprise. "You haven't heard? Why ever not?"

Scribe fumbled with his infolink and turned it on. "Oh," he said, "here it is, General." He bowed low and took the finished document from the desk, placing the link in the empty spot. Paulo looked at it and frowned. "By the gods," he exclaimed. "They took the city? Is this Carlton's work?"

"Yes, it has to be. He's claiming victory, at any rate." Dante shifted impatiently from one foot to the other. "Carlton has set up shop in Leader True-May's capital while he's stuck here. True-May's kicking up a real storm of furious protest. Not sure what he expects from us, but Cownden Lanser has reported he took up a spot in his office this morning and is raising hell."

"So what about the rest of the country?" Paulo's frown became a scowl. "And how is this our problem?"

"Father, of course it's an issue for us. If Carlton is getting stronger, we have to be prepared for war, nothing less. Put me in charge of this," Dante said. "We need to be ready and on high alert for any military action against Khandarken. Appoint me to head the troops."

His father gave him a long look. "That's all for now, Scribe," he barked and turned back to Dante as his scribe bowed and moved smoothly toward the far door. "I know you've been getting impatient, son."

Dante gave a sigh and took a seat in the rubber plastic chair in front of his father's desk. "Father, I'm not demanding to take over the entire military. That's a step that neither of us is ready for. But you aren't here enough to be aware of everything that is happening and someone has to be responsible. Let me take this. I'm ready for it and you've seen all the active duty you need in one lifetime. Stay on as General, I'm fine with that. Just give me the responsibility so I can take care of what needs to be done."

Paulo stroked a sideburn as he contemplated his

last surviving son. "I understand what you're saying, and for once I agree with you. I have to say my attention has wandered."

Dante barked a laugh. "You mean with your new female companion."

Paulo frowned but one corner of his mouth quirked up. "Speak with respect about Ms Hart."

He nodded with a smile. "I do, and I'm happy for you, Father. Mother died a long time ago, it's been many years of duty and loneliness." Dante could hardly remember his mother, but knew Father had never forgotten her. He was suddenly very grateful for his wife and their young son. Bethlehem filled his life and his heart with joy. One more reason to ensure Khandarken remained safe from incursions of the New Emperor's armies.

Paulo pursed his lips a moment. "This is a step I can take that doesn't require us to present a recommendation in writing before the Board of Representatives and listen to days and weeks of discussion and opinionated oratory."

Dante grinned. Father hated the bureaucratic process.

"It's a sound idea, son, and I concur. I'll do up the orders with Scribe this afternoon, and the authority will be passed to you."

Dante stood. "Thank you, Father. I'll do my best to meet your expectations in defending our country." His father got to his feet and extended his hand. "I needed the push, son. You did well to bring it to a head. It'll be a relief to hand on some of the responsibility. A promotion is in order if we are to do this right. Scribe will present you with the papers in due course."

Chapter Thirty Four

Nineteenth arrived at the Banderos compound the next day. As he stepped into the Great Hall, his gaze fell on Gerwal who was loading his lasergun. When he barked at two of their guards to bring up more ammunition from the cellars, Angel's brother halted in surprise, his mouth open at the unexpected sight. Then he grinned and walked through the doors.

"Father, you look well!" His gaze darted to where Angel stood at the desk arranging the charger for her voicelink.

She smiled, pleased to see one of her favourite brothers. "I'm glad you're back. As you can see, we're preparing for the worst."

"Yah." Nineteenth lost his smile. "That's why I'm here. I left Seventh in charge at the south station. We both thought it best that you have more support at the compound."

"How are things there?" Gerwal demanded. "I can't get any information out of First."

Nineteenth raised his brows. "The station has been repaired after the damage of the last attempted foray. The plexi on the main floor was boarded up as we thought that might be our weakest point of attack. We can still keep watch from the second floor."

Gerwal nodded. "Yah, sounds about right."

"Seventh has added five more men to his corps," he continued, "so twenty now, in case there's renewed action. Still not sure who was behind the last one, but I think we're ready for anything else that might come at us."

Alarm tingled along her nerves. "Do you think there will be another advance?"

He shrugged. "Who can say? Times being what they are, it's best to be prepared. On the other hand, I've heard some rumours."

"Like what?" She propped her hands at her waist as she waited for his answer.

"One of Nazurs men stopped at the station for the night. It was storming and too far from their barracks to get home. He ate with the guards and Seventh relayed the story he told."

Impatiently, Angel motioned him to continue.

"He said Orde killed the father. There was no high temp virus."

Gerwal's head jerked back as if he'd been struck. "Killed his father? That can't be…"

Nineteenth gave an emphatic nod. "That was his

story. Olaf Nazur, the father, didn't let Orde make the decisions he wanted to make, and there were constant battles between the two men. Then one morning Olaf didn't rise from his bed and Orde announced the father had died. No one saw what happened, but nor did anyone come down with the virus. Because it was never there in the first place."

Gerwal's neck turned a dull red as he gazed through the plexi down the field for a long moment, then loudly cleared his throat. "There's more to get done here. Angel, take all the documents from my office. Get them upstairs and hide them where they won't be easily found, perhaps in the attics."

"Yes, Father."

She paused on the stair as Nineteenth turned, gazing at Gerwal. "You look different, Father. Are you better?"

Gerwal gave a small smile. "I have to say yes. Not totally well, my back still bothers me at night. But I've made good progress, I'm relieved to admit. The pain was getting to me, and has left me weakened. Perhaps we can talk Hawker into bringing his assistant back again for more treatments."

Angel's cheeks grow warm. "I'm sure we could. Loyal says he'll come to see us as soon as he can."

"Loyal says that, does he?" Nineteenth sent her a sneaky grin. "What else does he say?"

Father frowned and looked at his daughter, but Angel ignored him. "He says the Khandarken reserves have been called up in the Western Territory since the invasion of Adar Silva. They're preparing for whatever Carlton might send their way."

Father nodded. "That's a good plan. Just like we are here. Nineteenth, try this." He handed him a lasergun. "I got a couple of new ones from the Hawker when he was here last. It handles much more easily than the old model."

As the men examined the new weapon, Angel snuck another peek at her voicelink but there was no news from Loyal. She would have to wait, with butterflies in her stomach, for him to appear in person. *What would Father have to say about their plans?*

She stiffened her spine as she entered his office and began to gather important papers from the lower drawers of his chrome and plexi desk. No matter what Father said, she would marry with Loyal the Hawker. It wasn't what she'd had in mind when she set out to recruit him for help with the Banderos organization. But it was exactly what she'd come to yearn for.

Chapter Thirty Five

First arrived in Sommerset amid a flurry of activity. Men with Empire insignias on their scruffy shirts worked in formation, removing rubble caused by what must have been raging fires throughout the city. Mule carts were lined up to be loaded with the dead bodies, clearing the streets house by house. The barracks on the edge of the city were full, so he sent his men to camp on the outskirts, while he and Fourth rode through the scarred streets.

"We need to find the Headquarters," he muttered. "Not sure I'm going to recognize them in their current condition. Ah, here we are," he said as they rounded a corner and came to a sudden halt. The Headquarters were in ruins, smoke still rising from piles of downed lumber. First took another look, realizing one wing of the structure off to the side was still intact. The doorway faced the empty yard at the back and Carlton's guards were set around the perimeter.

Several of the men immediately challenged them to go no further. First dismounted, handing his reins to Fourth. "Go back to the camp," he commanded. "I'll be a while. Come and get me at nightfall if I haven't returned by then."

Fourth raised his brows as he took the reins. "Yah, I can do that. What will you be doing?"

"Just do as I tell you," he barked. He turned to the guard and withdrew his ident from a back pocket, holding it out. "Advisor Judson Lanser is expecting me. We had arranged a meeting for today."

The guard took the ident and examined it at length, turning it front to back. It was an old document he'd gotten years ago when he'd briefly attended the Emperor's schools here in Sommerset. First decided the man couldn't read, but bit his tongue to keep from speaking. No need to poke the lion when he was finally close to getting what he needed.

"What did you say your name was?" the guard finally asked.

First took a deep breath in frustration. He hadn't said what his name was, now he knew for sure the man couldn't read. What was Carlton thinking, to choose a group of men to look after his security who didn't have the required skills?

"My name is Banderos," he said patiently. "First Banderos. Advisor Lanser sent me a note by messenger to meet him here today."

The guard nodded, gave him a searching look and waved another man forward to take his place while he entered the door of the servant's wing and shut it after him. There was a lengthy wait, while the guard left behind levelled a fierce glare at First, silently daring him to take one more step.

Finally the door opened and the guard returned. "This way," he called and waved him forward. First walked across the yard and followed him through the doorway, his heart beating heavily in his chest.

He was close, so close. *Was this meeting going to be different from the last?* There must be some purpose for the Advisor to call him back to talk. Surely he didn't waste his time with plans where he had no intention of following through. Judson Lanser must have found a reason to work with him.

First was shown to a small room at the back of the building, one high plexi window looking out on the dead grass and burned fence behind. He stood uncertainly as the guard left, closing the door. *Now what?* The room held two flimsy chairs and a small pallet, as if for a servant's berth. Perhaps that's what it was. After all, where else would the servants bunk? The smell of smoke and charred plexi was overpowering and he held his nose, breathing in through his mouth.

He finally used the tail of his shirt to wipe soot off one of the chairs and sat down. Still he waited. The sun had shifted slowly across the sky and the shadows outside had darkened before the door opened again. The same guard leaned in and waved him forward. "Come with me," he said and marched down a narrow hallway.

First was led to a large room with impressive stained plexi windows down one side letting in the rays of the setting sun. Judson Lanser sat at a desk in the corner, making marks with a pen on a parchment laid out in front of him. He glanced up.

"Come forward," he commanded, regarding him closely as he walked into the room. There was no chair on First's side of the desk so he stood awkwardly, waiting, as Lanser went back to his task. First glanced down. The parchment was a hand-drawn map of the countries of Khandarken and Adar Silva with the Catastrophic Ocean showing along the eastern shore. The Banderos and Nazur territories were indicated in sketchy lines on the western border leading into the forests below Jiran.

Lanser sighed and sat back in his chair. "I need you to show me where your land starts and ends, and who else holds territory there." He pointed his long yellow fingernail at the centre of the map.

First nodded and held his gaze. "To what purpose?" he inquired. "Why do you need to know? I understand you have taken Sommerset, but the southern part of Adar Silva is still unconquered. Why are you looking west at this point?"

The Advisor gave him a long look. "I'm interested in what you proposed last time we met."

First waited but the Advisor said no more. "How interested?"

Lanser snorted. "You won't get anywhere talking to me like that."

"The thing is," First leaned forward, bracing his arms on the desk. He realized this could be his last chance to strike a deal, and the Advisor was acting as if it didn't matter to him one way or the other. "I might not get anywhere with you anyway. You took your time getting back to me, and you have not proposed anything here today that would be of interest. What is your goal?"

Lanser gave him a level look. "Grab a chair," he said, pointing to several along the wall. "Let's look at this map. You show me what area you control. I'll tell you what I'm willing to do."

"I see." First stared at the map a moment. "Your map is clearly wrong and out of date, but I can fix that." He walked across to fetch a chair, satisfaction settling in his gut.

Finally, a hint of progress.

Chapter Thirty Six

Angel's voicelink vibrated and she rolled over on the pallet, feeling around for the device under her bolster. Loyal's particulars glowed on the screen, and she quickly tapped the button.

"Are you there, Angel?" His voice sounded deep and scratchy, as if he'd just woken up and hadn't used it yet today.

"Yes, I'm here." She wiggled with excitement to be in touch this way. "I'm still in bed, I was about to get up."

"Good. I didn't want to wake you, but my day looks so busy I wasn't sure if I'd have a chance to talk before I took off." He cleared his throat. "Thank you for coming to Sommerset with me that day. It was the highlight of my year."

She giggled. "You mean riding the Sparkling Wheel was the most exciting thing you've ever done?"

He chuckled. "No, sweetheart. Just being with you." There was a pause as her stomach quivered from the sound of the endearment. "It was a gift, spending that time together. I want to marry with you, Angel. I don't want to wait for an invitation to come back to the Banderos compound for a chance to see you again, or worry if you'll be free to spend time with me. My nerves are stretched to the limit."

Angel's breath caught in her throat.

Loyal coughed. "Are you still there?" he said.

"Yes. Yes, I'm here." She tugged the covers down and kicked them to the foot of the pallet as heat flooded her body.

"What do you think?" His breathing came heavy over the voicelink.

"I don't know…,"she said hesitantly. "That is, I've been thinking about it but I'm not sure…."

"Do you care about me at all? I know it's the wrong way to do this, asking you over the voicelink. I just never seem to get the chance to see you face to face for anything serious. Rascal was there, Adoni always about. I want to do this the right way. I should discuss it with your father, and I will when next I'm there, but when will that be?" He sounded desperate.

"Oh, Loyal…"

"I love you, Angel."

"Oh!"

Her gasp must have startled him because he said, "Are you all right? What's wrong?"

"Nothing's wrong." She shook her head, clasping

the voicelink in an iron grip as her fingers went numb from the pressure. "Not a thing. I would marry with you, Loyal. I'd like nothing better. And if Father says no, then I'll just run away from home."

His rough chuckle caused her nipples to tingle and heat to gather between her thighs.

"I hope that won't be necessary. I trust your father might approve, he's certainly been grilling me with all kinds of questions since I began meeting with him. But I promise I'll do a proper job of asking him when next I'm there."

His voice dropped lower. "I just don't know when that might be. Things are ramping up here, with a call out for the reserves and Major-General Dante Regiment is organizing our troops. I need to know you're safe. You have to be careful for me—no sudden trips into Hafford with only Runt and Rascal as escort, or rides out to one of the border stations just because you're curious about what is going on."

She felt herself bristle even as she softened at his obvious concern for her. "I'm always careful, Loyal," she said, a new crisp note to her voice. "And I go to Hafford on a routine basis. I have a job to do, too."

"I know, sweetheart. I'm not trying to tell you what to do." He paused a moment, as if to control himself. "I'd die if anything happened to you. For my sake, please be careful."

"I will," she promised, and took a hesitant breath. "I love you, too."

"Ahhh." His voice choked and there was silence

for a moment. "Thank the gods for that."

When Angel clicked off, she hugged the voicelink to her breast and rolled over in the bed clothes. The time she'd spent with him in Sommerset at the hotel rose in her memory like a warm cloak engulfing her with joy. He'd touched her so carefully, his fingers feathering over her skin as his mouth worked magic on hers. His hands had explored her body with slow care and attention before he rose above her. She'd been ready for him, so excited her heart raced…

There was a sound from the hall and she relaxed on her pallet. Before he clicked off, Loyal had checked that she still wore the beltlink, and Rascal kept his at hand as well. *Was she getting married now?* He'd asked again and she'd said yes! She never imagined… Well, she did imagine what it would be like to be married to Loyal, knowing she wanted to be with him every day, but never believing it would come true. And now she'd given her promise.

Tears gathered in her eyes. At that moment, she longed for her mother with all her heart.

Chapter Thirty Seven

First rode hard for the border. Excitement mounted, churning in his gut, and he had trouble staying focussed on his task.

"Where are we headed?" Fourth called. "You're taking the wrong trail for the compound."

"To Nazur territory," he shouted. "We need to get there fast. No time to waste." Advisor Judson Lanser had finally come through with the best deal First could have imagined. All he had to do was firm up the agreement with Orde, which should be easy enough. He'd already laid the groundwork, and handing over Angel would cement it.

Suddenly swerving, he headed along a track through the forest that would lead straight to the south border station. He heard shouts behind him, the neighing of a mount as his men followed.

He wanted above all to get this right—before it

blew up in his face. The south station loomed out of the trees as they drew near. There were more horses in the corral than he'd expected, and he eased his mount to a trot as he counted. Eighteen steeds, and there had to be at least five out on patrol, that was the routine. Why so many? Normally there were fifteen men at each station counting the patrol, and a few extra mounts in case of injury.

"Wait here," he said to his brother. "I need to check who's in charge and find out what the plan is." Tossing his reins to Fourth, he stalked up the steps and into the station, nodding to the guards as he went. Three guards, two with the horses, one at the entrance— that was usual. It was the number of mounts that was different.

He noticed the plexi had been boarded up. Made sense, some of it had been broken during the skirmish a week ago, and they had none to replace it in a hurry. But it meant the lookout had to operate from the second floor. It still worked, the trees had been cleared around the entire building long ago and it was easy to spot anyone approaching from a distance.

The watch had obviously already alerted the men in the station that he'd arrived. Seventh rose from his meal at the table to greet him. "First," he said. "You have quite a few men with you."

First smiled, a mere baring of teeth. "I've been to Sommerset and things are pretty tense there. No need to leave myself open to attack."

"True." Seventh narrowed his eyes. "You doing

the rounds of the stations this time?"

"Nope. Just called in to see if the repairs are done. I'm on my way to meet with Nazur. We need to work together if we're to survive in these times of unrest and Empire invasion."

"By the gods, that's true." Seventh sat to resume his meal. "Are you and your men hungry?" He gestured to the dishes before him. "There's hen stew and toasted pané. Even some astrofruit compote, they tell me."

"No. No time. But I wanted to check on how many men you have."

"Fifteen men here, and five on patrol," he mumbled around his mouthful. "Nineteenth and I organized it. Too much up in the air right now to leave anything to chance."

"Right. I thought as much. Which works out quite well, because I have need of five more men to accompany me into Nazur territory. Never travel light, I always say."

Seventh paused, his spoon halfway to his mouth. "I see. Well, there are some men sleeping in the barracks. They did nightshift and should awaken shortly."

"Good." First headed for the stairs. "I'll have a look." He bounded up the steps, knowing what he'd see. Sure enough, the extra men he'd recruited and left at the Banderos compound had been sent out here for backup. These were men loyal only to him— they had no history with Gerwal or the rest of the family. He woke the leader and pointed to the others he wanted, going back downstairs to await them.

"I think I'll have that dinner now," he said. "A quick bite before the men are ready to leave." He sighed expansively and relaxed in the chair as Seventh called to the cook for another meal.

Everything was falling into place, just as planned.

Chapter Thirty Eight

Gerwal took a moment to relax on his lounge in the Great Entry after a busy day doing the rounds of the entire compound. It was a while since he'd been able to visit all the areas and survey the various activities, and he took pleasure in the fact that he was finally well enough to do so.

The kitchens were in good shape. With a surprised grin, Thirteenth had welcomed him into the bakery where he and his wife produced much of the pané, biscuits and sandwiches for the residents. The cook, a small Jirani who'd been with him for years, gave him a grudging nod and showed him the racks of bear meat he'd bought from one of their territory hunters.

The men's barracks weren't full. Gerwal had learned from those still in residence that Seventh had sent a lot of the men out to the border stations to relieve the other workers and beef up security.

Seventeenth, who supervised the vegetable crops had been working in the fields with his men when Gerwal arrived, and had stopped to give him an update on the spring planting. He was short of staff, but reported First had ordered some of his farm workers to ride with him when he left the compound. Security was certainly top of everyone's mind. He was comforted that First was taking their safety so seriously, and decided perhaps his eldest son was doing a better job of managing the territory than he'd imagined.

His back was so much better, he could hardly believe it. It felt like a miracle, that those treatments the little Legitamian gave him should make such a difference. He hadn't totally recovered to his old self, and the muscles would begin to cramp after a few hours of steady work, but the improvement was remarkable.

Angel had gone out after an early sup to work in her garden. He glanced at the sky through the front plexi. It would begin to darken in a couple of hours, and before that happened she'd come in with a bouquet of some kind—flowers, herbs, it didn't matter. She delighted in those things and would insist he sniff the aroma and help her decide where to put the plexi container the branches would rest in for the next several days.

He smiled. Girls were different. Here he was, the father of twenty-six boys, nineteen of whom were still alive, and this one girl threw his life into constant chaos. He grunted. Not chaos exactly, she just put a different spin on things.

Where was his wife? Willa would bring him a bowl of brandy soon, and he'd relax and plan tomorrow's activities. First should be back from Sommerset shortly—he'd made another trip to find out what he could about Carlton's occupation of the city, and if there was a danger of invasion from Adar Silva. Gerwal had noticed some new men in the compound on his rounds today, troops that must have been recently recruited and wore a Banderos sash on their shirts. None of his staff knew much about them, and he wanted information from First as to where they came from and what role they would serve. Had they been trained? He certainly didn't recognize them. *Had he been out of commission that long?*

The front door opened, then closed a moment later. That could be First now, or perhaps Angel coming in with her flowers. But instead, a small group of the new men from the barracks with sashes on their shirts entered and approached his chair. He gave a brusque nod, eyeing them guardedly. "First isn't here," he said. "What can I do for you?"

One of the men stepped forward. "Mr Banderos, we have orders from your son," he said. "If there's any threat of attack, you are to be escorted to the cellars for your own safety."

"Yah? What attack?" He glared, but the same man seized his arm and awkwardly heaved him to his feet. His back gave a sharp spasm and he caught his breath at the pain. "What are you doing?" he shouted, struggling to pull out of the tight grasp. He lurched forward, tugging at his arm and reaching for his voicelink on the side table, but the man hung on.

As he fought to free himself, a second guard caught him from behind with an arm pressed tight across his throat and he was suddenly having trouble breathing. Another hand covered his mouth and pinched his nostrils.

Alarm rose like a tide in his chest as he wildly wrestled for freedom. But there were three men coming at him from all sides and he felt weakness set in as the air leaked from his lungs. His sight dimmed as he used an elbow to try to toss a blow at the attacker blocking his oxygen. He felt a stunning hit to the jaw that knocked a tooth loose and it rattled around in his mouth. *What was this? An attack from his own men?* He'd never imagined such a thing and the reality stunned him.

He fought harder as they pushed him stumbling down the stairs and through the tunnel to the cellar at the back of the manorhouse. The room was small and low, with rock walls and a dirt floor, the original stonework still visible around the base. They dumped him there. He landed in an ungainly heap in the middle of the space as the men left, slamming the door behind them.

Gerwal struggled for breath, his chest heaving as he spat out the tooth and felt around with his tongue for the new gap in his mouth. As his heart began to slow, he scrambled to his feet, ignoring the pain in his back, and seized the door handle. It was securely barred from the outside.

What had just happened? Was he being held here for his own safety? He doubted that mightily. *What about his wife, his daughter?* These men weren't his troops, they were strangers who had been recruited by his eldest son. And after hearing the news of what had transpired with Olaf Nazur at the hands of Orde, Gerwal didn't have any illusions about what was taking place here.

It appeared he was next in line to be permanently removed in the interests of an eldest son and heir.

Chapter Thirty Nine

It was late when the training exercises were finished and the troops returned to their beds in the barracks in Deep Creek. Loyal knew he would only be here weeks, rather than months like some of the other men. He'd already completed similar exercises some time ago. The goal was to get some training in early, so the reserves would be battle-ready if it came to that.

It was too late to contact Angel now. She would be sleeping the sleep of the innocent at home in the Banderos compound, surrounded by her father and brothers. His heart ached a little more each time he was unable to talk to her. It was like a slow death by torture to be separated from her like this.

He fell into a deep sleep, surrounded by the loud steady snoring of tired men. It brought back memories of when he was a young lad fighting with the resistance in the Last War.

The blind man had led them through the forest and along the river bank. "It's safe here, Captain," he said. "All we need to do now is find a way across the Violetta River. Our rebels hold the other side. There's a water raft hidden against the bank further along that waits for us, but stopping here for a rest is the best approach."

The captain nodded and the men sank to the ground. Loyal fell into a light doze, his limbs twitching in fatigue. It felt like only moments later the captain urged them to their feet. "Let's go, men," he said low. "Once we are on the other bank of the river, we'll be able to rest, find food and safety."

The blind man rose and helped the captain to his feet. "This way," the man said. "We'll follow the path." As the other fighters rose, Loyal staggered upward and stood swaying, his energy nearly exhausted. He took a deep breath, bent his knees and gathered the young girl into his arms. He could do this, he just had to try a little harder. He wasn't Jade, his father who left behind those who loved him. The girl's body was limp and she kept slipping from his grasp. He tightened his hold.

As they moved along the path, the captain lost his footing but the blind man grabbed his arm and kept walking down the river bank, talking kindly and pointing the way. They were all in bad shape.

"There it is," the blind man said. His voice was soft like a breeze yet Loyal could hear every word. He moved faster, and caught up in time to see one of the men pull a raft out of the underbrush at the river's edge. There were two oars strapped to the sides, and the blind man bent to grip a cleat and hold it steady against the strong current. "Grab hold," he said, and one of the troop stepped forward to secure it.

Then he turned toward Loyal, his expression sorrowful. "Time to let her go," he said. "She's gone now. There's nothing more you can do for her."

Loyal glanced down and tears welled in his eyes as he gazed at the girl's still face. "I can't leave her here," he choked. "Not after what they've done to her."

"You have to, son. You can't help her any more. She's gone. We can scratch a place to bury her." The captain gazed around as two men stepped forward, scrabbling at the rough ground with their hands. Soon a shallow indent appeared and Loyal stumbled forward, gentling lowering the girl into her makeshift grave. They scraped dirt and rocks over her until only her face was visible.

"Stop!" Loyal waved his hands frantically. "I can't

let you do that. Wait!" He peeled off his dirty ripped shirt and laid it gently over her face. Then he glanced up at the captain. *"I just couldn't…"*

"I understand," the captain said. *"Now we can finish."* He waved at the men and they quickly covered her with dead grass and leaves until there was no sign she'd ever been there.

They turned and walked away, the blind man in the lead. Loyal followed as tears leaked down his young face.

~***~

Angel snipped another branch of sagium and laid it in her basket. She had already harvested some germanium, and would add lavender to the mix. The blend produced a lovely scent in the linen closet amongst the sheets, and she often buried small sachets full of the herbs among her bedding for the sheer joy of smelling it at night as she drifted off to sleep.

She heard a muffled noise from the manorhouse and straightened to listen, gazing toward the side windows. When she heard nothing more, she went back to her work. In an hour or so, Father would have his bowl of brandy and she often joined him for a chat at the end of the day. But not yet. She had plans for this special herb blend, a gift for Loyal when next he came to the Banderos compound.

She smiled at the thought, her heart skipping a beat. They would marry and become a family. She just didn't know when, because they hadn't had the chance to discuss it between them.

She stopped to check her voicelink in case a message had come through without her hearing the signal. Disappointed, she slipped it back into the pocket of her robe. When she looked up, three men were filing through the garden gate toward her. They closed the gate and two remained there as the third approached in the soft evening light. She studied his face but felt no hint of recognition. These were the new men who had been recently recruited and wore the Banderos sash across their shirts. Before he left for the northern border station, Nineteenth had said First put out word looking for more troops to beef up their numbers as the Emperor drew nearer to their territory.

She gave a courteous nod. "How may I help you?" she asked. "First has not yet returned to the compound, but I understand from the messages arriving that he might be here later this evening."

The fellow broke out in a smile, but kept walking until he stopped right in front of her. He glanced at the basket she carried, then up to her face. "You might as well put that down," he said in a rough voice. "You won't be needing it."

"I beg your pardon?" She looked to the other men and back at him in surprise. "I'm busy at the moment. Perhaps you'd like to wait in the barracks for my brother to return."

He leaned forward to grab the basket from her fingers. "What do you have in here?"

"Herbs," she snapped, reaching to retrieve it from his grasp.

He simply seized her arm, tossing the basket to the ground. Then he dragged her toward the gate and the waiting men, walking through the rows of plants, his boots trampling the garden as if it weren't there.

"Stop that! Let go," she shouted, alarm racing up her spine.

He turned and grabbed her up against him, pinning her back to his chest and clamping a hand over her mouth. "You have to be quiet," he whispered in her ear. "Your brother gave us our orders to keep you safe in case there was an attack, and that's what we are going to do. Do you understand?" He waited, as if for her response.

She froze, her heart beating like a wounded bird in her chest. *Was there an attack on the compound?* Perhaps that was the noise she'd heard, although it wasn't loud and had stopped right away. *Oh, why hadn't she run to check on Father when she first heard it? Now it was too late...*

A second man bent to grab her ankles and she kicked wildly. He seized one and then the other, sandwiching her feet between his hands in a painful grip as they carted her unceremoniously toward the back of the manorhouse. More men waited there, men she didn't recognize, with horses saddled and ready. They tied a rag over her mouth, knocking her hair out of its loop so it fell loose to her shoulders. They heaved her onto a mount, securing her ankles to the stirrups. Someone tossed a blanket over her shoulders against the strengthening wind. Then, leading her horse in the midst of the body of men, they started down the field toward the compound exit.

She peered into the gloom, hoping she'd recognize the guard at the gate. If it was one of their own, she'd kick her horse or make him buck to get his attention. But the two guards standing at attention were strangers and they rode on through without a word being exchanged, heading down the track leading away from the compound.

Her heart felt like it would come right up her throat. She was having trouble catching her breath and the gag on her mouth just made it more frightening. *Who were these men, and why had they kidnapped her? Had something happened to First and his troops were now out of control? Where was Father?* He would be furious when he found out what had happened.

More alarming, where were they going? Down this track lay the south border station and the Nazur lands beyond. *Were they taking her there?* She didn't know Orde Nazur well, but had never felt comfortable in his presence. He had a habit of staring at her face, her breasts, her bottom. It made her shiver to think of being alone with him, and she had always been careful to be courteous and friendly and keep at least one or more of her brothers with her whenever he had visited the Banderos compound in the past.

Her mouth was dry beneath the cloth and she tried with difficulty to swallow. Her damp hands slipped where she'd clamped them around the saddle horn. She needed to relieve herself but had no way to let her captors know, and furthermore, nowhere private to conduct that function even if she could tell them.

She began to cry, tears of fear and then numbness, imagining the plants in her garden destroyed by the heavy boots of her captors as they dragged her out the gate.

Chapter Forty

First marshalled his men and rode out, leaving a cadre of his special troops to keep the south station available for his use. He'd already sent Seventh on to the west station to get him out of the way. However, there were other things to take care of to move his plans along, beginning with Orde Nazur. The second assault on the south station had been followed by another note addressed to him, hand delivered to the Banderos compound. This one was less threatening and more of a reminder. The alarming part was that Nazur's troops could cross his territory to reach the compound without alerting his own men.

We had a deal, it read. *I'm tired of waiting.*

Well, the wait was over. First rolled it around in his mind as he travelled. He had to bring Nazur onside, and at the same time pull the fangs of the viper. *How to do that and keep control of the situation at the same time?*

When they reached the Nazur border it was apparent things had changed. No longer could he ride up to the compound and be given entry. Orde's guards were patrolling the roads and trails, challenging them as he approached.

"Halt!" Two men rode toward them, several more holding back at the fork of the trail. "Who are you, and what do you want?"

Fourth rode out to meet them. "Banderos men," he called. "First and his troop are here to see Orde Nazur."

There was some consultation among Orde's men, then a runner took off toward the Nazur compound and the others formed an escort to herd them forward. Yes, things had changed since his last visit. Would Orde adhere to their deal?

When they rode into the neighbour's compound, Orde was waiting at the manorhouse but he wasn't alone. Eight men in uniform, Nazur insignias on their shoulders, were stationed around him.

First approached with care. *What was the plan? Were they going to kidnap him and force a concession?* He straightened his spine. Father would never allow that to happen, and the man wouldn't get Angel if he didn't cooperate. He shuddered as he remembered Father was no longer in control back at the compound. This was a part of his plan he hadn't accounted for—a trusted lieutenant, one of his brothers, stationed at the main base who had his back. Which one was the question That would have to be next on his list. But the list was long, and there was a lot to accomplish in a short period of time.

"Orde," he said, stepping forward to clasp arms

with the man. "Good to see you again."

Nazur gave him a dark look but offered his arm, gripping mightily so that a piercing pain shot up the tendon of First's arm.

"I thought we had a deal."

First nodded and glanced at the guards standing behind him. "We do, by the graves. But we have some things to discuss, and it's confidential."

Orde pushed his lips in a doubting gesture. "Uh huh. The deal is already arranged."

"Yah, it is." First crossed his arms across his chest. "Yet, it is even bigger than before. I've been working hard to make it so."

Orde's brows rose in apparent disbelief, but he turned toward the hall, waving his men to wait in the entry. "Come into the office, and let's hear it. This better be good because my patience is at an end."

First grinned confidently. "Lead the way."

~***~

Gerwal bellowed and banged his fists against the posts holding up the floor of the manorhouse. He kicked repeatedly at the footings, hoping it would be enough to shake the structure so someone upstairs would notice. Surely even a small shudder in the floorboards would alert someone in the house that he was being held. His fear was no one was there—that his wife and daughter had been taken, he knew not where.

He'd been down here for hours, although he

wasn't sure exactly how long. No one had come for him. *Where was his family?* If those men had touched his daughter, he'd kill them! He shivered and sank to his haunches, gazing helplessly upward toward the boards above his head. *How was he to get out of here?* The sad truth was, he probably couldn't. There wasn't a tool to be found in the place. The dirt floor had been swept clean of anything remotely useful other than the bodies of a few dead beetles.

He leaned against the rock wall, stretching his legs out in front of him. Was there any weakness in the walls? He had no light, but had crawled around the perimeter of the room feeling each crevasse and join. It appeared to be solid. He hadn't discovered a hole or flaw anywhere. If someone didn't find him soon, he was afraid of what might happen.

His mind turned to the years he'd spent building this territory. Days patrolling the fields around the manorhouse, and the forests and valleys as their holding grew. It was amazing he had so many children given how often he was out on the trails, days on end of short battles to head off the encroachment of other settlers, long negotiations to bring neighbours into the fold, attempts at trading with those more distant. There had been a number of small family farms with some land around them, cattle and sheep, big gardens that supported the children and workers. Gerwal had managed to incorporate most of them under his slowly encompassing roof—rationalizing that a bigger operation was safer and less volatile as Aqatain was defeated in what seemed endless battles and the Empire crumbled around them.

By the time Angel was born, the territory had tripled in size and he spent weeks at a time away from the manorhouse out on patrol. She would write letters and send the missives with her brothers to be delivered to him in camp at night. *Dear Daddy*, they would read, *and for Daddy only*. As if anyone else wanted to read those squiggly little notes. He snorted at the idea and repressed a grin, even as moisture gathered in his eyes.

Sometimes she would talk about needing him at the manorhouse. *Daddy, it's from your daughter Angel. Come home soon and fast. We all miss you.*

Many were about her concern for him. *Daddy, from your daughter Angel. Close the door and come home. Don't work too hard while you are away. See you when you get here.* There would be kisses attached at the end of each letter. How could she love him so much when he'd been such an indifferent father?

He rested his head on his knees as a shudder rippled through his body. He wouldn't give up, he refused to give up. As long as he had breath in his body, he would fight for what was his.

Chapter Forty One

First shifted in his chair and glared at Orde Nazur. "As you see, the agreement we worked out is still in place, but there's more. I've been to Sommerset to find out what the plans are. Emperor Carlton views our combined territories as a separate province and he's promised to appoint a Governor. Under his system, we'll continue to control our own land. I've negotiated a peace pact just as war is about to break out with the surrounding nations. We can avoid all that, and the dispossessed roaming our forests won't be our problem. They'll be under Carlton's control."

Nazur sat back and stroked his chin. "And how does this benefit us?"

First smiled. "We don't have to fight for our holding. Carlton has recognized our claims and will support us."

"I see." Orde frowned and ran his thumbnail along

the edge of the desk. "And when do I get Angel?"

"Soon." First waved his hand in the general direction of the Banderos stronghold. "We need to solidify our agreement and pin down the details with Carlton's man, Judson Lanser. Then I deliver Angel to you and we're locked into our contract. Two families controlling a tract of land larger than some of the Khandarken provinces, and an engraved peace agreement with the Emperor to ensure our security."

Orde stood, pushing his chair back. "Yah, I agree. So let's get on with it. The sooner we do that, the sooner I get my wife."

Standing, First pulled his knife from his back pocket. He snapped it open, held out his hand and looked the man in the eye. "Shake on it," he said.

Nazur didn't blink but extended his hand.

First slashed across both thumbs and they shook hands as bright red drops of blood ran onto the dark top of the old desk. "Done," he said. "We're committed. The next time I see you, I'll be bringing Angel with me. Watch for my runner with the notice."

As he turned to go, First ignored the churning in his gut. He was on his way, but there were many steps yet. What would happen when Orde realized the Governor appointed by Emperor Carlton was none other than his neighbour, First Banderos?

~***~

Angel woke when the horses came to a halt. Neck aching, she raised her head and gazed around. It was pitch dark, but the silhouette of the building in front of them was as familiar as home. The south border station was tall and narrow, built like a silo, with three floors positioned one atop the other. It occupied a hill overlooking the valley and creek below.

Her heart lifted. Surely here some of their own men would be able to free her from her captors and make this nightmare go away. The Banderos troops were a rough but loyal lot and would never condone this kind of treatment of the only daughter.

One of the riders gave a sharp whistle and the door to the station opened, light spilling down the steps. A couple of men emerged, each wearing a sash over their shirts. These were more of the new workers who had been recruited. They'd told her First gave them their instructions. *Then why was she being treated this way?*

"Finally got here," one of them called. "I see you've brought the package. Hope you behaved yourself and didn't accost her or First will have your balls."

The package? She glanced around as the men came toward her, untying her ankles from the stirrups. One pulled her from the saddle, tugging the cloth out of her mouth and squeezing her breast at the same time. She sagged, her legs useless. He caught her, throwing her over his shoulder like a roll of carpet and striding toward the doorway as his hand fumbled beneath the blanket to massage her hip.

Her anger rose in a tidal wave, wiping out the fear.

"Let me go," she said in an angry croak, her lips numb. "Put me down this instant!" She tried to kick against him but her legs weren't working.

"Hold on," he said. "I can see you can't walk, I'm just trying to help."

He jogged up the steps and stood her on her feet inside the doorway of the station, holding her upright with his grip on her arms. She blinked against the bright light. There were six or seven men lounging around the tables in the main hall, all examining her closely, yet she didn't recognize a single soul. Whirling, she faced her captors. "Where is Seventh? He's supposed to be here."

"He's been sent off to the west station," someone said, giving her a bold stare. "And your brother Nineteenth was sent north on patrol. No brothers here, I'm afraid, although we expect First back soon." He gave a smirk, his lips pulling tight.

Her heart jerked in her chest. She was at their mercy and she didn't even know who they were.

"This way," her captor said, opening the door to the cellar stairs. "First left some things for you stored down here."

He did? Her heart lifted momentarily, but the guard grabbed her by the arm and pulled her down the steps, arriving at the bottom to dump her unceremoniously on the dirt floor. He bent over her, placing his big hands on her breasts. "I've always wondered what you felt like," he whispered. His fingers squeezed and she let out a low cry. Pulling back, he waved at the pallet in the corner. "Help yourself," he said sardonically. When he closed the door, the small damp room went black.

Sobbing, she dragged herself across to the pallet and pulled the cover over, inhaling the musty scent. *What was going to happen now?* She shuddered at what she feared was to come with all the strange men at the station.

But it was quiet above her head as she fumbled her voicelink out of her pocket and flicked it on. The device hummed but died within seconds. She flicked it off and on again, but the light never appeared. Hands shaking, she stuffed it back in her pocket. *Why hadn't she powered it while she was in the garden?* Because she thought it was just a normal day at the compound.

However, the beltlink was still attached to her waistband. Wouldn't that work? She pulled it out and sent a desperate message to Rascal, then waited patiently for a reply that never came. She refastened the device in its hiding place and lay down on the pallet. If there was an answer, she would feel the vibration against her skin.

She dozed, waiting for morning

Chapter Forty Two

Angel woke to the sound of boots thumping on the floor above her head. She'd been dreaming, images flitting through her mind of the strange animals she'd seen at the Sommerset Fair, the feel of riding the Sparkling Wheel around and around as if she were flying. Then she'd grown warm as she dreamed of being with Loyal, the mild rasp of the whiskers on his chin against her neck as he kissed and stroked her, the way it felt when he'd entered her…

She smoothed hot cheeks as the emotions faded, and ran her fingers back through her hair. She had no brush or pins, but did her best to comb through the tangles. There was a rustling in the corner and she shuddered, hoping the rodents would keep to their own nest. The stale damp smell of the place was barely noticeable now, she'd been down here so long. Her breath caught in her throat as the door at the top of the steps opened abruptly.

As light tumbled down the stairs, she pushed herself to her feet and leaned against the wall, preparing to face whatever would happen next. She clasped shaking hands together and peered at the long legs descending toward her.

"Angel, are you there?"

It was First. She'd recognize his voice anywhere. Her heart thudded in her chest. At least she knew him, he was her brother and should be on her side. But now she was afraid to trust him. The conflict caused her stomach to heave as she tried to school her expression. "I'm here, First," she said. "Are you come to set me free?"

"Set you free?" The light was at his back and she couldn't see his face, but his voice sounded amused, as if she'd made a joke. The churning in her stomach ramped up a notch.

"You're not a prisoner," he said, moving into the room. "You're here for your own protection. Emperor Carlton has made incursions on our land and I had left instructions that if there was danger, you were to be brought here to ensure your safety."

"I see." She didn't, knowing that wasn't the whole story, or even the true story. "So now you're here, I can be released from this room."

"Of course." He stepped closer and took her hands in his. "But until the rebellion is quelled, you have to stay hidden for your safety. They'll never get this far before we beat them back, I promise. If it becomes any more dangerous, I have permission from Orde to take you to the Nazur compound. You'll be secure there until the fighting is over."

"What fighting are we talking about, First? I saw no threat, yet I was roughly dragged from our home and brought here as a prisoner."

"I'm sorry." His voice oozed concern. "My men are a little forceful, but remarkably effective. Do you have your voicelink with you?"

She startled at the sudden change in topic. "Yes," she said hesitantly. "But I need to power it."

"Let me see." He held out his hand.

Her stomach quaked at the idea of giving it to him. *How would she get in contact with Loyal without her voicelink?* "It's all right," she murmured. "I just need to power it up, and it will be fine."

"Let me see it," he repeated, his voice turning ice cold.

She slipped her hand in her pocket and wrapped her fingers around the device. *What should she do?* He stood before her, hand out, waiting. She wouldn't get past him to the stairs if she didn't cooperate. She pulled it from her robe pocket and laid the device carefully on his palm.

He flicked it on and saw there was no action. "Have you heard from Loyal the Hawker today?"

"No, no one."

"Right." He palmed his own device, tossing it carelessly in the air and catching it again with his other hand. "I think you should send him a message."

241

"Yes!" She tried not to let her excitement show, but it was difficult to hold it in. If she could only speak to Loyal, she was sure he'd come for her. "Can I borrow your voicelink?"

As she reached for it, he held it higher, just out of her reach. "On one condition," he cooed, his smile sickly sweet. "You have to give him the right message."

Her throat tightened so it was hard to force the words out. "What message is that?"

"Hear me out," he said. He paced to the stairs and back. "If Loyal Hawker comes to Banderos territory looking for you, it will be bad for both you and him. I have men patrolling our entire holding. All our brothers are indisposed at the moment, and it is only my men who are in control. They'll spare no quarter. So if you want Hawker to live, you'll give him the message I tell you."

Chapter Forty Three

Loyal left the training field, heading for the barracks where his gear was stashed under a pallet in the hall. There'd been no message from Angel since yesterday and he was having trouble concentrating. She'd called him just as he left the meal hall after mid day and he'd gone scarlet in the face as he jogged out the door and onto the field for privacy.

He squirmed at the memory. Her voice turned him on the minute he heard her speak. All she had to do was say his name. They'd talked about the trip to Sommerset and she'd giggled as he reminded her how they'd kissed on the Sparkling Wheel and then made love in his room. The sound had gone straight to his groin and left him stalking his way around the barracks to cool down before he headed out to join the other men for more fighting contests and arms training.

He ran straight to his bunk and lifted the pallet, fumbling around for his sack of belongings. His fingers wrapped around the voicelink, and when he flicked it on, a message appeared. His chest tightened at the sight. At last! He tapped the screen.

His anticipation cooled as he realized it wasn't from Angel. A call from her brother First, it seemed. He put the device to his ear. But it was Angel's voice he heard and his heart speeded up again.

"Loyal," she said, her voice slightly breathless. "I'm using First's device because mine has no power. But it doesn't matter because the message would be the same. I don't want to see you or hear from you ever again. Please believe me when I say this has all been a mistake. I have changed my mind about us. Do not contact me, do not try to see me. We are finished."

The message ended. Loyal stared at the voicelink as if he'd never seen it before.

"Any news?" Adoni appeared beside him, grin in place.

Loyal stalled for a moment, wondering what had just happened. *How could she do that? After the night they'd had together?* The magical memory was always right there in the front of his mind, causing his heart to speed and his cock to harden, leading him to forget what he was doing at every turn. Sudden rage swamped him, and he turned on his heel to leave.

"Hawker?" Adoni followed him to the door. "Anything wrong?"

Loyal didn't slow, just broke into a run straight across the field, heading for the creek on the other side. He ran until his breath wouldn't come any more, until he was gasping for air, until his heart thundered to find a way out of his chest.

He reached the creek and plunged into the cold water, clothes and all, his boots sinking into the mud. He gasped for air as the freezing water rushed up his body.

Her voice had been shaky and weak. That must indicate something. She couldn't intend to turn away from him, not when they cared so deeply for each other, not after taking that intimate step together in Sommerset. She couldn't mean what she'd said.

But his fear was that she did.

~***~

Carlton stepped out of the transport, having returned from his first tour of the reclaimed city. Headquarters was still a mess, a pile of burned rubble at one end oozed the smell of wet smoke. He sighed and straightened his back. An Emperor was not made by buildings, but by his achievements, and he'd conquered Sommerset. Soon they would have a victory march around the whole city, with the citizens out to watch, waving his flag. His smile spread.

He stalked into the servant's quarters, the only part of the great structure still standing, and headed down the hall to the room at the far end. At least that small section had survived and he knew he'd find Judson Lanser working away on the next stage of their plan. That was who he was, the organizer of the next part, always looking forward.

Lanser looked up at the sound of the door, and immediately rose to order refreshments. The room was a decent size, complemented by stained plexi windows down two walls. He collapsed on the lounge as a diminutive boy arrived with a tray of bowls and a steaming pot of spice-caf tea.

Lanser bowed, and reached to pour what looked like black liquid into the bowls. "How did it go, Emperor? Are things to your satisfaction?"

Carlton grabbed a handful of salted croquenuts and threw them into his mouth. He nodded. "Not bad. There are a lot of empty buildings and the troops have formed a perimeter, monitoring who tries to return to the city. Some citizens have leaped at the chance, now that the fighting is finished. I remember a lot of them from former days—Father's followers."

"Of course. Most of them will certainly be eager to align themselves with you as quickly as possible. We should hold a meeting—somewhere very public."

"Perhaps." He sipped his tea. "I thought more of a victory parade, with the troops fore and aft, the ornamental carriage, if it's still in one piece."

"I have news," Lanser said. His eyes narrowed in thought. "I've been working on this for a few days. From before the takeover, in fact. Here's what I've done and I hope it meets with your approval. You've been too busy with more important things for me to bother you with this."

Carlton sat up straight, a frown forming. "I'm never that busy. This had better be good."

His advisor gave him a level look. "It is. There is a family named Banderos that holds some land just north of the Adar Silva border."

As Lanser talked, Carlton's mind wandered to the map and he rose to lay it on the table in the centre of the room. "Show me," he demanded.

Lanser leaned over his shoulder. "As you can see, the map has been changed. That was the doing of First Banderos, the leader of the clan. It's somewhat interesting, in that he and his neighbour control a vast swath of forests and fields. It could act as a sort of insulation between Sommerset to the south, and the Jiranis to the north. And he's offered it up as part of the New Empire."

"Offered it up? What does he want?" Carlton gazed at the outline of the area in question. "It would be a huge advantage to control that area and keep the Jirani tribes at bay. But there's always a reason for someone making such an offer."

Lanser nodded. "First Banderos is your newly appointed Governor of the territory. He's your man now, and he'll do your bidding."

Carlton raised his eyebrows. "Are you serious?"

At Lanser's nod, he chuckled. "Cheap land," he said. "And we don't have to go to war to win control of it."

"Exactly." Lanser set his tea bowl on the edge of the table, running his finger around a line on the map. "And a sizeable barrier between us and the north."

Chapter Forty Four

Loyal had dried off from his plunge in the creek. He stripped his clothes off and quickly changed into uniform. He was in a cold rage, seething to get moving. "Adoni, are you with me?" he demanded.

"Likely," his assistant replied, eyeing him guardedly. "You just haven't told me the plan."

"Yah, sorry—I'm a bit scrambled here."

~***~

Three military troop movers took off from the field heading home, leaving the Khandarken men and their mounts on the vast plain north of the Banderos land. They were in south Jirani territory, near where the Shafoneur tribe grazed their herds. Governor Maude had been true to his word, providing a full troop of forty men to accompany Loyal and Damian Stuke on their foray to the Banderos compound.

Loyal levelled his hand over his eyes as movement in the distance caught his attention. "That must be the Shafoneurs." He made out a horde of riders coming toward them in no visible formation, their robes flowing out behind like sails. He whistled to Adoni and pointed, as several of the other men stopped what they were doing to stare in that direction.

"Jiranis," Adoni said, tightening the cinch on his saddle. "They travel like that—out of control.

Loyal chuckled and looked for his troop leader, a tall thin fellow named Lieutenant Heron, waving to get his attention. "It seems the Jiranis are about to arrive."

Heron spun around and peered down the field. "Yah, I see."

Loyal jogged to his side. "Have you dealt with them before? They're certainly different, but friendly."

Heron glanced at him and back to the fast approaching horde. "Never spoken to one, no."

"I have." Loyal turned to watch the front riders slow. Then he walked out to greet them, his arm raised in salute. To his surprise, Prince Shandro was in the lead, reining his mount to a halt as the others fell in behind.

Loyal bowed low. "Prince," he said. "I'm surprised to see you here. I thought it was the Shafoneurs who were being sent for this task."

Shandro swung down from the saddle. "Hawker,"

he said by way of greeting as they grasped arms. "Jiranis never sidestep a firefight."

Loyal laughed and watched a grin spread across Shandro's handsome dusky-skinned face. "I think I know the feeling," he remarked, gesturing at the other men. "Are the rest from the Penrhy tribe?"

"A mix. Penrhys, Shafoneurs. My brother and some of his men have joined us from the Moiselles out of interest to see what happens with the new emperor this time around. He's been engaged in combat with Carlton's troops in the past. We knew your men would be meeting us here. Is there a strategy set?"

Loyal nodded. "I believe so. I have a plan, but the greater priorities are still up in the air. Come meet Lieutenant Heron."

An aide started a small fire and soon they were squatted around it, tea bowls in hand as the talk went back and forth about how to proceed. Loyal shifted impatiently. "I have my own agenda," he said. "I'll need some backup to begin with, but should be fine on my own once the Banderos compound is secured."

Shandro nodded. "I heard you want to go through their territory and see what has happened there. Someone is out of communication?"

His face grew warm. "I left eight or ten voicelinks with the different family members. For some reason, none of them are in contact now except the oldest son, First. It's alarming, and with Carlton's troops moving around unrestricted nearby, I need to find out what has happened and if they're safe."

Heron glanced down and flicked a bit of dust off the sleeve of his jacket. "It's on our route anyway, Hawker. We can find out what's going on, then leave you there while we carry on toward Adar Silva. It'll be a reconnoitre exercise as much as anything. We could be at the north border station by tomorrow morning, if it's where you say it is. According to my map it should be an easy run." He tapped the funnel on his infolink.

"Okay. I'm in agreement." Shandro stood and stretched. "Let's move out."

Loyal glanced between the men as relief warred with worry in his gut. Finally, some action that should prove productive and get him a few answers about Angel and her father. Hopefully they were the answers he yearned for, not the ones he feared. He caught Damian's eye and nodded.

They rode until dusk when Heron ordered a stop to pitch camp. Loyal slept badly. The churning fear in his chest would not let him go—fear that Gerwal had forbidden his daughter to marry with him, that First had killed off more of his siblings, that Angel meant it when she said she wouldn't see him again.

Chapter Forty Five

By mid morning the next day, they were approaching the north border station. Loyal arranged with Heron for the troop to set up camp. He advanced on the structure with Stuke and Adoni at his side along with five men from the Khandarken contingent. As they drew near, he noticed there were more guards than usual around the facility as if there was the threat of attack. Well, it just made sense. With Emperor Carlton taking over Sommerset, the dispossessed were even more active and always unpredictable. When one of the brothers appeared in the doorway, shading his eyes to watch their approach, he felt a wave of relief wash over him that nearly felled him from his horse. He gripped the saddle with his knees and took a deep breath to calm himself. Now, perhaps some answers.

Loyal swung down from his mount and led it

through the gate, handing the reins to the attendant. Waving Damian and Adoni to accompany him, he gestured to his escort to wait. "Nineteenth Banderos," he called, "how have you been?" Maybe there wasn't a problem after all. But in that case, Angel's message was more ominous than he'd dared to imagine.

A slow grin formed on Nineteenth's face. "Loyal," he answered. "It's good to see you. We didn't know what had happened to you."

"Happened to me?" Loyal raised his brows as he walked up the steps and extended his hand. "I know we've been out of touch, but it was your voicelink that wasn't working, not mine."

Nineteenth shook his head as he seized his arm in a strong grip. "First took it, said it was needed to ensure the safety at the compound while he did the perimeter rounds."

"First took your link?" Loyal stalled as confusion circled in his head. Of course, the message from Angel had indeed come in through First's device. "He has his own voicelink," he said. "Why did he need yours?"

"He wanted some of his men to be able to contact him if need be."

"I see. Did you know that Gerwal's link isn't working?"

Nineteenth looked startled. "No, why would that be?"

"I don't know. Angel isn't in contact either." He didn't divulge that he'd received a message from her, just not on her device. The alarmed look on the brother's face told him more than he needed to know.

Nineteenth waved him into the entry. "First gave me orders to come here and stay put. There's been a threat of invasion from Emperor Carlton in the south, and certainly the dispossessed have been hovering like dogs on a scent. I thought it made sense. Seventh was sent to supervise at the west station for the same reason."

Loyal nodded. "Seventh isn't answering his link either."

"What about Rascal?" Nineteenth looked sternly into his face. "He was at home with Father and Angel, perhaps he can tell us…"

"No response," Loyal replied.

~***~

First stomped across the floor in the great entry and bellowed through the doorway. One of his men came running up the front steps in response. "Send runners to Sommerset," he shouted. "There will be a message from the Emperor's Advisor for me. I want it the minute it lands in their hands." He'd given Lanser his particulars for the voicelink, proud that possession of such a device made him seem a modern man. But they'd agreed between them not to exchange any important information through the link. Judson Lanser must be even more suspicious than he was in that regard, which just confirmed in First's mind that these links could not be trusted. Someone was always listening.

However, the exchange of information would be done by message, giving First a physical copy of his orders from the Emperor. Those orders were scheduled to arrive today and should include his appointment as Governor. He blinked rapidly, trying to repress the shudder of anticipation that ran down his spine. *Governor of his own territory.* What would the area be called? Perhaps it all became Banderos land at that point—First Banderos, Governor of the Banderos Territory. He cracked a laugh and caught the surprised expression on his aide's face.

"Get the men organized," he barked, turning away. "We should be ready to leave by morning. We'll be going back to the south border station to check on things there, then on to see Nazur. We'll be gone at least a week, so order up supplies." His aide left for the barracks and stores buildings on the other side of the compound.

First had sent someone to check on Gerwal, not wanting to show his own face down in the cellars. Apparently Father was still alive, weak but hanging on. Waiting to be rescued, no doubt. First was in two minds—kill Father now or let an 'accident' take him. It was arranging the accident that had him befuddled. How to make that happen in a way that was believable? His problem was his brothers. Fourth and Fifth were both onside, no questions asked. But the rest would be either hostile to his leadership bid or, at best, indifferent.

He didn't think he had it in him to kill them all.

And what would be the purpose? The compound and border stations ran well under the steady hand of the various brothers—Rascal, Runt and Baby didn't count. They were too young and hadn't taken sides as yet.

But they would as they grew older, especially if First killed all the senior brothers. He'd have to finish off the young ones too. The new men he'd recruited as his personal guard wouldn't be able to assume all the varied tasks and leadership roles that were needed to administer such a large organization. There must be a better way. The 'accident' was looking more and more appropriate, and would allow his family to support him without the anger or resentment that outright murder would cause.

He shut his ears to the low cries coming from the room where he'd ordered the youngest boys and Gerwal's new wife to be held, and settled down to a hearty dinner of llama meat and roasted vegetables. As he ate, he studied the room—the vases of flowers, all dead now, that Angel always set on the mantle above the fireheat; the handwoven throw the new wife, Willa, had procured for Gerwal's lounge; the wall of weapons including an old spear found when Father first began building here, along with more modern items like the laserguns brought by Loyal the Hawker. A lot of this he'd keep, it added to the charm and functionality of the place. Not the flowers of course, stuff like that made a man look weak.

Early next morning, the runners returned with a

parchment document folded and wrapped in waxed onionskin. First took it into his father's office, which he'd appropriated after Gerwal was secured in the cellars, and closed the door. He sat in Father's chair, staring at the package in his hand. Then taking a deep breath, he peeled it open.

The document looked formal, the wording legible, although he couldn't decipher it all and would have to have the scribe take a look and read it to him. But not now. He ran his finger over his name, First Banderos, inscribed in dark brown ink on the tan coloured sheet, and rubbed the Emperor's seal that was impressed in wax over the signature at the bottom.

He'd done it. Governor Banderos. Opening the bottom drawer, he set the document carefully in the cavity and shut it again, twisting the lock and pocketing the key. Time enough to make the announcement once the rest of his plans were in place. Angel still had to be delivered to cement Orde Nazur's complete cooperation.

He marched into the great entry and barked at his aide. "Time to go. Order the troops to prepare to ride out."

Chapter Forty Six

Nineteenth shouted to the cook for food and drink and took a seat at the table in the station hall, waving the others to chairs across from him.

"I think we need to get to the compound," Loyal said, "find out what's going on. I want to talk to Gerwal face to face. He must be made aware of any unusual activity in the area."

The brother nodded. "I'll come with you. I know First said to stay here, but Fourteenth is out on patrol and will be back shortly. He doesn't need me to help manage the station. Besides, I've been thinking it was time to send a runner, there's been no word from home since I left two days ago."

"Is that unusual?" Stuke frowned.

"There are always messages going back and forth," Nineteenth said, his brow furrowed in concentration. "Instructions from Father, reminders from Eleventh or Twelfth about where the herds are grazing, notes from the settlers looking for help or information. My concern is…" He silently rubbed his fingers across the table.

"That things are not normal at the compound," Loyal finished for him.

Nineteenth nodded. "I think we should be prepared."

Loyal stood, his heart pounding. "I have a troop of Khandarken soldiers with me, forty men, along with about fifty riders from the Jirani tribes. My problem is, I don't know the terrain well, but you do. You can tell us what we need to know as we go."

Nineteenth moved with purpose to the office at the back to leave a note for Fourteenth and returned carrying a large pack. "I'll bring my things—no telling how long before I get to return here. Let's move, I don't want to delay."

Nor did Loyal, by the gods. He'd been walking steadily toward this moment for what seemed a very long time. But he wasn't satisfied with that now. He needed to run.

As they rode, Heron and Shandro muscled their mounts in beside them to take part in the conversation.

"How many men at your compound?" Heron asked.

Nineteenth nodded. "About a hundred usually, but I know First has sent a lot of them out on patrol and he's been hiring men. About twenty, Angel told me, although it looked like more. It just depends if they're at the south station or home."

"Why the focus on the south station, when the Emperor would be coming from an easterly direction?" Adoni asked. Loyal gave his assistant a measuring look, realizing Adoni was more clever and observant than he'd ever given him credit for. He gave an approving nod and watched the man's face turn a fiery red.

"I've been wondering that myself," Nineteenth replied. "I think it has to do with this new arrangement First negotiated with the Nazurs. It's only a half day's ride from there to the Nazur border."

"What's our plan?" Prince Shandro forced his horse forward.

Heron raised his arm and pointed at a small row of buildings in the distance. "Is that the compound there?"

"No, those are settlers huts." Loyal turned back to the brother. "What if you approach the compound gate alone and see what kind of reception you get? You'll also see if it's your own men or these new troops who are controlling the entrance. Because if it's your men, you can find out what's going on." He knew in his gut that there'd been an upheaval of some kind. It sounded more and more as if First had done what Angel feared—seized control.

"Yah." Nineteenth rubbed his jaw as he considered. "There's another way through the wall but it's a little hard to find. Perhaps I should show you where that is before we make ourselves known to the gatekeepers at the main entrance."

They approached through the forest near a waterfall above the compound. Looking down through the trees, they saw the roof of the manorhouse and shapes of the outbuildings.

"Whoa," muttered Heron. "Bigger than I thought. It's going to be hard to get inside." The stone walls of the compound were high and thick, stretching off into the distance either side of where they huddled.

"That's the back gate." Nineteenth pointed to a gap in the wall below. "But it looks like there are guards posted. I'll talk to them, see what I can learn."

"I'll come," Loyal said. "Never know."

They rode down the steep trail leading to the bottom of the hill, then along the high wall to the gate.

"Ho there," a voice shouted. "Who are you?"

Nineteenth pulled his mount to a halt and dismounted. Loyal remained in the saddle, his lasergun held steady across his thighs. Best to be prepared.

"Hey, don't come any closer." A young face appeared behind the gate, shifting nervously. "What do you want?"

"I'm Nineteenth Banderos. I don't think I know you. Do you work for us?" Nineteenth moved slowly forward. "If so, you should know enough to let me into my own compound."

The face disappeared for a moment, as a conversation was conducted in low voices. Then he reappeared. "You have to go to the main gate," he declared, his voice unsteady. "Our job is to keep this gate closed. If you want in, you'll have to talk to our leader around the other side."

"I see. So, you don't have any authority to make a decision yourself."

"What? No, that's not true. It's just…" The fellow looked back over his shoulder, then waved them away. "You have to talk to the other men."

"Yah, I heard you." Nineteenth mounted his horse and rode off, Loyal following. They met up with Heron in the trees.

"Well, at least we know those men weren't yours," Loyal offered. "But we also can see the gate is poorly guarded. It shouldn't be hard to break through if needs be."

The story at the main gate was quite different. "Does First know you're here?" one of the guards asked belligerently. "We don't have any instructions to let the brothers in. We were told you all have your orders for patrol at the west and north stations. I guess you should return to your duties." His face was rigid.

"I've left the station under good control," Nineteenth shouted as he swung out of the saddle. "Now I need to talk to Gerwal! Open the gate and let me through."

"Not going to happen," the guard snarled, waving

his raygun in Nineteenth's general direction. "I don't even know if you're a Banderos brother. Stand back or I'll have to blast you."

"By the graves," he gritted. "This is my home, not yours. Now get the hell out of the way or I'll have to…"

A percussive blast shot from the muzzle of the raygun and Nineteenth fell back as his sleeve melted under the impact. He batted uselessly at the burning cloth, struggling to get his jacket off.

Loyal jumped down and grabbed the garment, peeling it from his shoulders. When Nineteenth pulled his arm out, he gave a howl of pain as the skin peeled back and hung in strings from the cloth. "Open the gate," he snarled, hurling himself at the metal rails, blood dripping from his hand.

The guard raised his raygun and Loyal shouted a warning, grabbing Nineteenth and hauling him backward. "Not like this," he muttered, dragging him toward his mount. "We are not going to win this way."

Chapter Forty Seven

Sommerset dawned clear and sunny. Carlton rose and bathed, then sent for Bieter, his assistant, to help him dress. They'd found an old uniform from his father's day at the Headquarters, abandoned in the servants' rooms after Aqatain fled the city. Carlton had a tailor fit it to his frame. The buttons were moved to allow for his more corpulent build.

His blood bubbled with excitement. Carlton had reclaimed the Empire that his father had lost. Aqatain's was the Old Empire, but this was the new one. The New Empire. It made sense, new emperor, new empire. Let the games begin. Perhaps he'd host the next Head Ball Games competition here once things calmed down. But that was for consideration another day.

Today was his victory tour of the city—and the populace was on alert. His Advisor had promised there would be huge crowds to welcome him back to his proper seat of government.

Judson Lanser appeared in the doorway, giving a low bow as he entered. "How is it going this morning, Emperor? Will we be ready on time? I've ordered the carriage to be brought around and it's waiting in the street. The horses have been groomed, and their harnesses decorated appropriately."

"I think about an hour," Carlton said, straining to see his image in the old foggy plexi mirror as he straightened his collar. "I've yet to break my fast."

"Of course," Advisor murmured. "I'll see to it in the dining hall. If you don't mind, I'll eat with you."

"Fine," he muttered, giving a tug as Advisor departed.

Bieter attached his neck cloth, then stood back to see the effect. "Very good, Emperor. Is there anything else?"

"My boots," he said, glancing down with a frown. "They need another polish, because these don't look right at all." He sat and stretched out both feet.

"Of course." His assistant knelt, carefully unpacked the polish case on the floor and soon Carlton's foot ware began to take on a high shine. One day he'd have new boots made—the kind Aqatain had worn, with carved and inlaid leather. But for now these would have to do. Always rein in the impatience, he reminded himself—one step at a time.

~***~

Carlton was tired when they finally returned to his

Headquarters, such as they were. The tour of the city had been a long three hours of standing in the swaying buggy, his arm raised in greeting as they passed up one street and down another.

There had been a lot of places where there was no one to greet him in return. Some parts of the city had obviously been devastated by the fighting, and burned ruins graced many of the lanes. But not all, and he'd been heartened to see the populace lined up in front of some of the houses to watch him go by. The children especially had been excited to see him, jumping up and down when his carriage appeared, and waving wildly as he passed.

In his estimation, it had been a great success, probably a better turnout than his father was ever given. Carlton had finally been acknowledged as Emperor by the citizens of Sommerset, the very centre of the Empire. After all this time, these years of struggle and toil, he was on his way to rebuilding his empire.

He collapsed on a lounge in the great hall, and propped his boots on a stool. "Bieter," he barked. "An ale, and perhaps some biscuits."

The next step was to enlarge his holding. The deal Advisor Lanser had made with the Banderos tribe to the north made more sense all the time. He gained territory without a single battle. And he'd heard there were roaming packs of dispossessed coming out of the mountains looking for a place to set down roots. They would be ripe for recruitment. Now he just needed a plan on how to pay for their service.

His assistant appeared in the doorway, tray in hand.

~***~

The battle for the Banderos compound began at dawn. The Khandarken troops led by Lieutenant Heron attacked the main gates, using lasers and rayguns to force the guards back. Once the area was largely cleared, they brought out the battering ram, a fallen log from the forest above the compound carried by twenty men as they tried to break open the gates. It was slow and dangerous work. The gates now sagged but would not be forced apart and the men had fallen under fire from scattered sentries hiding in the grass and hidden by the walls.

Prince Shandro ordered his men to build a ramp against the outside wall. He then sent his troops to climb it and hang over the top of the structure, strafing the guards who were regrouping to hold the entrance. Chaos ensued.

Meanwhile, Loyal along with Nineteenth, who was doped up on phang oil from Adoni's kit to dull the pain of his injury, was leading a group of men to take down the back entrance. The same young fellow appeared, nervously demanding they leave. But this time, a quick battering of laser fire encouraged him to lay down his weapon and step forward with his companions to release the lock and force the gate open.

By this time Nineteenth was staggering, although

still on his feet. "Let's go for the manorhouse," he muttered. "We'll probably find Angel and Father and can see how they are."

Loyal grabbed his shoulder and pulled him to a halt. "We need to secure the outbuildings first. Stay here with a couple of men and guard these boys," he said, pointing to the three who had surrendered the gate. "You're in charge, Nineteenth. Don't let them out of your sight."

As Loyal led his men toward the nearest barracks, he could hear the noise of the battle down the long field at the main gate. A few men were leaving the outbuildings ahead of them, moving cautiously through the grass and gardens to boost the numbers engaged in the battle. All the more reason to secure the other buildings while everyone was distracted.

They managed to take the barracks without lighting them on fire, although the door was off its hinges and scorch marks decorated the entry. Three more prisoners to add to those Nineteenth was guarding. As they made their way higher into the structure, Loyal heard noise from above. He found several of the Banderos brothers barricaded in a room on the upper floor.

"Thank the gods," Ninth said, emerging from the dim attics, Rascal on his heels. "We've been trying to pry the hinges off the door, but there wasn't a tool in sight." His fingers looked raw and red, and Rascal had a mark on his jaw where he'd obviously sustained a blow. "Thirteenth is here too, but his wife and children were taken elsewhere. He's in a real state."

"Well, I can use your help," Loyal replied. "Lead me through this maze. Help me find our way into these buildings and free anyone who's being held captive."

Thirteenth hadn't said a word, but turned with determination toward the stairs. "Damn window was too small to get out, and too high to jump from," he threw back over his shoulder. "Come this way and we can clear the stores buildings, and move along from there."

By the time they'd combed through all the outbuildings, two more of Loyal's men and three of First's guards had been killed. Loyal delivered more prisoners to Nineteenth, only to discover he had passed out. Ninth took over his role, locking the prisoners in the upper room of the barracks where he and his brothers had originally been secured.

"This way," Thirteenth declared, leading them out of the barns to a small building closer to the manorhouse. They glanced down the field at the roar of laserguns coming from the battle at the gates. Thirteenth crouched to run beneath the front window of the structure. "This is the Clone shed," he said low. "Bound to find some of the men in here." He fired his raygun at the handle of the door, then ducked as Loyal roared past him to kick it open.

Inside, a guard stood with his arm around a Clone, his shirt with a blue banner attached was undone and hanging open across his chest. He startled, then whirled to grab his raygun as Loyal gave him a blow to the side of the neck. He crumpled to the floor.

Loyal glanced around. Two more Clones, both slightly dishevelled, were seated on the lounge against the far wall, and another guard, this one entirely naked, lay on a pallet on the floor grappling with another Clone. In the end, Thirteenth's family was found in the back room of the shed, and two more men were added to the prisoner count.

Just the manorhouse left to search. Loyal's heart beat hard and he had trouble drawing enough air into his lungs at the hope he'd find Angel and finally get some answers.

Chapter Forty Eight

The battle at the main gate ended with men down on both sides of the compound wall. Prisoners were herded to the rooms at the top of the barracks, and the medic room cleared, soon to be filled with the injured. Fifteenth was still there, slowly mending from the deep burns he'd sustained weeks ago.

Heron approached the manorhouse from the front with his men, as Loyal led the brothers and Adoni to the back entrance. There was a brief battle, where the curtains caught fire in the Great Entry and a hole was blasted through a wall in the hall. There were only two guards left in the place, and once subdued, they were carted out to be added to the group already taken prisoner.

The brothers moved carefully through their home, the back rooms and into the upper floors looking for family. Loyal followed close behind, eager yet anxious to see Angel and find out what she'd meant by her message to him.

Gerwal's wife was found lying on the pallet in her room, weak and pale. The plexi window had been locked and barred from the outside. Baby was hiding under the bed, panting softly from lack of water. Runt stood behind the door holding a leg pried off the only chair in the room to strike down whoever entered. His face crumpled in relief when he saw his brother Rascal peer around the door.

Loyal accompanied Ninth on the search of the remaining rooms. To his bewildered distress, Angel was nowhere to be seen. *Had she left the compound before First's men took over? If so, where did she go?*

Water was sent for, and a light meal soon organized in the kitchens. Nineteenth was revived as the Great Entry filled with subdued conversation amongst the brothers and workers about what had just taken place. "But where is Gerwal?" his wife asked tearfully.

Ninth shook his head. "He must have gone with First to the south station."

"He wasn't well enough," Rascal stated emphatically.

"Nor did he do First's bidding," Thirteenth added. He moved to make room for Fifteenth to recline on Gerwal's lounge beside him.

Loyal looked around. "What have we missed? Doesn't anyone know where Angel is?"

There was a low thudding sound from below, and Loyal glanced at the floor. "Is there another level?"

"No, just the cellars." Rascal leaped to his feet. "I'll show you the way to the stairs," he offered and loped down the hall. Loyal picked up his lasergun and followed, heart pounding in an irregular beat. Damian Stuke came last. *Was Angel being held in the cellars?*

Rascal grabbed a handlight from the wall and led the way cautiously down a narrow set of stairs to a dark space with a dirt floor. "Careful," Loyal murmured. "We heard something down here, there could be more guards." All was silent around them as the three crept single file down a narrow hallway. They came to a pair of doors. Loyal opened the first one and Rascal shone the light in, but the space was empty of everything but a small huddle of broken old chairs.

Loyal brushed a web off his shoulder and grabbed the handle on the next door. The portal was locked, and he motioned for Rascal to shine the light on the mechanism. A deadbolt, which he quickly pulled back as he shot a questioning look at the young man. At Rascal's shrug, he dragged the door open, lasergun at the ready.

"About time." He heard a hoarse whisper, barely audible.

Rascal shone the light through the doorway. "Father!" He rushed into the dim space.

Gerwal Banderos lay on the dirt floor against the rock wall, unmoving. His eyes tracked their entry. "By the dogs of hell," he muttered. "I'm afraid I can't move."

"No problem," Loyal said, motioning to the men who had followed them down. "Carry him up, we'll see how he is. Are you injured anywhere, sir?"

"Just weak," Gerwal breathed. "No food or water for days now."

"Where's your daughter?" He hadn't meant to blurt that out, but the pressure to know was too strong.

Banderos jerked his head, turning to stare at him. "What do you mean?"

"I mean we haven't found her." Loyal barely gritted the words past his tight throat. "No one knows where she is."

~***~

By the time they got Gerwal Banderos up the stairs and onto a pallet amid loud noise and comments from the others, the medic had been pulled away from the other injured men to examine him. Soon the head of the tribe was sitting up against a bolster, sucking slowly on a bowl of weak tea laced with germanium honey. He carefully cleared his throat. "It was First's guards who restrained me and took me to the cellars," he choked out. "He must have Angel. She was in the gardens when the men came for me. Are you sure she isn't here? Have you looked in the back rooms, the servants quarters, the…"

"Everywhere, Father." Nineteenth cradled his heavily bandaged arm against his chest. "We've searched the whole compound."

Ninth shook his head. "We've looked in the attics at the barracks, the stores barns, even the Clone shed. She's not here."

"Where are your voicelinks?" Adoni asked.

"First," they all said in unison.

"The guards took mine," Gerwal muttered. "Is Angel answering hers?"

Loyal shook his head as he pulled his link from the harness. "Haven't heard from her in days." Heat climbed his neck at the memory of how he'd gone into a tailspin from the contents of her last message. He clenched his jaw. He'd hear the truth from her own lips, if he only could find her. *Could she have switched her affections to another man so soon?* Surely not. His gut clenched at the thought. Not after the wonderful and intimate time they'd spent together in Sommerset.

Fifteenth shifted on the lounge, rubbing a red patch on his cheek. "I heard what First and Sixteenth were arguing about," he said looking straight at his father. "The night Sixteenth died."

Gerwal slowly turned his head and stared at his son. "You heard them? How?"

The room had fallen silent as all eyes focussed on the two. "I was coming up the steps and Sixteenth was facing me. First didn't know I was there."

Gerwal took a shallow breath and inclined his

head. "And?" His voice was barely audible, his face flushed an unhealthy red.

Fifteenth pressed his hands tightly together. "First said, *shut up,* and Sixteenth said, *I won't shut up. You'll never be the head of the Banderos tribe. We'll all fight you for it to the last man.* Then he turned to walk away, and that's when First hit him on the back of the head."

Loyal watched Gerwal as he digested that information. His skin turned a strange mottled colour, and his fingers worked rhythmically on the bowl of tea he held. He stared at Fifteenth, as his mouth opened, then closed. Finally he croaked, "You're sure about that."

"Yes, Father. I heard it clearly."

"And why not say anything until now?"

Fifteenth flushed. "Because you wouldn't have believed me."

Gerwal's jaw bulged as he closed his eyes. "You're right," he muttered. "It makes me furious, but that's true."

Willa leaned forward to urge her husband to take a sip of tea, speaking softly to him to come with her for a bath.

Loyal glanced out the plexi window, noting the pitch-black night. "When can we leave for the south border station?"

"Not before daylight," Nineteenth declared.

Loyal frowned. "You won't be going with us."

"I know, but you can't leave till morning. It's a long ride. You should prepare now."

"Yah, cause I'm going at first light."

Nineteenth gave him a pointed look and nodded his head.

Chapter Forty Nine

First relaxed in his chair, savouring the bowl of brandy cradled in his hand. They'd reached the south station well before nightfall, leaving him time to relax and solidify his plans. He'd sent Fifth to the cellars to check on their sister and heard word she was fine. That boded well, she needed to be in excellent shape to impress Orde Nazur when he delivered her tomorrow.

He raided the clothes cupboard in her room before departing the manorhouse and brought her best robe, made of plantain and glitters. He remembered when Father bought that garment for her from a travelling hawker. He viewed the purchase as a waste—why spend money on such things? But it would certainly impress her betrothed. He noted the hem was muddy, as if it had been recently worn, yet he was sure he'd never seen her in it. Perhaps he wasn't home often enough to notice such things. or did she sometimes use it on her trip to Hafford to see her tutor, Wyway?

He shrugged and took another sip, enjoying the sensation as the liquor burned its way down his throat. This was his last mission as First Banderos. He would cement the deal with Orde, get rid of Angel, and travel back home to set himself up as Governor of the territory. By then Father would be dead, and he'd place the body somewhere outside the compound to be discovered by one of his brothers. Thus, the 'accident'.

He'd probably need some of his own expensive plantain garments soon—dress jackets with belted waists worn with high-collared shirts. Certainly, there would be a Governor's forum, likely held in Sommerset every year.

He heard a thump on the cellar stairs and glanced over. Fourth turned his head at the same time. "Why not let her out?" Fourth said. "She can hardly run away with all our men patrolling the place. It would certainly be more comfortable for her upstairs. It's damp down there, and cold."

First grunted. "We'll bring her up in the morning. She'll have to bathe and get dressed before we leave for the Nazur manorhouse." He was getting tired of having Fourth question his decisions. Probably best to send him out on border patrol after this was finished. Let him work the stations for a few years, till he grew used to the idea of who was in charge.

He rose, carrying the brandy bowl with him. "Well, I'm off to bed," he said. He was close to winning, so close.

~***~

Angel lay still on the pallet as her dream took hold. *She was sitting at her little desk, Mother at her side holding Rascal in her arms. "Write a letter to Daddy," mother said. "He likes it when he gets a nice letter from you." Angel pulled a small square of parchment toward her and set to work, a new nib on her pen.* Dear Daddy, *she wrote carefully across the top of the letter. Daddy was often away a long time when he rode his rounds of the land. She missed him when he was gone.* Please come home soon, *she added. Mother nodded and smiled at her.*

She blinked her eyes open and gazed around, but could only see the vague outline of the stairs against the far wall. There was very little light coming from beneath the door, which told her it was probably nighttime. She didn't know how long she'd been here, it was hard to keep track of time.

She fumbled for the cover and pulled it closer around her throat. The damp crept through her clothes and made it hard to stay warm. If only First would let her out…

She sighed. Her energy was low, and she was losing the will to fight. *Was she to die here?* Father would be sad. Would Loyal care? Not after the message she'd sent him to stay way. Perhaps he'd never even know what had happened to her. She'd told him to leave her alone, but there hadn't been a choice. First was nothing if not determined. If he'd killed some of his brothers, he wouldn't stop at the idea of taking Loyal's life. Tears leaked from the corners of her eyes into the hair at her temple. She brushed the moisture away with the edge of the cover. Maybe all was not lost. First didn't stay in one place for long. After he left, perhaps she could persuade one of his guards to set her free.

She closed her eyes and rolled her head to the side. A new dream, hazy at first. *Loyal had taken her for a ride on the Sparkling Wheel—up up into the sky and then down so fast her stomach fluttered with the drop. She turned to smile at him and he kissed her, his mouth hot and fierce on hers. Her excitement mounted. Would they make love? It had been wonderful, the way he took control of her body with such a gentle yet firm touch, his hands kneading her flesh. She'd been surprised at first, not recognizing the sensations that were triggered from his attentions. It was all so new, yet she was unafraid, eager to mate with him. His focussed gaze kept her pinned in place, his roaming mouth and hands exploring every nook and crevice of her body so that she was on fire even before he entered her. And then she came in a heavy wave of feeling…*

She woke as ripples of excitement slammed through her body. The sensation slowly faded. Opening her eyes, she looked around. She was alone.

Chapter Fifty

Dawn was still an hour away as Loyal prepared to ride out. The men were mounting up when Rascal waved wildly from his saddle. "Hawker," he shouted, "over here."

As Loyal walked toward him, the young man lifted the flap of his jacket and fumbled with something attached to his belt. When he raised his hand, a beltlink dangled from his fingers. There was a triumphant smile on his face as he tapped the button on the side.

Loyal ran, seized the device and searched the screen for messages. There only one—a partial text that read *…and I'm being held captive. I think they…*

"Adoni!" he bellowed. His assistant came running. "See what you can get from this."

Adoni took the beltlink and opened the back, fiddling with the pulser emitter. Then he clicked it shut. "I can't tell where she is," he said apologetically. "If we ride in the right direction and get closer to her, we should be able to pick up the rest of the message. Just don't know which direction that is."

Loyal rubbed his hands over his face in heavy frustration. *By the graves, could nothing go right?* At least now they knew for sure she was held against her will. But where? He waved Prince Shandro over. "I want to send you and the Jiranis to the west station, just in case she's there. I'm taking the rest of the men south."

As Prince Shandro saluted, Loyal turned back to Rascal. "Is there a trail that will take us all in the general direction of both stations? When we get closer, we branch off—Shandro to the west. By then the beltlink should be receiving clearly if we're anywhere near the spot where Angel's held. That will hopefully give us the information we need." Rascal nodded and pointed the way.

The men moved out in formation with Loyal and Rascal in the lead and quickly broke into a gallop, eating up the miles. The sun was still low in the morning sky when Rascal called a halt. "Hawker, here's where the Jiranis head to the west station. Runt can show them the way, and introduce them to the station patrol. But I've just received another vibration on my link."

Tugging it off his belt, he held it up to the light. "Okay, that's better. The whole message reads— *First's men took me from the compound and I'm being held captive. I think they mean me harm. Don't tell Loyal."*

Loyal gritted his teeth as his shoulders tensed. "That definitely came from the south," he said, trying to rein in his reaction as he examined the details on the screen. *Don't tell Loyal?* Was this just more of the same—she didn't want to see him again? His hands shook on the reins and his horse sidestepped nervously.

"Yah, it's from the south. But why would they mean her harm?" Rascal's face bore a fearful look.

"I don't know, but I intend to find out." Loyal spurred his mount forward. "Lead the way," he shouted, "we're running out of time."

Rascal raced ahead to find the track, taking them for miles through a thick forest only to emerge on the other side at the top of another hill gazing down at the back of the border station in the distance.

~***~

"They're getting ready to ride out," Adoni observed beside him. "We've barely reached here in time."

"I don't see Angel," Rascal muttered. "They're saddling the mounts, but only the guards are visible. Look at the sashes on their shirts—just like those we saw at the compound. This is First's own personal contingent. I wonder where they're going?"

"We'll soon find out," said the blind man, suddenly appearing beside Loyal. "But now's the time to be very careful. Don't want to rush into the middle of things and ruin our chances of success. It could be our last opportunity to find Angel."

In astonishment, Loyal slowly turned his head. During The Last War the blind man had walked with the rebel group of men, long days of slogging along the banks of the Violetta River looking for escape from the Emperor's troops and a way across the water to safety. Today he rode a black horse with white feet, a slash of brown on its forehead.

He wore the same grey robes, made of some thin fabric that drifted around him like a cloud in a light breeze. And his face—that beatific expression, eyes closed—was exactly the same.

"What did you say?" Loyal asked. No one else seemed to have heard the blind man or paid any attention to his presence.

"We need to be careful, Loyal." The blind man gestured to the activity below. "First is down there and he's on the warpath. We can take this place by storm, but it will need a bit of planning. Luckily we approached from an unexpected direction—good thinking on your part. They won't see us coming."

The man raised his face toward the sun and took a deep breath. "The guards are posted looking toward the Banderos compound in one direction and toward Nazur land in the other. Let's take advantage of that, shall we?"

Loyal nodded, but it felt like he moved in a dream or some kind of fog, with the blind man suddenly beside him, guiding his decisions. "Right, men," he barked. "We approach from three sides. A small party coming from the direction of the compound, and a second group from the other side where the guards are posted. See?" He pointed across the meadow, and Rascal nodded.

"I can lead that group," the boy said. "I know the way through the trees."

"Good, but you can't show yourself. If First sees you, he'll know the compound has been recaptured. It will alert him to what is coming." Loyal glanced around at his men. None of them appeared to notice the blind man's presence.

Loyal looked toward him and received a pleased smile in response. "Well done," the man said in his low modulated voice, that same tone that could be heard wherever Loyal stood, yet seemed to go unnoticed by the others.

He took a breath and shook his shoulders loose. "The plan is to approach cautiously," he continued to his men, "and talk to the guards but don't engage them in a firefight if you don't have to. Keep them preoccupied, with requests to enter, or to talk to First, whatever it takes. Only start a fight when they turn to support the men in the station itself."

The blind man nodded, and he welcomed the feeling of rightness that settled in his chest as the plan unfolded. "The rest of us will approach from here at the back," he said. "They won't even see us coming until we're upon them. The thing is, we don't want too much of a battle if we can help it. I think they hold Angel in there as captive, and I want to keep her safe. Understood?"

The men nodded and moved into position, Damian Stuke leading the first group back through the forest and eventually appearing along the lower track from the direction of the compound. Where Loyal and his men waited, they could hear the station guards hailing the group some way off, issuing orders to halt. As they slowly advanced, shouting their questions and demanding answers, Rascal's group suddenly appeared coming from the other direction.

The guards became agitated, dealing with strangers approaching from two fronts, and more men appeared in the station doorway. Loyal was closer to the structure now and recognized Fifth trotting down the steps to talk to the guards, then pausing and looking back as he saw the second group at the gate. He raised his raygun and fired into the air.

First appeared on the top step, stopping to take stock of the action below. There was shouting back and forth as First waved his arms and issued orders.

"Now, it's time," the blind man said in his low voice, just as Loyal raised his hand. He pointed his men forward and they began the silent descent of the hill and across the field to the back of the station. The main floor was heavily barricaded around the base and Loyal set his men to tear off the sheathing just as a laser roar sounded from the front.

They moved faster, using raygun blasts to burn the coverings off. Soon the men were pouring through the battered and broken plexi windows into the main level of the building, taking over the space floor by floor. Three men lay dead in the entry as Loyal leapt into the structure. "To the stairs," he yelled as another guard with First's sash tied across his shirt ran down the steps and fell to his death with a raygun blast to the chest.

They fought their way to the top, one more man down and one of their own wounded by the wayside. The third floor was empty. Loyal stalled in frustration as he gazed around. The garderobe was vacant, pallets stacked on the holder in the middle of the floor, an arrangement he'd seen in the other stations he'd visited.

He ran back down the stairs, to find his men milling around inside and out. Three guards with sashes were bound together and positioned in the corner of the entry. Fourth was tied to a chair, bleeding heavily onto the floor. But First was gone and Angel was nowhere in sight.

Chapter Fifty One

"Where are they?" Loyal roared from where he stood at the top of the stairs to the second floor of the station.

"Gone," Adoni replied. "First and Fifth, along with three of their men escaped through the field that way." He pointed out the plexi, facing east. "One of the horses is injured, I hit him with a raygun."

"Running to Nazur is my bet," Rascal said, appearing suddenly in the doorway and looking around. "Where's Angel?"

"I don't know!" Loyal couldn't contain his fury. He slammed his fist on the table, causing it to tilt dangerously as one leg splayed and collapsed. "Did they take her with them?"

"No," Adoni and Rascal answered together. "Five men, riding like hell for the Nazur border."

He waved at Rascal in frustration. "Try your beltlink."

As the young man fumbled for the device, Adoni walked across to the far side of the entry, pulled back a curtain and found a narrow door. He opened it and peered inside. It led to a set of stairs set tightly into the space leading downward, bathed in darkness. He pointed to Fourth. "What's down there?"

"Eh?" Fourth lifted his head in confusion and blinked rapidly. "Angel," he said and lost consciousness, falling sideways in his chair

"What?" Loyal spun on his heel. "What did he say?"

"Get a light," Adoni barked. One of the guards motioned with his chin toward a cupboard on the back wall. Seizing his lasergun, Loyal grabbed the handlight from a shelf and bounded down the stairs, slowing as he reached the bottom. He ducked his head to step into the low, dank-smelling space and shone the light around. At once he saw her golden hair spread across a dark pallet, her face turned toward the wall.

"Angel!" He reached her in seconds, kneeling beside the prone figure, feeling for a pulse at her throat and shining a light on the still face.

"Angel." He gathered her into his arms and collapsed on the pallet, cradling her against his chest. "She's alive," he rasped. "She's breathing."

Rascal landed beside him, holding her lax hand and slapping her wrist. "Come on, sister," he said, his voice unnaturally high. "Come on, Angel."

"Let me through," Adoni said. "Bring her upstairs."

"Yah." Loyal knew that was the right thing, he just didn't want to let her go. He surged to his feet and headed for the steps, cracking his head on the low beam as he went.

"This way." Adoni led him to the second floor where pallets had been laid out and some injured men lay moaning. Loyal gently placed her on an empty pallet and his assistant went down on one knee, feeling for all the pulses in her wrist and neck as Loyal and Rascal hovered at his shoulder.

Adoni glanced up. "She's fine," he said.

"She's not fine," Loyal thundered. "Look at her!"

"Yah, but she's just exhausted," Adoni said, giving him a pained look. "See, she's coming around, now that you're standing above her shouting at the top of your voice."

Loyal studied her face intently, saw her eyelids flutter before they opened and he stared into those dark blue depths. "Angel." He knelt at her side, stroking her cheek. "There you are."

A smile blossomed on her mouth, as she focussed on him. "I hoped you…" she whispered, and closed her eyes again. Loyal clamped his mouth shut in frustration.

~***~

They laid Angel Banderos on a travois padded with a pallet from the border station and headed single file back to the compound. Loyal walked for the first miles, striding by her side to ensure she was safe, she was warm, she didn't appear to be in pain. He finally mounted his horse and sent Adoni ahead to prepare a reception for her with the care she would need.

Fourth's wounds were bound as best they could with the medic kit at the station, along with the other injured men. They were all loaded on ponies or pallets and hauled along with the group returning home. Loyal ordered a contingent to stay at the station, promising to send reinforcements and supplies as soon as he could. They were to secure the station and protect it at all cost. Most of all, they were to keep a lookout for invasion from the west and Nazur territory, where First appeared to be headed.

"Our medic will know what to do when we get back," Rascal reported. "He's good, has healed all kinds of things. Even broken bones and such, he's …" He mumbled away to himself as he arranged a cover over his sister and tied it to the pallet.

It was a long day, and toward evening, Loyal dismounted again, insisting on spreading his jacket over Angel's still form to ensure she was warm. As he looked around, he realized in the melée resulting in the capture of the south border station, the blind man had disappeared again. Where had he gone? Or perhaps the question was—had he really been there at all? Loyal knew what he'd seen and heard. Although no one else seemed to be aware of the man, he welcomed the support and advice and realized at that moment he wasn't alone. He'd often wished for such a relationship with his father, but that hadn't happened. Yet the blind man appeared when he most needed him—to lend strength and wisdom, to help him make the decisions he needed to make.

He glanced at Angel's still face. His heart felt tender as if he'd taken a heavy blow to the chest during the battle, and perhaps he had. He still didn't know what Angel meant by the message she'd sent him, and Adoni's words persistently knocked at the back of his mind. There was no room for Loyal Hawker here, with all the brothers standing ready to take over from Gerwal, and Angel tied to the Banderos territory. Where did that leave him?

Chapter Fifty Two

First rode hard for the border, Fifth keeping pace at his side. All of his brothers were good horsemen but this one was fearless. First glanced back to find their three guards working diligently to keep pace.

Things were not going as planned and failure rode his shoulder like a hunter hawk, the claws biting deep into his flesh. *What had gone wrong?* Those men came out of nowhere to attack the south station, although he suspected Loyal Hawker had a hand in it. He'd spotted that yellow-skinned Legitamian riding with the group coming from the direction of the Banderos compound. That foreigner wouldn't have been there if Hawker hadn't arrived.

He'd been forced to abandon Angel in the cellars for the moment. Once he got things back under control, he could pick her off again and take her to Orde Nazur, just not today. Orde was going to be furious. It would be hard to keep him onside without delivering on the promises made. Perhaps a twist to the tale—he could say Angel had fallen ill and he'd left her with the medic. He planned to bring her in a few days when she'd recovered and was no longer contagious. *Would that tale work?*

It might. He could also send Fifth to the Banderos compound to collect his personal guards and bring them to him. With some support from Orde, he'd be ready to take back the south station. Then he'd have a headquarters to work from until he got things on track again.

As the plans formulated in his mind, calm descended. So long as he kept his head, all would be well. He shouldn't panic. At the same time, he'd made the right decision to run. If he were captured, there'd be no one to lead the troop to rescue him. Again, he realized the need of an assistant, a lieutenant he could rely on to have his back. *Was Fifth that man?*

He glanced sideways at his brother. Fifth was competitive, he rode neck and neck with First as they travelled across the land. Fifth hated having Fourth with them, unless he was willing to take orders. But there was something sly about this brother. Everyone recognized it, even Gerwal had been known to question his version of events and ask for a second opinion of what had transpired from one of the other brothers.

Near the Nazur border, they approached a narrowing of the track at a place where the banks rose high on either side of the trail. The only way through was single file. First dug his spurs into his horse's flanks, but Fifth moved faster and his mount leapt into the lead, crowding him out.

First held back his irritation and swerved to avoid his brother as he surged forward. There was a roar, and he glanced up as a shadow appeared above him against the strong sunlight. He caught the sharp silhouette of a big mountain cat leaping from the bank, legs outstretched.

First reined up in quick reaction, his horse rearing under him. The mountain lion flew, landing on Fifth's shoulders, its paws braced against his back. A roar erupted from its gaping maw as it sank its teeth into the side of his head. Fifth screamed and clung to the saddle, his mount racing into the trees ahead.

The guards fought for control of their steeds, rearing and shifting into each other in the narrow space. Realizing he had narrowly missed being targeted by the cat, First fumbled for his lasergun and tried to raise it to his shoulder. He couldn't shoot straight at the cat, Fifth would be hit, yet his brother's horse was already racing out of sight.

He let off a wild shot as he dug his spurs into his horse's flanks. But even before he reached his brother, he knew it might be too late. Fifth had fallen from the saddle. The cat had a heavy grip on his head, struggling to drag him through the grass. When First arrived, the animal looked at him over his shoulder before abandoning the body and leaping off into the trees.

The men milled around as First dismounted, tossing his reins to the nearest guard. Holding his lasergun steady, he slowly approached his brother where he lay on the ground. His horse whickered and shied away as First knelt to turn Fifth over. There was nothing to see where his face had been, the flesh ripped right off his skull so that only raw meat and blood oozed onto the dust under his still body. Fifth was dead.

~***~

At the Banderos compound, Loyal had the injured carried to the medic's quarters. Fourth was unconscious from loss of blood, but his heart rate was steady and he was expected to survive. He reclined beside Fifteenth who was still recovering from his burns. Then Loyal organized the men, setting guards around the compound and issuing the voicelinks he'd reclaimed at the south station to those who needed them.

When he re-entered the manorhouse, Angel had been taken to her room and the medic sent for. There was great consultation going on between Willa and Rascal in Angel's room, with Nineteenth hovering at the edge of the conversation, waiting for the medic to give his verdict.

"Sit down, Loyal," Gerwal muttered. "It seems the girl is going to be all right, they just have to decide how to treat her."

Loyal sat on the edge of the chair indicated, then

leapt to his feet again when Rascal appeared on the stairs. "What do they say?" he demanded. "Is she sick? Is she dying?"

Rascal shook his head. "She's sick, dehydrated, Willa is tending her—lots of mineral water, calla oil, vinegar to help prevent infection in her wounds."

"Her wounds?" He felt the floor tilt beneath his feet. He hadn't seen any marks on her flesh, but then he hadn't thoroughly examined her. How could he? "What wounds? Has she lost blood?"

"No, no, bruises mostly. Rough handling, I'd say." Rascal's face was pale. "Must have happened when they kidnapped her."

"Of course." She would have fought them. The very thought made him nauseous yet proud as he walked to the end of the room and back to try for calm. "When can I see her?"

"Not for a bit, she's not talking right now, anyway." Rascal gave him a sympathetic look.

"It's going to be all right, Hawker." Gerwal straightened in his lounge, shifting his feet on the floor. Adoni had just given him another treatment but he was obviously in some pain. With each treatment, he gave Adoni greater respect, which was interesting given his initial disdain for someone from Legitamia. "She's strong, Angel is. She's determined. It's hard to hold her back, right Rascal?"

Rascal gave a faint smile. "Yah, she is. Just like you, Father."

Gerwal gave him a retiring look as his son left the

room. Then he turned to Loyal. "Hawker, the question is—are you going to marry my daughter?"

Loyal turned slowly to stare into the older man's face. "Marry her?" He blinked. "I don't know, because I'm not sure if she will agree."

Chapter Fifty Three

On their way again without Fifth, First and his men were stopped at the border where Orde Nazur's soldiers had set up watch. "Halt," one of them called. "Who goes there?"

Impatiently, he reined in his mount. "It's First Banderos," he called.

The guards huddled together before one rode forward to meet him. "Why are you here?"

He bristled at the insolent tone, glancing nervously over his shoulder to see if their pursuers were catching up to them. To his relief, there was no one in sight. "I'm here to see Orde," he gritted. "We have a deal and I'm free to meet with him at any time. I don't know why… "

Before he could finish, the guard turned his back and rode away to talk with the others.

He shifted in the saddle. Had something changed

here? Was he no longer able to talk with Nazur and make their arrangements?

The guard returned, followed by two other riders. He gave a nod. "Follow me," he said. "I'm your escort, but your men stay here."

First felt his mouth drop. They expected him to ride on alone? "I always take my men with me," he sputtered.

"Not this time." The expression on the guard's face was firm.

Frustrated, he turned back and waved to his men. "I'll be a while. Meet me here in a day or two."

He rode west with the three guards, knowing his men would likely leave for other opportunities rather than hang at the border hoping he would reappear. What kind of leader said, *meet me in a day or two?* How would he even pay them for their services? Desperation rose in his chest to suffuse his face with heat. He'd lost almost everything that he'd held. With the south station taken, it wasn't a giant leap to imagine the Banderos compound had also fallen.

Where were his men? Likely scattered to the four winds. His brother, Fifth, was dead, that support lost forever. And Fourth? He didn't even know, but probably wounded or killed in the taking of the station. He tightened his thighs on the saddle, standing in the stirrups to stretch his legs and relieve the tension.

Orde Nazur wouldn't be aware of all this. He might know about the fall of the station, given his men were often seen roaming across the border to keep tabs on Banderos activity. But surely he couldn't know about the rest. Orde was his ace in the hole. He would provide him the backing he needed to fight for what was rightfully his. He straightened, frowning toward the horizon. There was the silhouette of the Nazur manorhouse and compound up ahead. He could make this work.

They rode into the corral as dusk fell, dismounting and handing their horses off to the workers there. First brushed the front of his jacket and hastily ran his hands back through his hair. No need to look like he'd just lost a fight.

"This way," the guard said, herding him with his body and so First was escorted up the steps to the manorhouse door, one man positioned each side of him. He was being treated as if he were under arrest. Irritation needled at his throat. The front door opened and Orde Nazur stood in the doorway, uniformed guards positioned at his back.

"First," he said. His face was blank, neither threatening nor welcoming. "Why are you here? You obviously haven't brought your sister."

He stiffened his spine. The man wasn't openly friendly, but they still had a deal. "I've come to organize that very thing," he said.

"I see." Orde stared at him a moment, then gave a nod to dismiss the two men who escorted First. "Come in and let's get down to work." He turned and First walked into the Great Entry of the Nazur compound. The door slammed at his back.

~***~~

At the Banderos compound, the men were ranged around the long dining table. Gerwal took the head, relaxing comfortably in his chair. Loyal Hawker, Damian Stuke, Lieutenant Heron and Prince Shandro Penrhy had each claimed a spot.

Shandro thumped a finger on the surface of the table. "I'm leaving tomorrow," he said. "We've gone as far south as the Adar Silva border and cleaned out some camps of dispossessed, with Heron's help." He cast a humourous look and Heron responded with an ironic smile. Everyone knew his troops outnumbered Penrhy's two to one.

"The war still rages south of Sommerset," Heron added. "Carlton's focus must be to clear out as much of the Adar Silva military as he can to secure his position. From what our aircart pilots say, the army has taken up a position in the hills to the south and the Empire troops are having trouble removing them from that line. Perhaps for now, the New Empire is contained."

"At least it keeps them from focussing on the land in this direction," Gerwal said. "We still need to be on alert for any activity at the edge of our territory."

"I can leave some men with you," the prince continued. "I know you don't yet have a handle on how many of the guards you have at your disposal, or which have Banderos loyalty."

Gerwal grimaced at this comment but remained

silent.

"Keep the men here as long as needed, Loyal," Shandro added, turning to address him. "Most are from the Shafoneurs. They aren't far from home and can return quickly once you release them. It'll likely take a bit to figure out the workings of this establishment anyway." He cast a sideways glance toward Gerwal.

Loyal nodded. "I appreciate it. There are guards around the perimeter of the compound and we'll be beefing up security at each one of the stations until things settle down. I've already received a commitment from Khandarken." He looked at Damian Stuke who had declared he would stay as long as he could, especially if there was any disruption arising from Carlton's men to the south. He took a sip from the bowl of clouded ale in front of him. "What we have to figure out is where First went and what his plans are."

Gerwal shifted in his chair. "I can contact Nazur," he said thoughtfully. "I don't know the son well, but it's possible I'll get an answer. The other option is to send in someone undercover. We might learn more that way." He tightened his mouth. "This is my son we're talking about, yet I no longer think of him in that way. Because of his actions, more of my boys are dead, and others seriously wounded. I don't know if Fourth is going to pull through. Fifth has fled and won't return, I'm sure. Fifteenth is lying in the medic hut with deep burns over half his body. And my daughter…" He choked as the other men glanced away or down at the table top.

Just then Rascal descended the stairs and Loyal's attention shifted. He half rose from his chair. "Is she…?" He didn't complete the sentence, but Rascal nodded and beckoned him forward. He bounded up the steps, oblivious to the chuckles around the table behind him.

Chapter Fifty Four

Rascal led Loyal down the upper hall to an open doorway and showed him through, closing the door softly behind him. Angel lay on a pallet by the plexi, covered in a throw of light woven fabric that shone pale blue in the sun's low rays. Her head was turned to gaze out the window at the garden below. He caught the subtle perfume of herbs and spices in the air.

He walked forward and stopped at the end of the bed, almost afraid of what she might say to him. "Angel?"

She turned at the sound of his voice. Her face was so pale it tore at his heart, her eyes surrounded by deep shadows like bruises beneath them. Slender fingers were clasped tightly together on the bedsheet. "Loyal." Her voice was no more than a whisper and tears suddenly filled her eyes, running down her cheeks.

"Ah, Angel. Don't cry." He knelt on the side of the pallet, gathering her into his arms as his heart seemed to compress in his chest. "Please don't cry." As the sobs increased, he held fast, pressing his cheek to her temple and smoothing his hands down her back. Her cries faded until there was just the occasional hiccup that shook her body. He pulled her tighter against him, rocking her gently.

"You're breaking my heart, baby," he said low. "What can I do?"

She pressed her cheek against his chest. "Just hold me," she murmured.

When the tears had stopped, he lifted her chin to gaze into her face. "Tell me. Did they abuse you? You know what I mean. Did they…" Somehow he couldn't put the fear into words, but when she shook her head such relief flowed through him he could barely contain it.

"No," she said. "Not that."

"Okay." He scanned what he could see of her body. "How did they hurt you? I know they did…"

"I'll tell you," she said. "Just let me rest."

"Yah, rest against me. As long as you want," he said, gathering her close.

~***~

When Angel woke, she found Loyal and her family gathered round the foot of her pallet. Obviously a conversation had begun among them. "Why do you think you were taken?" Gerwal demanded, his hands braced on the back of a chair. "I know why First captured me. I just can't figure out his plan for you."

Angel took a deep breath, gazing at the faces before her. Loyal looked awkward amongst her brothers. Had they come in when he was holding her in his arms? Her body warmed. "I think I was part of the bargain with Orde Nazur," she offered.

Rascal's face paled. Nineteenth looked determined and Loyal's eyes darkened as his face took on a thunderous expression. "Your brother traded you?" he exclaimed. "For what?"

Father took a step back in shock, his face a mask of outrage.

"I don't know what the agreement was," she replied, pushing herself higher against the bolster. "But I can guess. I heard the men talking when I was in the cellar. First had given them explicit instructions. They were supposed to protect me. He wanted me in good condition when I was delivered to the Nazur compound." She tried to hide the shudder that wound its way down her spine at the thought of what might have happened.

Father sputtered. "It must have been a deal to support each other in case of invasion. Perhaps against Carlton?" He shrugged. "First had already seized control by capturing me, just not in the way I would have expected." His face was haggard.

"I don't think that was it, Gerwal." Willa had silently entered the room, holding a parchment document in her hand. "Scribe was looking for some things in your desk and found this."

Gerwal stared as if it were a snake and kept his hands at his sides. "What is it?"

She pushed it toward him. "Have a look."

At his hesitation, Nineteenth took it from her fingers and passed it to Loyal. "Tell us, Hawker. What does it say?"

At Gerwal's nod, Loyal unfolded the paper and held it to the light. "By the dogs of hell," he muttered, glancing up. "It's a formal appointment by Emperor Carlton with his official seal on it. First was named Governor of your territory—yours and Nazur's—under the control of the New Empire. There's a map detailing the area."

Angel watched her father stagger and seize the back of a chair. "An agreement with Carlton?" His look pierced her. "And his sister was part of the deal that brought Nazur onside." Abruptly he sat down as if his legs had given out. "I never thought…"

Angel reached for his fingers as Nineteenth put his hand on Gerwal's shoulder. "None of us did, Father," she murmured.

Willa motioned to the servant hovering in the doorway and waited while he passed bowls of tea around. "Let's calm down, now," she said. "Drink your tea. We still have work to do."

Father gave his wife a piercing look, then glanced at Loyal. "Hawker, I'd like to have a talk with you later this evening. When you have the time."

Now what? Angel looked anxiously between her

father and her lover. How could things get any more complicated? She still hadn't had a chance to tell Loyal why she'd sent that message to him and he hadn't asked. Was he finished with her, as she'd claimed to be with him in the voicelink call? If so, he might leave before she had a chance to tell him how she really felt.

Her breath came high in her throat as she watched the men file from the room in a grim line.

Chapter Fifty Five

Loyal rode out to check with the guards he'd set up around the compound and was soon immersed in decisions to arrange shifts of workers to spell them off throughout the night. Riders arrived from the border stations and more men were quickly sent to replace them. The manager of the supplies building showed him what provisions were provided to each replacement team of guards travelling to the stations. They were running low on some basic items and the stores needed urgent replenishment.

Every decision was complicated—necessary, yet somewhat disorganized. Loyal figured the system would just have to do for now. There would be a time later where a new arrangement could be initiated. A team of workers were appointed to repair the main gates of the compound in the far field. Loyal asked them to take a look at the back gate as well and come up with some ideas for reinforcement. It had been too easily overtaken during the struggle to regain the compound.

When he returned to the manorhouse at Rascal's call to sup, the sun was already setting. Yet there was a great deal still to do. He walked in to find Gerwal seated at the table with all his sons who were present at the compound ranged around him. Nineteenth cradled his injured hand against his chest, and a bowl of brandy in the other. Rascal took a seat along the side of the table beside his brother Runt. Fifteenth had risen from his bed and was propped up in the lounge that Gerwal had recently vacated. Fourth teetered precariously on a cushioned chair beside his father. Thirteenth wore his baker's apron, happily sipping a tankard of ale. Ninth had left the offices, ink stains on his fingers. Seventeenth and Eighteenth were in from the vegetable fields, their fingernails black from their fieldwork.

Gerwal gestured to the only empty chair at the foot of the table. "Sit down, Hawker. Rest your feet. Somebody get him a drink." Soon a bowl of clouded ale appeared as Loyal eased into the seat. *What now?* All eyes were trained on him, though Fourth squinted to focus as if he were high on phang oil. What would Gerwal do with this son who had betrayed him, through everything that had happened?

"Now." Banderos thumped the table with his fist to gain everyone's attention. "We've had a family discussion and have come to a decision. "

"I see." Loyal took a sip of ale and sat back to await the news. Perhaps they were booting him out. In that case, it would be a struggle to whisk Angel away so they could marry together. He'd do whatever it took to take her with him. *But what if she really had changed her mind about them being together?* He'd demand to see her again before they forced him to leave, because he still had hopes….

"We are in agreement," Gerwal continued.

"I checked with Angel and she approves, too," Rascal added.

Loyal stared. *She agreed with what?* It was as if the young man had read his thoughts. His hand clenched around the ale bowl.

"So, we've appointed you, Loyal Hawker. Do you accept?" Gerwal gave him a piercing stare.

Appointed him? Accept what? He looked along the line of Banderos sons, gauging their expressions. Rascal and Runt looked eager, like young puppies. Ninth was thoughtful, Fourth had dozed off. The others were watchful, perhaps because they didn't know him as well. All except Nineteenth. He had that secret smile on his lips that Loyal had seen before when he was dealing with his sister.

Loyal released his ale bowl and leaned forward, bracing his arms on the table. "Do I accept what, Mr Banderos? I'm afraid I don't know what you're talking about."

Gerwal gave a slight frown, then put back his head and laughed. "Yah, I understand. That was badly done, wasn't it?" He glanced around at his sons, then at Loyal. "We want you to take over the management of the Banderos territory. We all agree you have the skill, you certainly have the contacts to help keep us safe. You have the training, of which we are in short supply. Perhaps you could remedy that while you're at it."

"Management of the compound?" he stuttered.

"Well, the whole thing. I want you to take my place," Gerwal said, waving his arm in the general direction of the stations. "Someone has to. The plan was that First, or one of the sons…" He stopped, glancing at the faces that had all turned to look at him. He nodded to his family, then glanced at Loyal. "That plan has failed, but we've come up with a better one. You take the reins, Hawker. We voted on it."

Loyal downed his ale and thumped the bowl on the table as turmoil churned in his chest. He slowly got to his feet. "I'll think about it," he said. "But first I have to talk to your daughter."

He turned to leave and heard Rascal behind him. "She's in her garden," the boy called.

Chapter Fifty Six

In Orde's office, First shifted on the hard wooden chair and surreptitiously wiped the sweat from his brow, drying his fingers on the leg of his pants. "So you see," he said again. "Our land will be protected. We just have to wait for Angel to get over the virus she's contracted. I didn't think it right to bring her here if she's still contagious. No point in everyone falling ill."

Orde leaned forward, resting arms on his desktop. "Who else got sick?"

"Uh." First thought a moment, nervously recalling that was the very question he had asked when Olaf Nazur died. "Just one or two of the men," he muttered. "Everyone is on the mend."

"Good, so not the high-temp virus."

"No." First gazed into Orde's eyes and saw patent disbelief. "I assure you," he said hurriedly, the sweat now dripping down his temples. "She's at the south station, which is only a half day's ride away. She can be here by tomorrow night or the next day at the latest."

"I happen to know," said Orde as he relaxed in his leather chair, "that your south station fell to a group of soldiers a day ago. Who were they, anyway? Not your men, obviously."

First stuttered, "I don't know who they were. A group of dispossessed, I thought. They're out of control all around us. that's why we need the Emperor's backing. You could help me regain the station." He tried to gauge the other man's expression. "Let's head out first thing in the morning. Angel will still be there and you can bring her home after we…"

"Good idea." Orde stood and gestured toward the door. "Let's go to the corral and see how many men and horses we can contribute to the cause."

First slowly got to his feet. "All right, yah. I have three men waiting for me at your border."

Orde walked ahead of him through the doorway and down the stairs. "This way," he called. First hurried behind, glancing down to place his boot on the last step. When he looked up, he gazed down the barrel of a raygun. There was a loud nose, and his body jerked at the impact, then he was falling…

~***~

The garden gate squeaked and Angel glanced up as Loyal walked through, carefully latching it behind him. She paused in her work, stomach clenching, then patted the earth around the sagium she was replanting, sticking a stake into the ground to tie it upright. Loyal was here, and from the expression on his face he wanted some answers.

"Angel, what happened here? Who did this?" Loyal stood, hands on hips, as he frowned at the mangled rows of plants.

She rose from her knees, brushing the dirt from her pants. "It was the guards when they kidnapped me. They walked over everything. I'm not sure…" She gestured at the row of germanium. "Perhaps some of these can be saved." The plants looked as if a herd of cattle had roared through, trampling the stalks and breaking the heads off.

He gave her a piercing look from those pale blue eyes. "You were here in the garden when they came?"

She nodded uncertainly. *Had Father talked to him yet about his new plan, and was he now the head of the Banderos organization or had he turned it down?* He looked pale and lines of strain showed around that beautiful expressive mouth.

"Let me," he said, gesturing to the row of plants. "Give me the spade and just tell me which ones to put where. Perhaps we can rescue some of them."

She passed the small shovel over as he pointed to the bench. "Rest there, Angel. You aren't ready to do this work. Let me."

Her heart fluttered in her chest at his care for her garden. It touched her, warmed something inside that had been left cold and dull from the events of the past days. Yet, he wasn't even asking about the message she'd left for him. Perhaps he didn't want to know. He bent to prop up a small broken rosemary bush.

"Loyal," she murmured, her throat tight. "I didn't want to send that message."

He straightened abruptly, his pale gaze pinned to her face.

"First made me do it."

He stared as he lifted one hand to rub a spot over his breastbone. "But did you mean it?"

Tears formed in her eyes. She seemed to cry at a moment's notice these days. Impatiently she brushed them away. "How could I, after the time we had together in Sommerset?"

His face flushed dark as his hand pressed harder on the spot in the centre of his chest. "I don't know, but I need to hear you say it. You sounded as if you meant what you said. Is that how it was? Have you changed your mind about us again?"

"I didn't change it the first time." Her tears came faster. "First told me he would kill you if you came onto our land. I had to protect you, don't you see?" Her fists clenched in agony.

"Ah, Angel." He took a step toward her as she seemed to fall in his direction. He caught her up in his arms. "I love you. That statement broke my heart."

She was engulfed in his arms. "I'm so sorry," she sobbed. "I didn't mean…"

"It's not for you to protect me," he said. "That's my job—to protect you. Do you love me? Because that's all that matters."

"Yes, oh yes. I was afraid you wouldn't forgive…"

"Of course I will. I want you, Angel. I want to marry with you."

"I want that too," she whispered against his shirt. He stopped her words with the soft pressure of his mouth.

It was dusk when they left the garden together, walking hand-in-hand toward the manorhouse.

Chapter Fifty Seven

"So, things have calmed down somewhat," Loyal said over the voicelink. "I don't know yet what it will mean for the Banderos organization with Carlton ensconced so close in Sommerset, but I guess we will deal with that over time."

Maude cleared his throat over the link. "You're staying there, then?" the Governor asked.

"Yah, Gerwal offered me a position to take over from him, and I've accepted." He had reached the main gate of the compound in his mindless stroll, and turned to walk back up the field. In spite of how many people lived here, the compound was so large it was easy enough to gain privacy for a conversation.

"Does that have anything to do with the daughter—what's her name? Angel?"

Loyal's neck grew warm. He was just glad that Maude couldn't see him through the link connection.

"Could be," he said. "We're going to marry."

"Ahh." Frank Maude paused. "Good. I plan to be there for that event, so give me a couple of days to prepare for the travel."

Loyal stopped in his tracks. "You want to be here?"

"You're my nephew, of course I want to be there."

"Thank you, Uncle Frank," Loyal stuttered. "We've never really acknowledged that relationship in public."

"Well, no. But that's because we've always dealt on a professional basis. A wedding is different. You'll want family there. I'll bring your mother with me. We can recruit Father Unwin from Deep Creek to conduct the service. I doubt he's ever been in an aircart before." He gave a chuckle at the idea of the aged priest travelling by air. "Are your cousins, the Farmers, coming?"

Loyal gazed across the field at the vegetable gardens in the distance, where Seventeenth and one of his brothers laboured. "I haven't told them yet," he said low.

"Well, you'd better get on it. They'll want to attend."

Loyal's chest constricted as he contemplated his family coming to the wedding. The ceremony was something he'd wanted to get accomplished as soon as possible, so he'd have the right to be with Angel. He hadn't thought about the event itself. She would be surrounded by her family. Now he was being offered the same blessing.

"Listen," Frank added. "I'll organize the travel from this end if you can manage to put us up for a few days. What do you say?"

Loyal gazed around at the buildings before him, the large manorhouse, a couple of barracks with family housing beyond that. "There's room here, Uncle Frank. Have you seen the place?"

"No, never have. That's another reason I want to come down. Get a look at the land."

"Yah, that's a good idea. I'll set the date and let you know."

Loyal clicked off and slid the voicelink into his pocket. He stood a moment, taking in the landscape—gardens, fields, numerous buildings, the high wall surrounding it all that meandered up and over the hill behind the manorhouse in the distance. He, Loyal Hawker, controlled all of this.

The Banderos brothers were slowly becoming more open with him as they worked together to solve the immediate problems of the security and safety of their land. He was amazed one or more of them hadn't tried to grab the reins for themselves, but it seemed the three older brothers had been the most aggressive about it. He didn't know where First and Fifth were, but the question of what to do with Fourth was still on his list of issues. The fourth son was not well, and was currently being nursed in the medic's hut along with Fifteenth. Time would tell what steps would need to be taken.

Now, among a myriad of other issues, he would turn his attention to organizing a wedding. He headed back to the manorhouse to talk with Angel and get her thoughts on what should happen.

~***~

Father Unwin waited patiently in the Great Entry with his formal stole arranged around his neck, a kindly smile on his wrinkled and weathered face. Loyal shifted from one foot to the other. His dress uniform was digging into his neck and he stuck a finger in to loosen the collar. Abe Farmer stood at his shoulder, Uncle Frank beside him. Mother, Maude's sister, had come in the entourage, and looked more cheerful than he'd ever seen her.

Nineteenth and Rascal had ascended the stairs a half hour ago, and they still hadn't appeared with Angel. *Had she changed her mind?* His heart skipped a beat at the thought.

Just then he heard footsteps on the stairs and Rascal appeared dressed in a dark wool suit, slowly descending toward the crowd. Nineteenth came right behind him, Angel clinging to his arm. She looked stunning. He could hardly get a breath, his lungs labouring for oxygen. She was dressed in a lovely gown of an old-fashioned design, with glitters along the neckline and down the bodice. It was a deep gold colour, just slightly darker than her hair which was coiled on the back of her head in ornamental loops. There were flowers caught in the curls.

She stopped before him, let go of Nineteenth's

arm and took his hand.

He leaned in and caught the scent of her body. "You look like an angel," he whispered

She gave him an impish grin and the tension eased inside. Everything was all right. She was here, ready to become his wife.

~***~

Loyal took Angel's hand and kissed her fingers. The ceremony had been very touching. Father Unwin presided at the church in Deep Creek and had been posted there for many years. He'd married Loyal's aunt and uncle long ago—Jade's sister Letitia to Gregoff Farmer, before the Last War was ever thought of. He was a deeply spiritual man with a wonderful sense of humour. He was also practical, and the wedding was accomplished in record time, to Loyal's vast relief.

He turned Angel to face the woman behind him. "This is my mother," he said, glad mother had arrived the night before to meet everyone.

"Ms Hawker." Angel smiled and bowed, her hands pressed together against her forehead. "I'm very pleased to meet you once more, Ms Hawker."

'Thank you, my dear. I'm pleased to meet you as well,' Mother said, giving Loyal a wink. 'And it's not Ms Hawker, call me Marika. Welcome to the family, dear." She turned to him. 'Loyal, you've done very well. I'm pleased to see you take a wife, although it will be tough for you and me to live so far away from each other.'

Loyal wrapped one arm around her shoulders, while still keeping hold of Angel's hand. 'It won't be too bad, Mother. We're coming to Khandarken to visit once things settle down here, and we'll spend time in Deep Creek with you. There's nothing to stop you from travelling here to see us, as well.'

Angel's forehead creased in confusion. 'Are you related to the Governor who is here, Mr Maude?'

Loyal chuckled as his mother gave a pleased smile. 'Yah, they're brother and sister,' he said. 'I know it's a lot to take in, but I'll help. Come meet the others.'

She tugged on his hand. 'That makes him your uncle.'

'Right. And my cousins are here—Abe and Beth Farmer.'

'Well, I know that. I met them before." Angel laughed as they approached. "You could be Abe's twin, you look so much alike, with the white blonde curly hair and tall build."

"True, sometimes people get us mixed up."

She blushed. "I don't think I'll do that."

"You'd better not." He pulled her against him and settled a firm kiss on her mouth. The crowd gave a loud cheer as some musical instruments were tuned up in the corner of the entry. The dancing was about to begin.

Chapter Fifty Eight

Upstairs, Loyal backed Angel into her room and locked the door. "Finally," he said.

She giggled, fingers pressed to her mouth.

"What's so funny?" He released the clips on his uniform jacket and shrugged it from his shoulders, laying it over the back of a padded chair.

"You," she said, plopping down on the side of the pallet. "I got somewhat confused down there with all the visitors. Who was Julianne, Abe's wife?"

He nodded. "Her name is Julianne Adjudicator. Her father was Little Harry Adjudicator, although he's dead now."

"Right. Why was it a bad match between them?"

Loyal pulled in his chin. "Who said it was a bad match?"

"Just some gossip I heard," she murmured. "Someone mentioned it."

"Well, Julianne's father was involved in a scheme to overtake the Farmer talc mines, that's probably what they were talking about. But she didn't have anything to do with it."

"Oh." She pulled one of her long gloves off and laid it beside her on the bed. "Who was Beth's husband, the big dark-skinned man?"

Loyal laughed and grabbed her hand, slowly pulling off her other glove. "His name is Dante Regiment, and he's the Major-General of the Khandarken military. His father is the General."

"The older man of the same colouring, with the scars on the side of his face."

"Right, that's him. Scars from the Last War. The final technical blast, according to Dante. His eyesight was affected as well."

She smiled. "It was nice to see Damian Stuke again, I like him. His wife is beautiful. What was her name?"

"She is lovely, her name is Fanny Master, but you're lovelier." He pushed her down on the pallet. "Quit trying to distract me with questions. It won't work, you know. I only have one more job to do tonight and nothing's going to stop me."

"What job is that?" she asked softly.

"You. You're the job." He nuzzled her throat as his fingers fumbled with the snaps on her dress.

"I was hoping you would say that," she murmured. He reared back. "You were?"

"Yes. I've missed you so much."

"Ahh." Something compressed in his chest. "I've missed you too. There were days when… Well, never mind that. Can I get you out of this dress?" He tugged on the sash, pulling the bow loose and tossing it aside.

"Let me do it." Impatiently, she pushed at his shoulder. "It was my mother's dress and I don't want it ruined."

"No, it's my task." He felt a smile forming at the stubborn expression on her face. "You can undress me once I've finished here."

She let out an exasperated sigh and flopped back on the pallet.

"There's a good girl," he said and slid the dress off her shoulders and down her arms. She giggled and he laughed, hovering above her as he laid his mouth carefully over hers. At last, he thought.

He kissed her thoroughly, until her clothes were bunched at her waist beneath his impatient hands. He raised his head.

"At last," she said, staring up at him with those dark blue eyes.

"You read my mind," he replied.

Chapter Fifty Nine

Advisor Lanser appeared in the doorway. Carlton brushed Bieter's hands away and seized the tails of his cravat. "I'll do it," he muttered. "Just finish with my hair."

Bieter grabbed the hairbrush but the more he brushed, the wilder Carlton's hair became. His assistant dropped the brush on the shelf and removed the lid on a small tin of hair wax. Dipping his fingertips into the concoction, he rubbed his hands together, then smoothed them through the jet-black curly hair. Carlton stared in the plexi mirror while his grooming was completed and his hair became tamed. He motioned impatiently and Bieter backed toward the door.

"What is it, Judson?"

The Advisor stepped hesitantly into the room. "There's news," he said.

Carlton huffed an impatient breath. "What kind of news? From where?"

"From the Banderos land, not good news." Deep lines furrowed his brow.

"All right." Carlton gave his cravat one last tug and turned from the foggy plexi mirror. "Tell me."

"I had inserted a couple of our men into First Banderos' new group of guards."

"Right. Good move." Carlton clipped his belt closed and patted it flat against his stomach. "Don't tell me they've deserted. Perhaps First wasn't paying proper wages."

"No, not that. First led a group of his men west, toward the Nazur land. But his guards were stopped at the border, and not allowed to accompany him to see Mr Nazur."

"Hmm." Carlton smoothed an unruly sideburn.

"One of them has arrived here with news."

Carlton glanced at Judson's reflection in the plexi. "And?"

"The brother, Fifth, died on the way to Nazur's place, a mountain lion attack apparently."

Carlton nodded. "There have been lots of reports the lions are getting more aggressive."

"Yah, so the guards waited for First to reappear at the border, but soon they were told by Nazur's men that he had been shot. First is dead. We've lost our Banderos territory to a different strongman, they say. A new man arrived with a horde of tribesmen and a troop of soldiers from the Khandarken military and took over the place from one end to the other."

Carlton frowned. "What about all the brothers? Did they just let it happen, a stranger taking over their land?"

Lanser shrugged. "No word on that. But our insulation between Sommerset and the northern peoples is gone, evaporated. Our Governor is dead."

Fury rose like a tide in Carlton's chest, as beads of sweat gathered on his brow. "Send in another undercover man. Find out what's happening there. I don't see the father and all his sons letting a stranger drop in and just take over what they'd managed to build over the last many years."

Lanser shook his head. "The whole new guard has been dismissed. They were all First's men and with him gone, no one trusts them apparently. Those men have joined the dispossessed in the hills around the city or are roaming the streets of Sommerset looking for work."

Emperor Carlton waved his arm wildly to silence the string of meaningless words. "We have to get it back, Judson. There's no choice. That land was our security from Khandarken and Penrhy interference. And First was our man. Go out there and recruit this new strongman, find out who he is and what he wants in order to work with us. We need that territory under our control. Do whatever it takes to get the job done. We have our own military right here in Sommerset. Time to step up and secure our holdings."

From the Author -

I love to write, and my readers are the life blood of why I write. If you enjoyed this book, please consider giving a review. Even if it is just a few sentences, it makes all the difference

You can contact me at my website
www.sylviegrayson.com,
Leave a review at Amazon
Or email me at sylviegraysonauthor@gmail.com.
All comments are appreciated.

Sylvie Grayson

The Last War series is a stunning portrayal of a new world created from fire and consumed at the edges ...- sci fi and fantasy at its best...

The Emperor has been defeated. New countries have arisen from the ashes of the old Empire. The citizens swear they will never need to fight again after that long and painful war.

Bethlehem Farmer is helping her brother Abram run Farmer Holdings in south Khandarken after their father died in the final battles. She is looking after the dispossessed, keeping the farm productive and the talc mine working in the hills behind their land. But when Abram takes a trip with Uncle Jade into the northern territory and disappears without a trace, she's left on her own. Suddenly things are not what they seem, and no one can be trusted.

Major Dante Regiment is sent by his father, the General of Khandarken, to find out what the situation is at Farmer Holdings. What he sees shakes him to the core and fuels his grim determination to protect Bethlehem at all cost, even with his life.

Ms Grayson has created a fascinating new world with a lot of the same old problems. Sci fi and fantasy rolled into one with a sure hand and enormous imagination

From the mud and danger of the open road to the welcoming arms of the Sanctuary, from attacks by the dispossessed army to the storms of the open sea, Son of the Emperor takes us on a wild ride into danger and on to the dream of freedom.

With the Emperor defeated after a seemingly endless war, the citizens pray they'll never need to fight again. But already unrest is growing in the north of Khandarken.

After Julianne Adjudicator's father disappears, she seeks to escape the clutches of her vicious stepmother Zanata, who has posted a reward on her head. The Sanctuary, near the Legitamia border, is rumoured to be the safest place for a woman in need of shelter in a sometimes hostile world full of unrest and roving dispossessed. But when Julianne seeks asylum, it soon becomes clear all is not as it first appeared.

Then Abe Farmer arrives at the Sanctuary seeking medical help and she seizes the opportunity to leave. Abe isn't interested in taking a young woman with them, as he and his injured bodyguard struggle to return to the Southern Territory. Yet when he discovers her fate if she stays, he finds he has no choice. But the journey becomes more dangerous as they encounter the army of the New Emperor. Caught in the middle of a firefight, they flee toward the Catastrophic Ocean. Can Abe keep her safe till they reach home?

From the mud and danger of the open road to the welcoming arms of the Sanctuary, from attacks by the dispossessed army to the storms of the open sea, Son of the Emperor takes us on a wild ride into danger and on to the dream of freedom.

…a whole new world with some of the same old problems - fantasy at its best…

The Last War is over and the next one is about to begin.

From attacks by Emperor Carlton to conspiracy in the ranks of the police, Khandarken is in more danger than at any time since the end of The Last War. But when the Young Emperor makes an offer, can Chief Cownden Lanser resist? Khandarken's future hangs in the balance.

The Young Emperor has been backed into a corner. He holds a bit of land in Legitamia where he marshals his troops, but the skirmishes they've launched to expand his empire have had limited success. Now, his ambitions are aimed at overthrowing everything Khandarken has cobbled together since the Last War.

Cownden Lanser, Chief Constable of Khandarken, is a private man with a close connection to the Old Empire that he doesn't divulge to anyone. Although he's dedicated to his position, things are not what they seem in the rank and file of the police.

Selanna Nettles is a sookie, trained in Legitamia but working near her family in the Western Territory of Khandarken, healing the injured mine workers and the dispossessed. But her life takes a startling turn when Chief Cownden Lanser hires her to attend a set of high-level meetings in Gilsigg.

When these three meet up in Legitamia, the result is explosive. Not just for them but for the future of Khandarken. The Emperor makes Cownden an offer that might be everything he's secretly dreamed of. How can he refuse?

The Last War series is a stunning portrayal of a new world created from fire and consumed at the edges… sci fi/fantasy at its best…

Fanny Master is running for her life. Can she trust a criminal enforcer to keep her safe?

The International Head Balls Games are about to begin at Deep Creek. Tension rises with Adar Silva, Khandarken, Jiran and Legitamia scheduled to take part. Damian Stuke, an enforcer for a gamer in the Western Territory, still has nightmares about being captured and tortured during the Last War. When his sister marries the Chief Constable of Khandarken, his life has to change.

Training for undercover work in Deep Creek in the midst of the Games, he encounters a fascinating woman with a small child and a hidden agenda. But as he discovers what she's hiding, his protective instincts kick into high gear.

Fanny Master's parents have been assassinated, and she is forced to run for her life. A member of the Khandarken political elite, she doesn't know who is after her, but she'll do almost anything to remain under the radar. That could include using someone else's ident and adopting their child, a child who might be from another world.

As Emperor Carlton ramps up his plans for invasion, the assassin makes a new attempt on Fanny's life. Damian is her only hope. Will he save her from her unknown enemy, or is he still working for the other side?

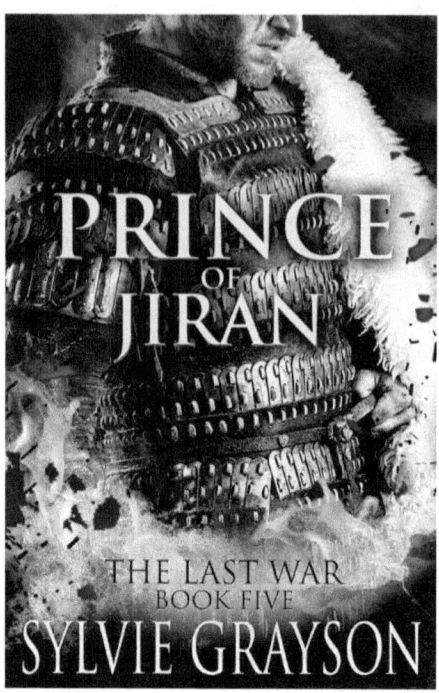

A Penrhy prince caught between duty and desire. Can he win the impending battle?

Shandro, Prince of the Penrhy tribe of Jiran, has a goal to uphold the family values in spite of his father's conniving moves as he deals with the hotbed of competing nations surrounding them.

Then he's is sent on a mission across the mountains into Khandarken to bring back Princess Chinata, a bride for Emperor Carlton's Advisor. In exchange, Jiran and the Penrhy tribe are given a peace agreement, protection against invasion by the Emperor's troops. This seems a good trade, as Carlton is hovering on their borders with his need for more land. However, not far into the journey, it becomes apparent someone is not adhering to the terms of the peace accord.

Near the tribal border, Shandro and his troops have come under direct attack from unknown forces. He digs deeper into Chinata's background to find strong ties to the New Empire. Is it too dangerous to bring Princess Chinata into Jiran? Or as her escort, does Shandro become her defender against the Emperor's troops?

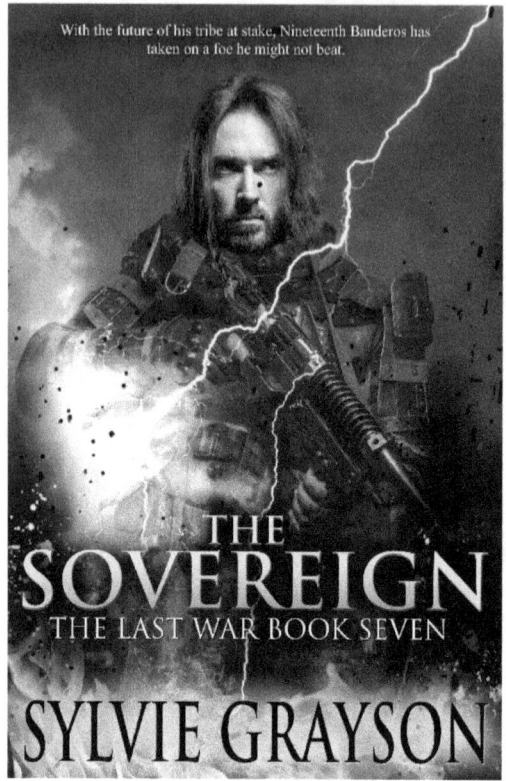

With the future of his tribe at stake, Nineteenth Banderos has taken on a foe he might not beat.

With the future of his tribe at stake, Nineteenth Banderos has taken on a foe he might not beat.

The ever menacing Emperor has overtaken the city of Sommerset, the seat of power from the Old Empire. Now he's been approached by a local strongman, offering to work with him to seize the Banderos territory.

Nineteenth Banderos has been given the task of heading up a Foreign Legion for the dispossessed, but his plans take a detour when he meets the Shafoneur Sovereign who has plans of his own. Nineteenth isn't one to turn down a challenge, especially if the reward might include the chance to marry a beautiful young Shafoneur girl he's fallen for.

Unfortunately, a war with Emperor Carlton looms on the horizon. Allied with the Shafoneur tribe, Nineteenth is not about to let a neighbour claim their land, but that is not the only threat he faces. Can Nineteenth protect his family and his new alliance?

Contemporary romantic suspense from author Sylvie Grayson...

Some secrets are too dangerous to keep...

A thrilling novel of romantic suspense from author Sylvie Grayson.

After losing her husband to a deadly illness, Julia Butler is determined to look after her family, but this is the 1930's and times are tough for everyone. As the endless string of jobless men trudges past her farm, she does her best to hang on. Then two strangers suddenly appear at her home. They are hiding something that places her family in danger, and nothing will ever be the same.

Dr. Will Stofford has become disillusioned with women. In an effort to heal his broken heart, he leaves his brothers behind and sets up his medical practice in the Kootenays where no one knows him.

Meeting Julia throws his plans into chaos. Will can't turn his back on a challenge and he won't rest until he solves this puzzle and puts things right.

In the 1930's, can a country doctor and a determined widow save the lives of these abandoned strangers?

When a police detective falls for his main suspect, life gets complicated…

When Chloe Bowman woke to find her husband gone, never did she imagine it would take so long to find him, or that in the midst of the search she'd discover she didn't really know this man at all. She soon realizes she has been left alone with her young son and a time bomb on her hands. Then the earthquake throws everything into question. Lurking in the shadows is the mysterious Rainman who travels under an unknown name.

Police Detective Ross Cullen was already investigating Chloe's husband when he disappeared. Although he's powerfully drawn to Chloe, Ross also knows that when one member of a family disappears, the first place to look for the suspect is among those closest to him. No one was closer than Chloe.

But the deeper Ross digs the less he knows, and the more he's attracted to the young wife as she struggles to put her life back together.

Can Ross break through the Rainman's disguises to solve the case so he can be with Chloe?

Can Rain solve his last case without getting his girlfriend arrested?

Rainier is a survivor. He's made some mistakes, and now he's paying for them. As a condition of his probation, he must work with the police on investigations where his skills might be useful. There is one more case to solve to complete his commitments. Then he'll be free. As he heads undercover to work this last case, Sophia arrives in town. She is a childhood crush who means a great deal to Rain, and she is obviously terrified of someone.

Sophia has made a bad choice in the past, and now she's in hiding to avoid dealing with it. Still, it follows her, and Rainier is the only one she can trust to help her deal with it.

Rain's problem? The clues he uncovers on his final case all seem to lead directly to Sophia. Can he solve the case without breaking his heart or pointing the police in his girlfriend's direction?

Jake never expected his investigations would prove deadly.

Sylvie Grayson delivers another thrilling romantic mystery that will keep you on the edge of your seat— a gripping story of suspense with characters that you'll root for and a plot that pulls you in.

After years of taking courses and jumping through hoops to get licensed, Jake Murdoch is more than ready to open his private investigator's office. Leah Bonnar, a family friend and childhood irritant who blames him for a past disaster in her life, steps in to volunteer as his assistant. Given he's not making money yet, he needs her help to get things up and running. Yet as the cases start pouring in, she organizes the hell out of him. Jake is attracted to Leah, and grudgingly grateful for her help in equal measure. Despite their history, their relationship heats up.

But in the midst of one of his investigations, Jake steps on the toes of a couple of very determined con men and Leah is sitting right in the crosshairs of their revenge. Can Jake find the evidence he needs to stop the criminals, while protecting Leah from their efforts to bring his investigation to a halt?

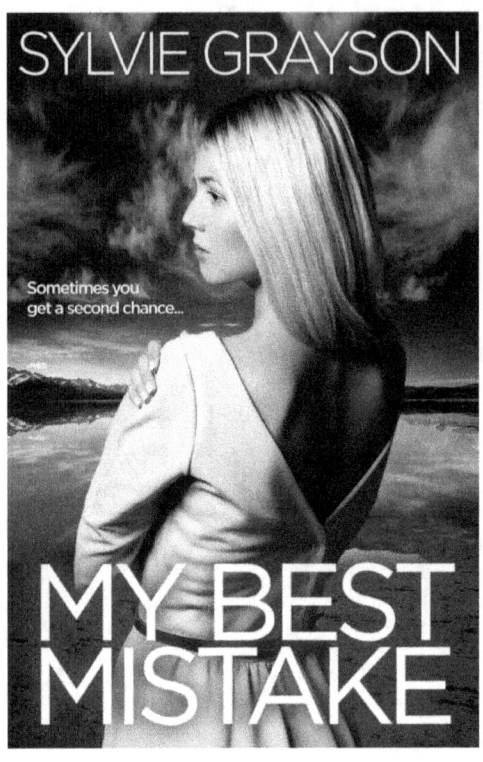

Jordie let her get away the first time. He's determined it won't happen again.

Jordie was heartbroken when he returned to town to find Jenny had married another man. Now she lives beside him, and he'll either go crazy or do what he should have done before - claim her for his own.

Jenny is back and she's angry, her husband cheated

and she can't let it go. But when her boss dies and someone comes after her, who will she turn to? With her cousin living right beside her it's becoming harder to ignore the chemistry they have always shared. Can Jordie help put her life back together?

Emily moves to a new town to hide her secret, but it follows her. Can Joe protect her from her past?

When Emily Drury takes a job as legal counsel for an import-export company, she does it because she needs to get away to safety. Joe Tanner counts himself lucky. He's charmed a successful big city lawyer into heading up the legal department of his rapidly expanding business. But why would a beautiful woman who could easily make partner in a high profile legal firm give it all up to come to Bonnie? As Joe realizes she has become essential to his happiness, his first reaction is to protect her. But he doesn't know the whole story.

Can Emily trust him enough to divulge her secret? Will he learn what he needs to know in time to stop the avalanche that's gaining speed as it races down the hill toward her?

Katy Dalton's friend has disappeared with her money and bad things start to happen. Can Brett Rome save his father's company, and the woman who causes chaos in his heart?

Katy Dalton needs her money back, but Bruno has stopped answering his phone and bad things start to happen.

Brett Rome is frustrated. The last thing he wants is to leave a promising career in hockey to come home and run his ailing father's trucking company. What he discovers is a company teetering on the very edge of bankruptcy and a young woman demanding the return of her money.

But danger lurks in the form of Bruno's dubious associates. What secret are they hiding and why are they willing to kill Katy? Can Brett put this broken picture back together, and is Katy part of the solution or the problem?

As the Great War drags on, can a prairie farmer put his life back together?

It's 1918, and prairie farmer Shane Narraway and his brothers are doing their best working the land to help feed the Allied troops overseas. As the war drags on, it is a tough time of hard work and deprivation for everyone. But Shane's bigger goal is to marry Emily Waddell. Emily has just arrived in Canada and already lost her family and her dreams to their first harsh winter. She's looking for a way to create a new life for herself. With the war news worsening daily, his brother fighting in Europe, and the outbreak of the

Spanish flu, Shane's life is about to unfold in ways he never imagined.

Sylvie Grayson wrote a romantic and touching story of two beautiful souls. A seriously good novella!

ABOUT THE AUTHOR

Sylvie Grayson loves to write about suspense, romance and murder, in both contemporary and science fiction/fantasy. She has lived most of her life in British Columbia, Canada in spots ranging from Vancouver Island on the west coast to the North Peace River country and the Kootenays in the beautiful interior. She spent a one-year sojourn in Tokyo, Japan.

She has been an English language instructor, a nightclub manager, an auto shop bookkeeper and a lawyer. Now she works part time as the owner of a small company, and writes when she finds the time.

She is a wife and mother and still loves to travel. She lives on the coast of the Pacific Ocean with her husband on a small patch of land near the sea that they call home.

If you enjoyed this book, please consider giving a review.

You can contact me at sylviegraysonauthor@gmail.com
or visit my website at
www.sylviegrayson.com and follow my blog or sign up
to receive my newsletter. You will be the first to hear the
latest on new book releases, contests, book giveaways and
author presentations.

I'd love to hear from you. You can leave a comment on
my website or contact me directly at
sylviegraysonauthor@gmail.com
or find me on Facebook at
https://www.facebook.com/Sylvie-Grayson-Author-
103310004539962
or on BookBub at
https://www.bookbub.com/profile/sylvie-grayson